Zura Maids

Zura Maids

FEMRITE PUBLICATIONS LIMITED
KAMPALA

Zura Maids

Apio Eunice Otuko

FEMRITE - Uganda Women Writers Association
P.O. Box 705, Kampala
Tel: +256 414 543943 / +256 772 743943
Email: info@femrite.org
www.femrite.org

ISBN 978-9970-480-19-7

Cover and Layout design by Bonnetvanture T Asiimwe
bonnetvanture@gmail.com

Dedication:

In memory of my father, Dr. John Baptist Otuko
For Arthur, Jesse, Venus, Noah & Innocent Ebil.

Acknowledgment

I owe a great debt of gratitude to FEMRITE and the Danish Center for Culture and Development (CKU) for the opportunity to participate in the Novel-Writing Mentoring project, and to Glaydah Namukasa for her generous comments, suggestions and encouragement while revising the novel.

I was also lucky to enjoy the patience and expertise of Professor Arthur Gakwandi who mentored me during the project, and Hilda Twongyeirwe who read the first manuscript and provided very useful comments. I know that behind the scenes, at FEMRITE, there were people who were involved in editing, typesetting and proofreading, and I will forever remain grateful. Thank you Tino Akware, Edna Namara, Hillary Bell, Eira Javerot, Chris Conte, Regina Asinde and others I have not mentioned here but who spent their time making Zura Maids a better book.

In a special way, I thank my family for their encouragement even when the first draft sat gathering dust on the shelf since 2008. Thank you mother – Grace Otuko, My sisters Monica Adong, Peace Otuko & Babra Otuko. You were always happy to read the first draft as it took shape. I thank my husband Fred Ebil, and our children Arthur Okello Ebil, Jesse Odoc Ebil, Venus Atyang Ebil, Noah Ebil and Innocent Otuko Ebil for encouraging me.

In praise of Zura Maids

"In this powerful first novel, Apio Eunice Otuko breaks new ground for the African novel..."

Arthur Gakwandi, Author of Kosiya Kifefe

"Zura Maids is well-constructed, suspenseful and frighteningly believable... The author's approach has a lot of compassion and dignity."

Chris Conte, Editor of Crossroads

Zura Maids explores experiences of victims of human trafficking, using fictional characters. It entertains the reader as it also tickles them to come up with effective solutions to the problem.

The New Vision, August 2017

"A striking literary debut that creatively explores the reality of human trafficking in today's global village."

Glaydah Namukasa, Author of Voice of a Dream

CHAPTER ONE

"My name is Lena. Lena Ayugi. For the last time this April morning, it is my pleasure to remind you about me," Lena said, staring at the painted replica of the famous terracotta Luzira Head that hung high up on the rear wall of her ward. "This fine new day is a great day for me. In a short while, I will no longer be called Prisoner No. UG50." She waved at the Head.

Other painted replicas of the 1000-year-old piece of antiquity hung on the walls of all the wards and offices of Luzira prison. The wardresses often bragged about it to whoever cared to listen; how the original sculpture, which had sat in the British Museum since 1931, had been excavated from Luzira prison compound, how having replicas in all wards and offices was a great tribute to the site where it was uncovered. Lena had learnt from Wardress Akurut that the reason why the replica was in wards and offices was because Luzira prison missed its treasure. "Why should it make millions of pounds for the British Museum when it is ours?" Wardress Akurut had commented during one of their casual conversations.

"It's a new day, a second chance in my life. For the first time, since I met you, I really don't mind your stupid grin." Lena sneered at the Head, and then walked to her bed – a thin mattress spread on the floor – to pick her treasured possessions. She felt a tinge of excitement rush through her body as she reached for her battered copy of the Holy Bible. She had finally served her two-year jail term in Luzira Women's Prison on the peninsula overlooking Lake Victoria. Today she would be released. This day, Thursday, was Freedom. This day, Thursday, was family reunion.

The excitement of the anticipated freedom had kept her awake most of the night. She was up before the wake-up bell. She did not wait for the banging of iron rods on the metal plate of their doors, which the wardresses did with glee to force those who ignored the bell out of bed. She had forced herself to lie back on the bed while she waited for her cellmates to go out to their various day's work. She was in no mood for any conversations on her day of freedom.

She held the Bible to her chest for a while, thanking the group of priests and nuns who had visited prisoners and given her the coveted gift. The good book had been her best companion in Luzira. She had spent long hours reading and re-reading the books of Job and Ecclesiastics; pondering over the verses of suffering that related to her situation.

Lena felt that the world had wronged her. The world had no right to keep her away from her loved ones. The world had no right to violate her body the way it had done. The world had no right to deprive her of her freedom. She held the Bible tight to her chest and let the words of hope and freedom seep deep into her heart and mind.

She glanced at the wornout beddings on her paltry bed: a dozen of embroidery she had made during the two years of regrets and boredom lay neatly folded at the head of the bed. Next to it, a black and white photograph of her family still lay face up on the special spot she had reserved for it. She placed the Bible on the bed and grabbed the photograph; her siblings – all four of them – forever smiled back at her. She stared at their faces, wondering how the ugly world had treated them since she left. She hoped they were safe from the rebels. She said a prayer she always recited whenever she thought about them. 'Dear God, I believe with all my heart that you have protected my siblings from the rebels.' A pang of guilt raced through her mind as she stared down into the innocence in their eyes. If only she hadn't left home. If only she hadn't left them alone.

In her first days of prison, her fellow inmates had coveted the photograph because it reminded them of their own families. Lena regretted that she had let their grimy hands touch it. Their fingerprints had left ugly marks on the faces of her dear siblings. But she was glad she had saved what remained of their sweet faces; her most cherished possession in prison.

She had devised means of saving the photograph without offending its admirers' insatiable appetite to touch. She had approached wardress Akurut for help. Two days later, Akurut had introduced her to the prison's Art and Craft workshop where she learnt that an inmate could gain skills such as hairdressing, weaving, tailoring and woodworking. She secured scraps of timber which she assembled into a rickety wooden frame where she kept the photograph.

She had enrolled for woodwork and weaving not because she wanted to acquire skills but to fill her jail time with something productive. Interestingly, she now hoped that with those skills she would start a better life once she walked out of the suffocating prison walls. She thought about her few possessions in the backpack which had been in the prison store for the last two years. She couldn't wait to reclaim everything. Prisoners who served their term were often released in the morning hours. Lena hoped she would not wait for long.

She balanced the photo in her hand, not sure yet if she wanted to put her family in the backpack once she reclaimed it. She thought they were too precious to be stashed away with everything else. What if she misplaced the bag? What if the bag got snatched by thieves believing it valuable? What if she forgot it somewhere along the way? Besides, the bag would suffocate the sweet lives. It was not good at all for the living. Her siblings were alive and the living needed good air to sustain the life in them. Yes – her siblings must be alive. Every day, she spoke to the smiling faces on the picture. They kept her strong. Kept her alive. Their smiles were inscribed in her heart.

She decided that the Holy Bible would be the safest place for the photograph on her journey home. It was the one less likely to attract any thieves. Who wouldn't fear to steal the Word of God? Gently, she removed the wooden frame and placed the photograph in the middle pages of the Bible. She was ready to go home. She did not know whether any other prisoner would be leaving that day or whether there would be new ones coming in. All she knew was that probably the high walls of Luzira women's prison would soon house 431 inmates. Not 432.

She held the bible tightly in her armpit and walked out of the ward. She sat at the edge of the veranda from where she would see the wardress on duty come out of the office to summon prisoner No. UG50. Waiting for the wardress' final command would be easier with an open sky to gaze at.

A lake fly flapped its wings and fell on her lap. She let it say goodbye. This April morning the lake flies still danced around the enclosure in the same way they did the first night she arrived, slowly beckoning would-be watchers' attention in lazy circular motions. At night, they gyrated around security lamps. Lena leaned towards the hovering flies and swatted them with her free hand. They looked different this morning. They were more cheerful and friendly. Surely they knew about her Freedom Thursday. Yes. They were celebrating her Freedom Thursday.

She heard footsteps approaching and looked up. It was one of her wardmates, Martina Maa, the sixty five-year-old on a fifteen-year term for child abduction. Lena always admired the thick crown of Martina's shoulder-length grey hair and the large deep-set eyes that brightened the aging droops of her heavily bleached, orange-yellow-red skin. She was not fond of Martina Maa though, because of her uncanny resemblance to the old hag Esther, who had lured Lena from her home three years earlier.

Martina had an overbearing presence; cursing and complaining nonstop about the living conditions in prison, demanding special treatment from the wardresses, throwing it in everyone's face that she was a wealthy woman with high placed connections, telling stories of the luxuries she missed in life.

"I am happy for you, Lena dearie," Martina said, patting Lena on the back. "You know how I hate this place dearie, and what I wish for myself, I wish for you too."

"I thought you were working," Lena said.

"Dearie me, I had to see you off first, my dearie Lena. And to remind you that you can use my help when you are out there. I want to be a good woman, dearie Lena. My offer still stands. A job for you in my company."

"But I will be fine."

"Lena dearie. I won't force you to accept my help if you don't want to. All I ask of you now dearie, is to place a few calls to my business managers asking them to come visit me. I am worried about my businesses. I haven't been visited for two months now.

Please, help me dearie."

"I don't think I can help you. I won't be able to call."

"Dearie, dearie me! The last person who visited me was the company lawyer. His name is Tony. I ordered him to bring me this year's audit report. I haven't seen him or anyone else since then. I need to know what's going on with my business. Please help me dearie. I will give you some money to help you find them."

Lena looked up at Martina. She noticed the occasional look of sadness on Martina's face and for the first time, she felt her heart softening. She could help Martina. For all those times that Martina had gone back to the cell laden with chips, chicken, milk, soda, bread, biscuits, sausages, and shared with her, she would help; after all, it was just a phone call.

Lena sighed. "Ok. Give me their contacts."

"Dearie, dearie me! Tell your family about me." Martina slipped a folded piece of paper into Lena's hand and hurried away towards the Workshop.

"Lena, it's time," wardress Akurut shouted from the compound.

Lena hurried back into the ward and picked her set of embroidery. As she moved out, she paused in the doorway and waved at the nine empty beds of her fellow inmates. She was glad to be free of the squabbles that often broke out among the inmates over small things like a missing cup or comb. She would not miss anyone. Not even Martina Maa who always shared delicacies with her. Though she would miss the Katikkiro of the ward; wardresses called the Katikkiro a dependable captain because she spied on fellow inmates, keeping a sharp eye on them and reporting those planning to escape. The woman had such resilience. She often got scratches, trying to stop cup and comb fights gone nasty though she retaliated by clawing back and yelling out how she looked forward to concluding her twelve-year sentence. Lena pitied the Katikkiro because she couldn't fathom being incarcerated for twelve years. Her own two years had seemed like an unending journey.

"Goodbye ladies," Lena addressed the empty beds.   "Don't worry; your time for freedom will soon come. You too, Katikkiro, one day your twelve years will become twelve seconds."

She hurried towards the administration building, where she met wardress Akurut.

"Afande, I have some things in the store," she said.

"You need to get clearance before you can collect your things," wardress Akurut said. "Once you get your civilian clothes, hand back the uniform then go to the cashier and sign for some money for your transport back home."

"Thank you, Afande."

"Well, I haven't done anything."

"Thank you for the transport money."

"Not me. It's the prison routine."

At the store, Lena emptied her bag to confirm its contents. Yes, the oversized old blue gown passed onto her from her deceased mother's scanty closet was still intact, so was her pale blue dress. She picked the dress to change into and put the rest back into the bag, including the embroidery. She zipped up the bag, picked her bible and went inside the changing room. She took off the uniform and wore the blue dress. It had grown shorter down the years, but she didn't care. This was her dress. Her Freedom dress. She was happy to finally be free of the yellow uniform. Free of the black stripes that had marked her a convict, with 'No. UG50' stamped on the front and back of the dress.

Before she had been sentenced to the two-year-jail term, she had fought to keep the plain yellow worn by inmates still on remand because in her desperation, plain yellow was a colour of hope. For her, plain yellow promised the possibility of being declared innocent. But she was declared guilty and doomed to wear the yellow uniform with black stripes!

She grabbed her possessions and walked out of the room. She handed back the uniform to the office and signed the Prison Release register. She then went to the cashier and signed for 20,000 shillings.

"Thank you," Lena said to the cashier and placed the money inside her Bible. She looked up and smiled at the Luzira Head. The Cashier asked her to wait for an officer to escort her to the gate. Lena waited outside the cashier's office.

Outside, Lena looked at the clusters of inmates; some in yellow uniforms with black stripes, others in orange, and a few in plain yellow, picking rubbish. The oohs and aahs issuing from the different groups were mingled with the occasional incessant laughter of other inmates searching in old newspapers for articles they thought were rib-crackers. A few inmates: the very weak and sick, were just basking in the morning sunshine discussing the latest gossips that had filtered in from new inmates and wardresses.

More clusters of inmates were spread out along the compound of the twelve blocks of wards. She glanced at an inmate in plain orange, the colour designated for those condemned to death. Even when Lena had spent two years in prison, she had never gotten used to the idea that someone could wait for death in such a manner. She felt that whereas she waited with impatience for the end of her jail term, celebrating each passing day, those serving death sentences must dread the dawn of each day for fear of the noose. How could a human being wake up each morning only to wait for their own death? To walk to their own death? To see their own death coming?

Lena said a silent goodbye to the nagging routine of the bell that had marked her life in prison: waking up, sleeping, working in the different sections, collecting food from the kitchen to the ward; and the dehumanizing daily head counts.She still felt she did not deserve jail. She had committed the crime in self-defence!

It did not matter to her that the magistrate had chosen not to believe her innocence. What mattered was that her attorney, Arthur Mubende, that good man, had believed her. Only a week before, he had come to see her, and ascertain with the prison authorities that this Freedom Thursday would mark the end of her jail term.

Arthur Mubende had chosen to believe her. He did not mind that she had been in a brothel. He had told her so himself. He did not mind that the world had made a prostitute of her. He believed her when she told him she had been deceived, that instead of the housekeeping job, she had been forcefully held in a brothel somewhere in the sprawling slums of Kawempe, along with fifteen other girls. He believed her when she told him that after six months of sexual slavery she could not take it anymore and so she had decided to end the ordeal with a cigarette lighter a client forgot in her room.

The brothel had burnt down. No one was hurt, but she was charged with arson, and after a slow six months' trial she was found guilty. Arthur had tried to convince her to build the case of her innocence around the illegal businesses of human trafficking and prostitution that her accusers were running, but she refused.

It simply was too shameful. Back home, people would get to know about it and laugh at her siblings and compose songs about her. No. She did not want to bring shame upon her siblings and her parents' memory. There would be no fighting back, she told him.

They lost the case and she was sentenced to two years imprisonment. Two years of jail and no news of her family. Throughout her time in prison, Arthur had wanted to find her siblings and tell them about her incarceration. She would not have any of that. They were too young and hopeful to be told anything like that. Her crime was too shameful for their ears. Silence was the only choice.

Wardress Akurut came. Lena smiled as she followed her to the gate. There were four guards on sentry duty. One sat at his desk inside a small room sunk in the wall of the gate. Lena handed him the release form. He studied it, occasionally glancing at her. He then opened a large book with names of prisoners, looked at Lena for what seemed like eternity, and then said, "Here, sign."

***

Martina watched Lena until she was out of sight. However much she loathed being locked up, a part of her was thankful to prison. Her personal loss of freedom had made her confront the truth that she was in the wrong trade, that her kind of business was causing suffering to young girls. Since she joined Lena in the prison cell and got to understand her story, her conscience had been awakened.

Lena's 'crime' of attempted escape from slavery had hit Martina hard. It had brought her guilt, shame and regrets. It made her think of all the girls who were suffering under her Zura Maids business. Sometimes she felt a heavy, invincible spell of 'good' envelope her. Goodness that made her promise herself she would kill part of her Victoria Group of Companies. That she would sacrifice Zura Maids establishment.

Often, Martina got haunting dreams. Nightmares that transformed her world into that of thousands of helpless slave girls her business had sacrificed. She dreamt of barren, grey and lonely lands filled with scrawny girls clawing in desperation at the thick, plastic strings that held them prisoners against dead mahogany trunks as huge black vultures circled above, waiting.

Whenever Martina had the dreams, she would be tempted to confess to Lena that her business might be responsible for Lena's misfortune. She struggled with the desire to repent. Words pounded her mind: "Kill the Zura! Kill the Zura. Kill the Zura!" But she wouldn't kill the Zura, for it was more than half her estate. Killing it would tantamount to murder of the entire Victoria Group brand. The VG was a dream. The Zura was her success story, her life. Her legacy. No, she wouldn't kill the Zura. Maybe sometime later, she would appeal her sentence, fight for freedom and remodel the Zura.

When she had learnt that Lena's time in jail was almost up, she had offered her a job in the VG. She wanted to compensate Lena's innocence that had been severely battered. To compensate for what all the girls in Zura Maids were going through. Martina hoped that would lessen her guilt. The choice had been Lena's to make, but Lena had refused the offer. Martina still couldn't understand why the girl had refused the offer. Why had Lena refused her job offer? Could it be that Lena had discovered the kind of trade she was running? But...it couldn't be. She had been so careful to keep the details of her business a secret from Lena. From anyone.

Martina felt fresh pangs of guilt as she remembered the sincerity, the innocence with which Lena had communicated her crime. She sat down and replayed in her mind the conversation they had one day during her first week in the ward.

"Hi, I am Lena, two years on arson charges."

"Dearie me, Martina Maa, here. Glad I'm not sharing space with a serious criminal. Dearie me, I am in for child abduction."

"Abduction?"

"Whose house did you burn down?"

"A place where I was being held hostage. A brothel. I burnt it so that I and my friends could escape."

"A brothel." Martina tried to place in her memory any brothel fire earlier. She couldn't recall any. That was strange; this was information she ought to know because she was in the same business. So why hadn't she heard of any brothel that had burnt down in Kampala?

"And you, whose child did you ab—"

"I didn't abduct any child. I was framed, possibly, by my business rivals. Dearie, dearie me! Hmm. They abducted a rich girl from Entebbe, drugged her and dumped her on my doorstep."

"Do you know them? I mean those who framed you."

"No."

"Well, for me I know who caused my troubles. A woman called Esther. She came to our village promising girls housekeeping jobs in Kampala. But she sold us into a brothel."

"Dearie dearie me."

"I should never have left my siblings alone. I should never have left my brother with such responsibility. He was only fourteen. I should never have believed old Esther. What hurts me most is that the hag, the beast, must still be getting more innocent girls from villages. I wish I could stop her right now. Right right now."

Martina shook her head to shut out Lena's words. She still wondered whether Lena's slavery experience was linked to her Zura Maids establishment. She knew it was possible for brothels in search of cheaper sources of housemaids to unofficially tap into the Zura recruiting network in the countryside. Perhaps Lena was brought by one of her agents and then sold out to some unknown brothel that she later burnt down? But in no way could dearie Lena have been linked to the Zura. If she had been, there wouldn't have been any chance for her to escape being shipped overseas. Dearie Lena was skinny and pretty, with a strong will and a calm spirit; qualities which deserved to be exported very far away from home.

The bell called inmates for the ten o'clock head count. Martina cursed. All prisoners may go rot in hell, all those lowly prisoners she was confined with, and the scum who called themselves wardresses! She wanted nothing to interrupt her moment of deep thought. Her moment of wishing dearie Lena had accepted her help. She planted her hands down for support, and rose to join the rest of the inmates hurrying to the wards.

Inside the ward, the wardress called for silence and began roll calling.

"Present," the inmates answered one after the other.

"Present," Martina said and waited for dearie Lena's voice. For her soft 'present.' She remembered Lena's saddened face, the three lines of frown permanently etched on her forehead. The teary eyes that sat behind beautiful long lashes. The glorious beautiful black skin that concealed prison difficulties and scarcities. She saw the lacerations. The scarred back, shoulders and buttocks: scars speaking of wounds that had been inflicted by her captors when she burnt down their brothel. Her sad and hollow laugh.

Dearie Lena sitting like a dummy, barely opening her mouth.

Martina already missed Lena. She hoped it would rain at night. On several nights, tropical rain drumming on the jail roof soothed her into sleep. That was what she needed. Rain.

CHAPTER TWO

"Stay out of trouble." An elderly guard on sentry duty waved Lena off at the gate.

Lena breathed a sign of relief and walked out of the gate. She turned back and waved at the Luzira Head pasted high at the centre of the pillar on each side of the prison gate. The great gate grated shut on its rusty hinges. She stood outside the walls, her bag on her back and her battered Bible clutched to her chest. She was out of prison. Once again she belonged to the free world.

Her eyes followed a shadow of clouds racing across the Luzira enclosure. It cast itself on the women's section, and then slowly glided over the jacaranda trees that lined the gravel road snaking through the rest of the complex. It came closer, straddling the tall wall that separated the women's prison from the Kampala Remand Section, then inched its way above the Murchison Bay Prison and finally the Upper Prison. She lifted her face to say goodbye to the picturesque clouds presenting against the April blue sky. It was a beautiful day, and she was going to see her siblings.

The winds lifted the dust on the road that connected the prison to the rest of the world. Lena squinted through the dust. Unlike other inmates she had seen leave prison, she had no one to pick her up. To hug her. To congratulate her upon achieving her hard-won freedom. She longed for the warmth of her siblings. If she hurried to the bus terminal in downtown Kampala, she might catch the midday bus to Lira. The ride along the bumpy north-bound route could take at least five hours, so she could reach Lira before dusk and catch a truck to her village. But first she had to find Arthur Mubende, say goodbye to him and thank him for standing with her.

It dawned on her that she would need more money than she had, to travel to Acokara. She would need to eat! She flipped through the Bible and extracted the 20,000 shillings the cashier had given her. This was the same amount old Esther had paid for her when she boarded a bus from Lira to Kampala, three years back. She hoped the fare to Lira hadn't increased since that time. She placed the note back in the Bible. She had no money to pay for a taxi to take her to the bus terminal or to connect from Lira to Acokara.

She considered hurrying back through the prison gate to see Akurut and ask her for some help. Perhaps she could ask Arthur Mubende to help her. She shook her head at that thought. She had to conserve the little remnants of pride the brothel had left her.

The free world ahead of her ceased to be welcoming and instead seemed daunting. She wished she were back in her ward. Then she remembered the money Martina had given her to make calls. She placed her backpack on the sandy road and shoved a hand into it. She rummaged through the contents and pulled out the piece of paper Martina had given her. A fifty thousand shilling note fell from the paper folds. Lena stooped and picked it. On the paper, four names and telephone contacts stared at her. She would make the telephone calls to Martina's people and still remain with enough money for her journey home.

She picked up her bag and hurried forward. She ignored the taxis that sped past, filled with passengers heading to and from Kampala city. Occasionally, a taxi conductor would stick his head through the window behind the co-driver's seat and beckon her to board. She ignored them. She wouldn't dare waste the money she had on a journey that was walkable.

She had heard from inmates that walking to Kampala city from Luzira only took an hour. If she kept up the pace, she would reach the city in time, and then proceed to the Buganda Road Court, where she hoped to find Arthur Mubende before catching a bus to Lira.

She kept glancing over her shoulder to ascertain that she was not being followed; that her prison term had indeed ended and no mistake had been made; that no guard was coming after her to take her back into prison. A day more behind those gates would kill her.

She kept to her left, following the busy traffic towards the city centre. Almost a kilometre into her journey, she realized she was running late. She would not be able to meet Arthur at the courthouse and still be in time for the bus to Lira. She stopped and looked at the stream of cars; the taxis, the Lorries, the Starlets, the Vitzs, and others whose names she couldn't read in the few seconds she glanced at them before they sped on. If she had more money, she would hop onto one of the numerous commuter taxis. Perhaps she would even jump onto a special hire taxi and be at the courthouse in seconds. But…couldn't she just try her luck asking for a lift?

For the fifth time, she flagged down a car; shaking her arm with urgency, hoping that the driver would stop and not speed past her as the others had done. The man swerved to a halt next to her.

"What on earth is your problem?" He shouted at her.

"I am sorry sir, but could you please give me a lift to town?"

she said, looking straight at his face. She saw his eyes run over her; head, chest, legs and down to her dusty feet which peeked out of threadbare black sandals. She felt awkward. "Could you give me a lift, sir?" she dared again.

He looked back at her with a smile that made her wonder whether she was doing the right thing. Fresh fear enveloped her. The man was a stranger, and she did not want to expose herself to danger. She thought of turning away and continuing with her journey on foot but she decided that if he agreed to take her, she would be careful. She would not take the seat next to him. She would take the backseat.

"Unbelievable," he said and threw his hands up in the air then chuckled, "Is wandering on the road and putting motorists at risk your way of asking for a lift, beautiful one?"

She cringed and looked around at a small crowd of motorcycle riders and pedestrians that had started clustering close by. She hadn't noticed she was wandering in the road.

The man noticed her frightened gaze and gestured a dismissive wave at the crowd, "Idlers," he muttered.

"I don't have money." Lena said, ready to walk on if he asked for payment.

"I don't ask women for money." He moved to the front passenger seat and opened the door, ushering her in with his hand. "Just get in."

Lena hesitated, looking at the backseats.

"Get in here."

Still, she hesitated.

"Do you want a lift or not?" he said, a tinge of irritation in his voice.

She got into the car and sat. He shut the door before getting into the driver's seat.

"I'm Fred." He smiled at her, easing the car into mainstream traffic.

"My name is Lena."

"Eh Lena, you speak good English. Where did you go to school?"

"Oyam for my primary and secondary. Gulu for my university," she said and caught him looking at her in the rear-view mirror. He wore a stupid grin on his face. She licked her cracked lips and frowned at the dirt covering her pale blue dress. She wondered if she would be safe with this strange man.

"Nice name. Is that all?"

Lena was quiet.

He scratched his chin. "You know, not for anything really, but to know where I can drop you off or if indeed I can be of any further help."

"I am hoping to take a bus to Lira today," Lena said and immediately regretted giving her details to him.

"Haa! You seem to be in a hurry, beautiful," he said. "Jinja Road is always bad at this time of the day."

Lena looked straight ahead and noticed they were stuck at the tail end of a bumper-to-bumper line of assorted cars. She noticed he had switched off the engine and reclined back in his seat. He was squinting against the thick gas fumes emitted by the different running engines. Ahead, a newspaper vendor hopped from window to window, trying to sell what was no longer news at that time of the day.

The fumes irritated her too. She remembered the fresh lake breeze she had often enjoyed in Luzira and wondered how long they would have to wait in the jam.

"This jam is a bother, beautiful one," the man said. "I will never get to the embassy in time. My father will be mad tonight."

Lena raised her eyebrows at the rear-view mirror.

"You know," he gave her a side look. "My old man loves travelling and is really looking forward to this trip to South Africa tonight."

Silence.

He need not bother her about his family. She wasn't interested.

He looked at his watch and clicked his tongue. "But trust these guys at the embassy.They close at midday on Fridays. That means I have barely fifteen minutes remaining to get there."

The newspaper vendor had caught up with them; he waved a copy at the driver's open window. He was a kid. Maybe thirteen, maybe fifteen. Bloody riots over market ownership and Bodies floating on the Nile screamed on the cover page.

"The boy needs to survive," he said, and reached into his shirt pocket. He selected a five thousand shillings note, gave it to the boy, and then received a copy of the paper, and his balance. He reclined back in his seat and read the newspaper.

Lena was glad he had finally let her be. She pondered the Bodies floating on the Nile headline. It reminded her of the bodies that scattered on the ground during the rebel war back home in Acokara. She was barely seventeen then and in the middle of an intractable war that would twist her life in the wrong direction. As she remembered the ghastly experience, she clutched the Bible in her left underarm and crackled her long, lean fingers in anger. Had it not been for the rebels, her life would be quite different. Even fulfilling. She shivered as she remembered her village-mates of Acokara whom the war had reduced to paupers in a hastily-setup camp for displaced persons.

Over three thousand families were wasting away in a field of crammed rotunda-shaped, grass-thatched mud and wattle huts perched on the edge of the defunct railway sub-station like a burst of mushrooms. Her mother's small hut was sandwiched in the middle of this sprawling settlement. To the east bragged a little cluster of earth bunkers that had been set up by a small group of government soldiers sent to guard the camp. To its west, tens of civilian huts of the new arrivals into camp linked the rest of the camp to the main road that connected Acokara to the rest of Uganda. Lena thought these formed the real frontier to rebel attacks. Their proximity to the main road made a shy shield to the camp and the nearby army detach. It was here that families tied their surviving herds of cattle and goats.

The war still raged on by the time she left. She wondered whether the camp had suffered more attacks from the rebels while she was away. She thought that she would die if she reached the camp only to find that the rebels had come and abducted her little brothers, or taken her sister as a forced wife. "Oh no. God forbid. Why am I even thinking of this? My siblings are all safe in the camp. This journey will soon end and I will be with them again," she mumbled as she covered her mouth to shut out the emotions that were threatening to erupt.

She remembered the few weeks after moving to the camp. Her mother could no longer maintain their small herd of cattle, so she sold the animals and used the money to fund Lena's education in Gulu University. Lena had hoped to get a good job after university education. She dreamt of better housing for her family, housing in safer locations. She longed for that job – the job that would pay her enough to put all her siblings in school. But a displaced persons' camp in a remote village was not the place to look for such a job.

Uncle Okello, her maternal uncle who lived in the never sleeping suburb of Teso Bar in Lira town, and his wife, agreed to let her stay with them as she searched for a job. Lena jumped at the opportunity. "Only temporarily," Uncle Okello's wife had stressed.

Lena packed her bags and relocated to Uncle Okello's.

After a couple of weeks, Uncle Okello's wife gathered the household for a meeting.

"Free board and keep isn't doing Lena any good," she announced, quickly waving off a protest grunt from Uncle Okello. "Going back to the village will be the best way to remind you, Lena, of the urgency of getting a job. In the midst of scarcity, you will work harder to find one."

Lena fell on her knees, pleading to Uncle Okello for a few more months, a few more weeks, a few more days. But no matter how much Uncle Okello pleaded with his wife, she remained unrelenting.

Dejected, Lena returned to Acokara.

For weeks, she remained inside her mother's hut, hiding away from the rest of the camp dwellers, crying out her embarrassment. Later, her mother reminded her that being back with her family was okay. She would help look after her four younger siblings. "We are in a war situation; every extra pair of hands is most welcome. You ought to be grateful for being alive in the first place."

Her mother's words sank deep into her heart. She cast aside her disillusionment, dug a hole in the floor of her mother's hut and buried her degree certificate there. What good was a degree in the middle of war where all one needed was survive?

She socialised with the women and girls in the camp and led

several wood-gathering expeditions into the much-feared forest of Alyec Otoo, a home believed to be for leopards. She dissuaded teenage girls from eloping and counselled mothers against giving their daughters away to soldiers in exchange for food. With time, the ghastly camp conditions were not so bad after all. She felt useful, even happy.

But her happiness was short-lived. The rebels killed her mother.

Lena still remembered the last moments of her mother. On that fateful day, the Lord's Resistance Army rebels attacked their camp and set it on fire. The family gathered outside the burning hut and as they were thanking God for enabling them escape the fire unhurt, their mother said she had forgotten something valuable inside the hut. She ran back inside and never came out. They never found out what it was that their mother died trying to save.

The responsibility of heading a family was abruptly thrust upon her. She didn't elope with a man to Lira or Gulu town as many girls her age did to escape the misery and scarcity of the settlement. She didn't go for the option of a better house, a better life in town. Her father was dead, her mother dead, and there were four siblings to look after. She took the reins of the family in her hands. Together, with the help of other members of the camp, they built a new hut. She had to keep her siblings safe, feed them and bring them up into adulthood.

Then hell came to Acokara in the form of an old woman. Everyone called her old Esther. She came with a bale of old clothes that she donated to the camp children.

Old Esther announced job opportunities. She was looking for girls who could work as domestic servants in Kampala. A job that would pay very well, she had said. Tens of girls immediately enrolled. Desperate to offer her siblings a better life, Lena, too, enrolled despite her brothers' and sister's protests. Okulu, the fourteen year old in whose hands the family would remain, tugged at her arms.

"But Lena, you went to school. Even to university. People who go to university cannot be servant."

"Don't worry. I am actually going because once I am there in Kampala, I can maybe get a better job. And once I get a better job, I will get a good home in a safe place. Then I can come take you all with me to Kampala."

An overwhelming sense of sadness crept into Lena's heart. For the millionth time in three years, she cursed herself for succumbing to the vulnerabilities of poverty. She wondered how her siblings were doing, how they were surviving, and if they had survived. It had been three years since she left. She cursed that time she hugged each of them, promising them a better life in just under a month's time. At that time, she was yet to know that instead of the housekeeping job old Esther had lured her with, she would be forcefully held in a brothel. She was yet to know that she would be turned into a prostitute and end up in jail.

Lena pulled out the photograph of her family, and looked at it again. She thanked God that in the three years of her absence, she had not heard any news of rebel attacks on Acokara camp. But maybe it had been attacked... how would she know when nobody from home ever visited her?

From the corner of her eye, she saw Fred looking at her but she didn't care. In a few hours she would be with her siblings, laughing with them, hugging them, loving them. In a few minutes she would see Arthur Mubende, that good man who believed in her.

A bout of coughing issued from the driver's seat. Lena turned to look at him. He was still looking at her. She realised he had coughed to get her attention. He reminded her of Martina Maa who always coughed to get her attention.

"Excuse me sir," she blurted. "Could I borrow your phone briefly?"

"Anything for you, beautiful one," he said and passed her his cellphone. "Don't mind about the credit. And when you are through with the call, let me know where to drop you off."

"Thanks." Lena received the cellphone and ignored his annoying endearments.

Traffic started moving slowly.

Lena retrieved Martina's piece of paper from the bag, careful not to expose the bag's contents. Mukwano was the first name on the list. She punched the phone buttons, thankful for the strange man's kindness. Two years of being locked away from modernity had robbed her of simple things like making a phonecall. Mukwano's number was not available.

Lena punched in the second number to a Mr. Tony. She noticed Fred was grinning at her in the mirror but he quickly looked out at the darting vehicles moving in the opposite direction. She heard his brief laugh and knew that he was enjoying a poor woman's desperation. Lena worried that she might not have enough time to dial all the numbers. The call was taking too long to connect and Fred was pulling over to the roadside near a building labelled Embassy of South Africa.

She was not familiar with the city and she was not sure of the distance she still had to get to the city centre. She wanted to ask him to give her a little more time with the phone, and to ask him how she could get to the city centre from where they were but he was already jumping out of the car.

"I will be back in a flash," he said. "You may wait in here if you want." He nodded knowingly to the security guard standing outside and disappeared into the embassy perimeter walls through the small security gate at the front.

Alone in the car, Lena regained her confidence. She interrupted the dailing process of the second number before trying the third and then the fourth numbers. All the numbers were not available. She felt sudden nausea and realised how draining her morning had been.

Minutes later, she felt a presence and immediately looked to the right window. Fred, arms folded, stood staring at the contents of Martina's paper which sat open on her laps. She picked and folded it up before stuffing it inside her bag. She in turn glared at him through the open window and said, "A friend of mine needs me to urgently contact her workers. But never mind. Their phones are all off. Thank you sir for your kindness."

He reached for the cellphone. "Always glad to be of any help, beautiful."

"I will now find my way around," she said, and made to open the door.

He entered the car.

"Are you sure you know the way, beautiful?"

"No. But I guess I can always ask."

"Then, may I wait for you to ask?" He laughed.

"Please help me with directions to the Buganda Road Court," she said, letting go of the door.

"Oh ho, beautiful! I thought you were headed to the bus

terminal?"

"Yes sir, but I want to see someone at the court first."

Fred shrugged. "And by the way, I am Fred, not sir. Just stay comfortable. I will take you to Buganda Road Court."

He made a turn and headed for the road opposite the embassy building. "Buganda road is just about two minutes away."

"Thank you."

"Did you say you are from Lira?" Fred asked.

"No. I am from Oyam," Lena said.

"And when did you come to Kampala?"

Lena stayed silent. She assured herself that she didn't have to answer all his questions. She leaned forward as her eyes began to trace familiar buildings. At once she knew they were already on Buganda Road.

"Well, maybe I could see you… say… later in the day?"

Lena's attention was on the court grounds ahead. "You can drop me here, sir. I am going over there." She pointed in the direction of the court.

"I must say I enjoyed your company, and wish you the best. Hope to see you some time. Maybe."

"Thank you so so much, sir." Lena jumped out of the car and hurried away before Fred could say another word.

CHAPTER THREE

Lena strapped her backpack in place, clutched her precious Bible and moved towards the Courthouse. She would find Arthur Mubende, let him know she was all right, thank him again, and then find her way to the bus terminal. She took quick steps to the front porch. The doors to the Court halls were open. She entered through the main entrance. A policeman stood at guard, though he was paying more attention to whatever was happening inside the hall. This was how the guards always behaved during her trial; they put all attention on the actions inside the courthouse rather than on what was happening outside the hall.

She looked to the right, at the rotating glass door for the Court staff and caught sight of a man clad in a cloak. She took uncertain steps past the guard, towards the unfamiliar interior, where the man in a cloak had just disappeared. She paused by the rotating door, wondering whether to just enter or wait outside for anyone who would help her find Arthur Mubende.

She felt a tap on her shoulder and turned to meet a mean-faced court guard, not the one she had just by-passed. She cringed as his stern eyes swept over her.

"Can I help you?" the guard said.

"Y-yes, sir."

She looked around her and saw men and women freely walk in and out of the glass door. Fear crept over her. Why would the guard single her out for questioning?

"I am looking for my attorney. His name is Arthur Mubende."

"Did he tell you to find him here?"

Lena recalled the many times during her trials when Arthur would emerge out of the building to receive her from the prison bus. She would follow him, a prison guard in tow, to one of the rooms at the back of the hall from where he could prepare her for the hearing. He had never told her to find him there, but it was the only place she used to find him.

"Yes, sir."

The guard shook his head and said, "Hmm, there are no offices for lawyers on this building."

"But this is where I always found him. He always came through this door."

"Come; let's check if we will find him."

She followed him through the rotating door to the long, narrow corridor where several heavy ancient wooden doors lined the passage on both sides. It was the same corridor she used to walk through with Arthur during her trial. Several doors to the right, at the back of the hall, a large label stated The Barrister Pool. She stood beside the guard as he tapped on the door of The Barrister Pool before clasping the door handle. He opened the door and led her inside. The room was large, the same size as the Court hall from where she had received her final conviction two years earlier. But this was different, with a single row of files, bookcases, and several swivel stools lining up the entire length of both walls. Eight or nine workstations spread out across the room. Lena wondered whether it was a library.

The place teemed up with smartly dressed young men perusing the large volumes of files and books. Lena became more conscious of her dirty blue dress.There was just no way she could stay there a minute longer. As she turned to leave she heard the guard speak.

"There," the guard said. "Ask those people, but make it fast. We don't let visitors linger in here just like that."

He waited by the door.

Lena approached a young woman perched on the stool nearest the door. No, she did not know anyone called Arthur Mubende. Try the gentleman in blue by the third workstation.

Lena hurried towards the man in blue. He had already noticed her.

"Are you in trouble girl?" He had a high-pitched voice. He pushed away a red volume of The Laws of Uganda, and turned to face Lena.

"No, sir." Lena whispered. Every minute made her more and more conscious of her dusty appearance. "I am looking for Arthur Mubende."

"Are you a relative?"

Lena was disturbed. She wished the man could lower his voice. She didn't need more attention than she already had.

"No, sir."

"Are you a preacher perhaps then?" He tapped the Bible Lena still held glued to her chest. "Trying to convert our Arthur?"

Lena glared at Mr. Blue Shirt.

"No. I neither preach nor convert. He was my attorney two years ago. I just came out of jail. Today." She was running out of patience. She wished Mr. Blue Shirt knew she had siblings to go to.

He ran a studious look at her.

"I am on my way out," he said after a while. "I will check if he is back."

He stood up, relieved the chair of his black jacket and hauled it over his left shoulder. He picked his briefcase and made for the door.

Lena thanked her stars. She said a quick thank you to the guard and followed Mr. Blue Shirt out of the room. In the corridor, Mr. Blue Shirt paused and retracted his cellphone from his coat pocket. He swiped it several times before turning to Lena. "Sorry girl. Your Arthur is not reachable. You might want to try later."

Lena felt her heart tumble with disappointment. Throughout her journey to the Courthouse, it hadn't crossed her mind that Arthur might be away.

"Could I have his telephone contact, please?"

"Of course. And just in case you wish to see him, he will most likely be here tomorrow."

He pulled out a business card from his shirt pocket, scribbled Arthur's telephone number on it and gave it to Lena.

Lena whispered a thank you and hurried out of the building. She really needed to see Arthur and she didn't feel that getting his telephone number was enough consolation.

Outside, she scoured the parking yard for Fred's car. Not that she expected him to be there waiting for her, but she sure needed a lift to rush her to the bus terminal.

Lena felt mixed emotions surging through her; she felt angry, she felt afraid, she felt apprehensive about her reunion with her siblings. And now, more than ever, she needed Arthur. She needed him to prepare her for the reunion with her siblings. She swallowed hard. Somehow she would have to find her way to the bus terminal. Somehow she would have to find her way with her siblings.

She walked outside the gated compound to where a group of bodaboda motorcyclists waited for passengers.

"I would like to go to the bus terminal," she said to one of the cyclists.

"Which one?" Several of the men chorused.

"The one with buses to Lira," she said.

They burst into laughter. She stood rooted to the spot, wondering why they were laughing. She noticed their laughter had attracted other street users who stared at her. She hoped, by heaven, that her appearance was not publicising Freedom Thursday.

"Sister," the one she had approached was quick to say, "That will be Namayiba Park."

"But sister," another quickly chipped in, his chest swelling with authority. "Have you seen any bus on the road today?"

"Bus owners are on strike today. Come, let me take you to the new taxi park. You can use a taxi instead of a bus," yet another suggested, starting the engine of his motorbike in anticipation.

Fifteen minutes later, Lena hopped off the motorbike, dug into her backpack and drew out Martina's money. She paid the fare and was surprised when the cyclist didn't complain about the fifty thousand shillings note when his share was only three thousand shillings. He gave her the balance and rode off.

Inside the new taxi park a warden informed Lena that she was late; the last taxi to Lira had just left. Lena watched him scratch his neck, his green apron upon which the words 'Taxi Warden' were scrawled, fluttering in the early afternoon wind. What she wanted was a miracle. She wanted this man to tell her that the last taxi to Lira was yet to leave.

"Do you think the buses will work tomorrow?"

"Maybe they will. Maybe not." He turned away from her and darted to an elderly woman, thrusting out his dirty hands to help her with the bundle of luggage on her head.

Lena felt the last bits of energy drain from her body. Hers was a tale of losing the two proverbial birds – one in the air and one in the hand. Sweating from the afternoon sun and wondering what she would do with the coming night, Lena stood in the park. She did not know Kampala at all. She had heard about the frightening tales that tricksters, conmen and street children played to strip unsuspecting travellers of valuables. Hunger gnawed at her stomach. She longed for the beans and posho she had left behind in prison.

She scanned the park for as far as her eye could see. Several green-uniformed wardens were scattered throughout the terminal. From afar, it was difficult to identify her warden. He had seemed friendly, even with his bad scratches. If she could find him, she would ask if passengers were allowed to stay in the park overnight. If not, then she would go to the nearest police station and ask to stay the night. As she pondered the possibilities, she found herself longing for the safety of her prison ward.

"Still here?" a voice roared.

She smiled. It was her taxi warden.

"Yes," she said. "I wish to spend the night around here and catch another means in the morning. Is it safe?"

"Well, yes I guess," he said. "Follow me."

They walked to a small waiting shade.

"If you have the means, you can rent a hotel room over there." He pointed to a nearby brick house whose walls closeted the park on one side. "Or stay here until you make up your mind."

**

Lena awoke to the repeated honk of cars. She jumped off the bare floor that had made for a bed and stretched her limbs. She had spent the night among strangers, most of whom had been failed by the striking buses. Many still snored on the jackets they had strewn on the floor of the waiting shade. An elderly couple and three children, probably their grandchildren, were still fast asleep, their bags firmly secured as pillows under their heads. Lena groaned. Here she was on day two of her freedom, but she had slept worse than a prisoner.

She looked at the eastern sky that glowed with the silver tongues of the rising sun, marking her first Friday of freedom. Freedom that would let her see Arthur Mubende and her siblings. Freedom that would let her be Lena Ayugi. She had marked her directions very well; she knew how to get back to the court, and how to get back to the taxi park. Namayiba bus terminal was just opposite the taxi park. She hoped there would be buses. She went back to the courthouse to try her luck once again with finding Arthur Mubende.

Lena gazed at the clock that towered above the building on the court grounds. She had so far used twenty minutes since leaving the taxi park. As she turned into the compound, she saw a prison bus in the parking yard. Male prisoners stepped out, handcuffed in pairs. They matched towards the court hall, prison guards following closely behind them. Civilian men and women hurried along, following the prisoners; probably family members and lawyers. The rotating glass doors of the courthouse endlessly let in streams of suited men and women, some already garbed in their traditional bar cloaks. They all reminded her of Arthur and the times of her trial. She maintained her vantage point in the parking yard and studied their faces as they aimed for the glass doors. She searched for Arthur, for that kind, handsome man that had stood by her during her trial.

No, none of the faces belonged to Arthur. None of the faces

looked familiar.

Wait! Mr. Blue Shirt. She hurried forward, straining her eyes to ascertain the features of a gentleman who had just emerged from the building. He halted a few paces from the glass door and shouted into his phone. Lena immediately identified the high-pitched voice and scuttled towards him.

"Excuse me sir." Lena approached him as he turned to get back into the building. Today he wore a light-blue shirt and dangled his black jacket.

"Ahaa, who do we have here? Coming for our Arthur again, ain't you?" He clicked his tongue.

Lena nodded in affirmative. "Good morning sir."

"I thought I saw him somewhere in court. Did you try calling his number?"

"No."

He swiped the screen open, dialled a number, and then held the phone to his ear. He talked into the phone before turning to her. "What is your name girl?"

"Lena. Lena Ayugi."

He repeated the name down the line.

"He will be here any minute," he said and asked her to follow him to The Barrister pool.

As she waited, she wondered if Arthur would have time for her as he had during her trial. And did he generally treat all his clients that way: give them all the attention that existed in the world?

During her trial, Lena always looked forward to an occasional visit from Arthur. As an attorney, he could come to the prison five days a week if he chose, from Monday to Friday. He could visit any time between nine in the morning to four o'clock in the evening.

But he always chose Monday because that way, he avoided the hustle and bustle of the crowded visiting days.

He was a busy man. A kind man whose handsome face was always bright with what Lena thought was perfect goodness.

She considered him the champion of pro bono services. He had done his best with her case. This she knew because her accusers had wanted a severe punishment for her. But Arthur fought hard to see her sentence reduced to two years. Moreover, he was ready to do more. He was ready to appeal the ruling but she refused. Her accusers were so rich and powerful that she didn't want any more confrontations with them.

The more Lena thought about Arthur Mubende, the more she became apprehensive that he might not pay any attention to her, after all she was no longer his client. She was just like any other free human being who didn't need his attention. But she owed him. Attention or not, she owed him a thank you. And she wanted to see him. Maybe... maybe for the last time, she thought.

CHAPTER FOUR

Arthur Mubende kept his word. In less than fifteen minutes he was welcoming Lena with a firm handshake.

"Congratulations," he said with a broad smile. "It's been two long years. I am proud of you, Lena."

"Thank you, sir." Lena hid her excitement behind a smile.

"It's a pity I got caught up in a web of urgent cases. I had wanted to pick you up from Luzira yesterday. It must have been hard for you."

"Oh, no. You didn't have to pick me up. You've already done a lot for me. I don't even know how I will ever repay you, sir."

Arthur stared at her. Her eyes were misty with emotions. Arthur noticed that Lena's happiness was clouded with sadness. The girl had matured in prison. She had a determined look about her, so obvious that it couldn't be hidden by the mixed emotions. He admired the courage she showed by putting up a brave appearance on the court premises. Many of the ex-convicts he had worked with dreaded stepping back on court grounds ever again. He reached into his shirt pocket for his vibrating cellphone and stepped aside to answer the call.

"Sorry, Lena, it's rather a busy morning for me. Two of my clients are having their cases heard shortly." He flapped the jacket of his cellphone in place. "Can you wait for about half an hour?"

Lena nodded and sat back on her stool.

"It won't take long." Arthur hurried away to the courtroom.

It was not until almost eleven O'clock that he hurried back to Lena. Lena smiled when she saw him dash through the doors. He had been gone for so long.

"Sorry I kept you waiting. The hearings took longer than I had anticipated. We will have an early lunch, and then you can tell me what I can do for you this time," he said.

"I can't say no to lunch because I am really hungry. But I hope I will still be in time to catch a bus to Lira."

"You sure will," Arthur said and led the way out of the building to the parking lot. "The road is clear of jam at this time. We will go to Kati Kati Restaurant, they have very good food."

They had lunch at Kati Kati. He watched her feast on a large grilled tilapia and potato chips. She put the cutlery aside and ravished the fish with her hands, filleting pieces and throwing them one after another in her mouth.

"I can see that they starved you of fish as though you didn't live by the lake shore," he said, smiling at his own joke.

She paused with a chunk in her mouth and smiled. She plucked the fish eye out and added it to the chunk in her mouth.

"This is the most delicious part of the fish," she said.

Arthur nodded. But his smile faded away in an instant.

"Are you okay Arthur?"

"Yes I am. It is just that you remind me of Molly, my sister. We lost her eleven years ago. The eye was Molly's favourite part of fish too."

Lena swallowed the food, raised her face to look at him, and then reached for her bottle of soda. She was drinking a Fanta. She took a sip before resuming meticulous filleting of her fish.

He took a sip from his Highland mineral water bottle and watched her eat. She did not raise her eyes off the plate. He knew that it was probably her first meal since she came out of prison. She had no relatives or friends in Kampala. It was obvious that she couldn't possibly have any money. He had learnt a lot about her during her trial. It was by sheer luck that he had landed on her case. A day earlier or later, the girl would have been at the mercy of Court Prosecutors.

He had discovered she had no known relation except four younger siblings and some equally poor distant relations, in a remote camp for the displaced in northern Uganda. One of the reasons he had singled her out to represent pro bono was that he hoped her case would provide answers to some questions he had been struggling with for a long time. Unfortunately, he had lost the case, and she had gone to prison. Now that she was out, he hoped she could help him.

"I am really glad you came to see me," he said.

"I needed to thank you, sir. But I also wanted to ask you something," she said, her eyes now fixed on him.

"By the way, you can call me Arthur. Go on, ask."

"Anyway it's not that important. I realise I don't have all the time for conversation. I need to leave soon."

"It's okay, go on. Ask."

She pushed the plate of bones aside and went to wash her hands. She came back and took her bottle of soda in her hands. She didn't drink from it.

"Thank you so much Arthur. For everything. Everything. The food was delicious."

"No problem. No problem at all. You wanted to ask me something."

"Why did you decide to help me? I mean I had no money... nothing."

Arthur cocked his head to one side. "Well... but what did my help do anyway? We lost the case. You went to prison."

"No. You helped me. If it were not for you, they would have given me more years perhaps. So I've been wondering why you decided to help me."

"Well, I helped you because I... I have a cause. I once had a sister. My young sister, Molly—"

"Molly. You have mentioned that name before."

"Yes. She was twelve and in primary seven at Buganda Road Primary School. One day, eleven years ago, she did not return from school. We searched everywhere. We are still searching. It was right before that infamous story of child trafficking broke in the news all over the nation. We have only lived with suspicions and speculation. Some said she was abducted and maybe trafficked to God knows where. Some said she was perhaps sacrificed. I chose to believe she is still alive. And I am still searching, and in the process, helping boys and girls who suffer similar fate."

"I am sorry," she rested her arms on the table and cupped her cheeks within her palms.

"Well, there are many young boys and girls out there who need help. A lot of help." Arthur took another sip from his bottle. He didn't think anyone would ever really understand what drove his interest in such cases as Lena's. There simply were too many injustices going on with impunity in the country. He could not just close his eyes and pretend. And since pro bono services were fast becoming lip service in the legal trade, he was always available to offer his help to those who needed it. He knew Lena had told the truth about her enslavement. After she was convicted, he tried to trace for the other fifteen girls she had been enslaved with but they had either escaped or hidden themselves very well.

Or their captors had re-enslaved them and successfully covered the evidence. Now he depended on Lena for any additional information that would probably work to his advantage.

He told Lena of the two newest cases on his file. He had just received the case of two scrawny, ten-year-old boys who had been trafficked and dumped on the street. The boys had been brought into the city from the eastern arid plains of Karamoja seven months back. They were enslaved to beg on the streets of Kampala. Every day they came to the streets to work while their trafficker watched them from a distant vantage point. At the end of the day, they surrendered every coin they received, and if he suspected they had not surrendered all the money, he caned them and denied them their daily pay – a plate of food and a rag to sleep on at night in their tinned house at the fringes of Katwe slum in Kampala.

With pain, Arthur narrated the mysterious disappearance of his sister. How his family searched all the morgues around Kampala for answers. How they engaged the police in a fruitless search that only served to fuel further desperation and anger.

His mother remained inconsolable.

His father remained angry.

The whole family never came to terms with the loss. He vowed to find his sister, to find out what happened to her. He vowed to avenge her suffering. To avenge the suffering of all those unfortunate children wasting away in untold slavery. He wanted answers; he wanted justice.

After the story about traffickers broke out, he started giving pro bono services to victims of kidnap and human trafficking. He had figured out that probably Molly too had been kidnapped and trafficked somewhere. But many years down the road there had been no leads at all. It was so disturbing that more young girls and boys were falling victims.

Lena's case had excited him. Baffled him. Even angered him. How the magistrate could fail to see Lena's innocence shocked him. To Arthur, it had been plain to see the girl was a victim of a crime; she could only escape by burning down the safe house in which she was held. How any magistrate worth his salt could not see that, angered him. But now that she was out, she needed support to live a normal life again.

"So, you see why I am really glad that you came to find me?" he said.

"I understand."

"I needed to come to terms with what could have happened to my sister. I needed to follow up on villains who destroy children's lives. I am yet to conclude that, Lena."

"I see," she said. "And I hope your sister is alive and well and that you will one day find her."

"Hey, it's freedom for you. We must not be mixing your celebration with sad memories."

"I understand, Arthur. The story of Molly is a story of any child. It is my story too. We are not mixing any issues here."

"That is thoughtful of you."

"Thank you."

"You must be eager to go find your siblings."

"I am dying to see my siblings. Thank you so much for the lunch. I sure needed it," she said.

He glanced at his watch. "The bus owners refused to put their buses on the roads yesterday. If they are working today, then there will be so many people waiting to travel. I am sure it will be a struggle to get a seat. You may as well stay and try tomorrow.

And do not worry about your accommodation and transport. I will do what I can."

"Thank you… Arthur, but you have done enough for me already. Besides, I can't take another day without seeing my siblings. It's such a miracle for me that I have seen you. I don't even know how to thank you enough."

"Would you like to press charges on the lady who took you away from your village?"

"Lady? She is not a lady. She is a devil. A monster. That woman Esther? I would strangle her if she crossed my path again."

He laughed. "If you did that, you would loose your freedom again."

"These past three years, I have spent countless days and nights just thinking about her. Thinking about that gang she sold me to. Thinking about all of those filthy men who used me. The hurt. The incarceration. The humiliation."

"I understand, Lena. But let's face it. All those memories should not ruin your possibility of a new start. Personally, I have great respect for you. You are a strong girl."

"I can only say thank you for all the help you gave me. You treated me with utmost respect other inmates only dreamt of."

"I can help you further; I still think those people have to pay." He studied her, hoping that she would agree with him. He had to be careful though. He would definitely understand if she did not want to go through the pains of revenge and revisiting memories. He wondered whether she was thinking about what he had just said. Hopefully she would trust him. She had once fallen prey to a con artist who made a slave of her. He didn't want her to misunderstand him.

"I don't know what to say about that. For now, I really need to see my siblings first. Besides, I don't think I am ready to face that whole process."

"I understand."

"May I ask for a favour for a former inmate of mine?"

"Go on."

"One of my cellmates was an elderly lady, a business woman called Martina Maa. Very wealthy. She has no family, so her business is under the care of her employees who haven't visited her for close to two months. She is worried about her business. She asked me to contact her employees urgently. Someone helped me with a phone and I tried their numbers yesterday, but they were all off. Could you please help me call them again?"

Arthur pulled out his cellphone, unclipped the cover and asked for the contacts. He tried each one of the four numbers, but they were off.

"Hmm. Still off."

"Are they within Kampala?"

"I think so," Lena said.

"Well, if she is that desperate, then you could find out more details from her, like the name of her business, location, office line, then you could go there in person and see them."

Lena stiffened. "Huh, that would mean going back to Luzira!"

"Well, if you think she cannot reach these important people without you, then that may be the only option."

"I think I may have to do that later. I don't know when. But she gave me some money so I think I will go back eventually. Do you know how much it costs to travel by bus to Lira these days? Is it still 20,000 shillings?"

"I am not sure, but it shouldn't be more than 30,000 shillings."

He reached for his wallet from the inside pocket of his coat, opened it, counted out 100,000 shillings and gave it to her.

"Oooh, thank you so much, Arthur. But I can't take the money. Besides you have already helped me more than enough."

"I know that you will need this money. It does not matter if you do not need it now." He placed the notes on the table.

"I will have to pay back this money someday."

"No no, you don't have to pay back anything. Now come, I will drop you close to the bus terminal. I have another meeting in 30 minutes."

He stood up, waited for her to move, and then he followed. He felt he hadn't explained to her exactly what he wanted. He had not spelled it out that he needed her help to investigate the brothel businesses in Kampala, starting with the one where she had been. He could not tell her. And now he was not sure he would ever see her again, but truth was that she needed time off, to be with her siblings and go back to her normal life. He might have to find another way to go about his interests.

CHAPTER FIVE

"I am going to Lira." Lena smiled at the young uniformed tout courting her to board Soul of the Soil, an old rickety bus that plied the north-bound route.

"A seat for this lovely sister," the tout announced and led Lena to the bus conductor issuing tickets at the bus entrance.

"Sister pay here, then board," the conductor said.

Lena paid and took her ticket.

"Go find yourself a seat," the conductor said, stepping aside to let her in.

Lena passed by the tout who was now shouting out to the sea of pedestrians on the nearby sidewalk, "Last bus to Lira! Last bus to Lira! Travel with us, reach safe and sound!"

She entered the bus and headed for the last row, dropping onto the seat with exhaustion from her rush to the terminal after Arthur had dropped her off. Her light blue dress had long lost its colour to dirt and sweat. A middle-aged woman glanced at her, tucking to safety the hem of her not so pretty skirt that had spread out to Lena's seat. Lena relaxed as she wedged her Bible firmly under her left armpit. She thought about Arthur and wondered if he had noticed her shabbiness. If he had, she had not noticed. He was just that good man.

The seats were rickety, rusty and visibly dirty. Lena worried that the bus could easily throw them off the road, especially along the bumpy stretch after Karuma Falls bridge. But the physical state of the bus was the least of her worries.

Her major concern was that the bus would reach Lira late into the night. That meant she wouldn't be able to continue to Acokara camp immediately because there wouldn't be any means of public transport going into the countryside. Where would she spend the night? She thought of Uncle Okello in the never sleeping suburb of Teso Bar in Lira town. If she decided to spend the night at Uncle Okello's, it would take her less than ten minutes from the Lira bus terminal to his home - that is if she hired a bodaboda. But could she afford bodaboda luxury when her siblings were probably living on nothing?

Besides, Uncle Okello's wife was partly responsible for her misfortunes. Lena had never forgiven her for throwing her out of their home years back, when she was desperately hunting for a job in Lira town. When the indomitable Mrs Okello, the ultimate decision maker in Uncle Okello's household, put her feet down, one's fate was forever sealed. No, she wouldn't dare go to their home ever again.

She had heard that Uncle Okello's wife hated poverty and never wanted to mingle with the poor for fear that the thin line separating her from them could blur. To her, poverty was contagious, and she preferred to keep a distance from it. She considered the likes of Lena and her siblings to belong to that unfortunate stock.

Lena looked at the tough woman next to her. The woman immediately returned a glare and moved herself further away from Lena. Lena frowned as she sat back in her seat. The poor, ignorant woman didnot know today was her happiest day in many years. That she had gained her freedom and was on her way to her siblings. What more could one want other than freedom? To be free to decide when to sleep, when to work, or perhaps where to go - that was the ultimate shoreline of freedom.

As the bus engine rattled along Bombo road, Lena found herself going back to the deep thinking mode prison had bred in her. A faint smile played on her lips as she recalled the distant figures of bare-chested fishermen who daily rowed their way into the surrounding islands of Lake Victoria. She would watch them turn into silhouettes against the rising sun as they docked their tiny canoes. The men staggered under the weight of their harvests ready to feed the world with fresh fish. From her vantage point, Lena always watched these fishermen and thought they were some of the happiest people she ever saw. She admired their freedom and longed for her own. The day had finally come. Now she, too, was free. She had earned her freedom and she would use it well. She would decide her next steps at the end of her journey. In Acokara.

She was aware of every passing minute of her journey. The bus was taking ages. Now and again, the bus stopped and passengers alighted to ease themselves in the nearby bushes or to buy snacks from roadside food markets – mostly goat and beef muchomo grilled on long pointed sticks. Roasted cassava and gonja were Lena's favourites, but she fought the urge to spend even a coin. After all, prison had taught her to eat very little.

The journey to Lira took six and a half hours, well into the night. In the bus park, Lena and several other passengers took solace within the safety of the bus for the remainder of the night.

***

Yawns, coughs and shuffling limbs mingled to announce daybreak. Lena, too, awoke from her sleep. She rubbed her eyes and peered through the window at the outside world. In the east, the night sky had already given way to the morning light. Business was already going on in the park.

She stared at cocks caged in stalls, ready for sale. They reminded her of the caged life back in Luzira. She felt pity for the inmates she had left behind.

The long hours of sitting made Lena's body ache as she got up to join other passengers to disembark.

She was on home soil.

She walked directly to the truck stage for Acokara of Otwal Sub County, Oyam district. Her home district. She paid the truck conductor 10,000 shillings.

Up the truck, she perched high atop the bundles of the merchandise that filled the trailer. She barely had space to squeeze herself among the passengers, most of whom were merchants on their way to the weekly market in the massive internally displaced people's camp of Acokara. The merchants carried bales of second hand clothes, groceries and little drums of paraffin, and other items.

The truck bumped along. Lena wedged her legs firmly between the bundles of merchandise. The road meandered forever on the 62 km stretch.

"The road is terrible," a merchant lady seated next to Lena shouted. "This time we may take about two hours to Acokara."

"Yes," a male voice echoed in agreement. "And it was the same last week. This is the most unusual year. The rains are heavy and they have come down early."

"Bad for roads, good for farms," the merchant lady said.

"Not exactly," another lady joined in. "It depends on the road you are talking about. If it is an ill-maintained murram road like this one, I agree. But one can never blame it on the rains."

"Eh! Blame it on your politicians," an elderly man seated at the tail end of the truck yelled. "They eat what is meant for the road one way or the other."

Lena enjoyed the discussion and silently agreed with each of the merchants. The travellers split into two loud groups with each member shouting their opinions without paying attention to who was listening. They gesticulated with their hands to stress their points of view. Lena watched them as she silently prayed for safety on the bad road. Other travellers occasionally threw in jokes to spice up the journey and neutralise the tempers that accompanied the aggressive conversations.

They reached Corner Iceme, a spot known to be constantly under rebel attacks. Everyone went silent. The travellers crossed themselves and moved their lips in silent prayers. The revving engine of the truck sounded so loud in the sudden silence. Lena, too, quickly crossed herself. Like other travellers, she scanned the undergrowth on each side of the road for any unusual movement. Lord, please keep us safe, she mumbled.

After a few kilometres, she began to relax. It was the beauty of the woods, she realised. It caught her attention, dimming the fear that had gripped her from Corner Iceme. Nothing could compare to it. She gawked at the luscious April greenery that renewed the blackened stalks, lucky enough to have survived the dry season fires. The countryside was beautiful. Here and there, wild grapes were bringing forth sweet scented flowers; shrubbery was thickening in places under a neat pattern of canopies that lined the roadside. Squirrels, rabbits and edible rats darted back and forth as butterflies danced around the flowery plants, creating a paradise of its own.

Lena loved this. She wished the beautiful scenery could stretch to Acokara. But how would she be wishing that when she had in her mind the vivid picture of the sprawling encampment which housed thousands of displaced people seeking safety from rebels? How could she even think of associating beauty with Acokara camp?

The little paradise that had existed before the mass displacements had dissipated to give way to rows of low-roofed mud and wattle huts, each housing a family regardless of the size. Forests of odugu, itek, okango and all those robust trunks of trees had been cut down within a fortnight of resettlement and used for building and cooking. Lena remembered how she and her neighbours' daughters would walk far away from the camp to find firewood. Yet it was always dangerous.

She remembered with nostalgia her late Aunt Tino's tale of how leopards once invaded Alyec Otoo forest. The forest stood thick and proud on the eastern fringes of Acokara beyond which peeped the rocks of Omoro in Acholi land. Aunt Tino had endlessly retold the story of how she relocated from Alyec Otoo forest to Acokara village in the early 1980s.

Aunt Tino had built a hut in the fertile forest of Alyec Otoo and lived there alone for many years. One day she returned from a two-week visit and found the smoked limb of a goat she had left over the fireplace in her hut gone. She scrutinized the surrounding and found marks of leopard grips on the wall. The leopard had probably smelt the meat, forced its entry through the air vent that ran round the top of the wall just below the roof. Whichever craftsman had built the hut in his attempt to provide Aunt Tino with a roof had not thought of keeping out intruders. When people heard of the leopards, no one ventured into the forest again for a long time.

Everything changed when villagers were displaced into the camp during the war. People started invading Alyec Otoo forest once again, desperate for materials to build their huts and light their fires. They cut down trees for timber and firewood, slashed the obia to thatch their roofs, and cut the nearby vegetation to create settlements. Lena suspected that Alyec Otoo forest might have been stripped bare in the three years she was away. If so, there would not be any leopards or whatever other animals terrified people. And with the trees and vegetation in Acokara gone there would not be any more butterflies or rabbits or edible rats.

Lena thought about her family. She looked forward to the end of the journey so she could get answers to all of her questions.

CHAPTER SIX

On the third day of her freedom, Lena stood at the eastern entrance of Acokara camp. A skinny old man sat at the doorway of his dinky hut, his hands cupping his chin. She passed a group of youths, drunk and reeking of arege, probably gambling away their scanty belongings on a game of cards. Naked children covered in days of dirt ran around in games of 'catch me' and 'hide and seek', while their mothers with smoke-tinged eyes fanned flames beneath blackened pots of whatever meagre soup they cooked.

She recognized a few people from afar; Abang the youthful widow, whose husband had died in one of the rebel attacks, Maria, the elder whom everyone referred to as grandmother, Ayoo, one of the wives of Muzee Olum, the camp leader. Ayoo busied herself serving arege to a group of men seated by her hut. Many people still had on what was left of the clothes they had worn three years back. Lena blinked back tears of humiliation and walked on.

Further, at the eastern side of the camp the nearby army bunkers sent out a false wink of reassurance as soldiers manned their posts. Lena noticed a sudden ripple of excitement among them as an officer pointed in her direction. She recognised Jaffrey, the sadistic army private, notorious for raping camp girls and bullying civilians. Jaffrey was a skinny, middle-aged monster with a stern-face and bad temper, a brute no better than the rebels themselves.

Lena remembered the grisly complaints of rape and brutality against Jaffrey that had marked the early days of camp life. At first, people reported the cases to the Afande Commandant, hoping that he would punish Jaffrey. They hoped that Jaffrey would be forced out of the camp, to prison perhaps so that women and girls would be safe at last. But the camp circumstances proved everyone wrong and Jaffrey right. They came to learn that Jaffrey had the Afande Commandant in his power but no one knew why that was so.

The Afande Commandant simply waved off families who complained to him about Jaffrey. No, he could not help. He was not able to discipline Jaffrey or any other soldier. To silence the victims and their families Afande Commandant threatened to relocate the army and leave the camp unguarded. Elders in the camp begged the army to stay and offer the camp protection from the rebels.

The victims and their families stopped complaining. The camp leader, Muzee Olum, would even send girls to the bunkers whenever Jaffrey and other soldiers fancied moments of pleasure. That way, both forced and casual sex with soldiers became a part of life. Anything for protection from the rebels. Sometimes the soldiers indulged too much in pursuing girls, leaving the camp to fall to fatal raids of the rebels, such as the one in which Lena had lost her mother.

As she looked at the excited soldiers Lena wondered if Afande Commandant was still the same one who was in charge three years back. She stared at the army detach. And yes, the mean Afande Commandant was still there. He, too, stood craning his neck to look at her.

Jaffrey walked towards Lena. She knew he meant to meet

her. She looked away and hurried further into the camp. She had to find her hut and with it her family.

A young mother with her baby strapped to her back pointed at Lena. "People, that looks like Ayugi," she said as she rushed out towards Lena.

"People! It is Ayugi," she shouted and threw herself at Lena in a bear hug.

Lena hugged her back. It was refreshing to be home with her people. She laughed as a flurry of feet rushed towards her and excited shouts of recognition engulfed the camp. Women ululated. Children shrieked with joy at the rare opportunity of happiness exhibited by their mothers. Lena waved at the young men playing cards. They had paused in their game to share in the rare moment of happiness in their territory.

Jaffrey caught up with her and panted out his "hello" as folks who had surrounded Lena gave him way.

"A happy moment Ayugi," Jaffrey smiled, his gaze roaming over her body.

Lena felt a slimy blob of disgust in her mouth and fought to hold it back. She had only just arrived to a happy welcome. She would not allow Jaffrey to spoil the moment. She held her head high and pouted her mouth. She stayed still to show him she was not afraid of him.

"Remember me?" he said.

"Not worth remembering I think." She sneered. Jaffrey was not any different from the men who had humiliated her and thrown her into jail. She looked past him at the crowd that murmured in surprise at her nerve. She felt sorry for these people who now held back in fear.

"Not worth what?"

"You heard me." Lena spat out. "I have more important things on my mind than recalling faces that do not matter."

The crowd pushed back.

"Come with me!" Jaffrey made to grab her hand.

"Don't you dare!"

"Listen to her!" Jaffrey chuckled, turning to look at the crowd.

"Young woman." Muzee Olum walked forward. "You may have gone to University, and now you are living and working in Kampala, and you might want it your way. Here, we are a peaceful people. We follow instructions. If Afande Jaffrey gives you an order, you you-you obey."

Lena noticed Muzee Olum's limbs shaking with fear. She felt sorry for him. She looked at the ring of people cowering further away and felt a well of tears forming. She blinked and then turned her glare back to Jaffrey who stood waiting for her to follow his orders. She wanted to slap the roguish smile off his face.

"I am warning you; if you touch me, you will have to end up killing me!"

From the corners of her eyes, she saw three soldiers, including the Afande Commandant, walk over.

Jaffrey blinked several times in disbelief. His face quivered with humiliation. He too had noticed the three soldiers.

"How dare you?" he said, pointing a finger at Lena. "No one else speaks when I speak. No one says no to me. No one says no to my orders, you hear?" He raised his hand to lash out at Lena.

"Tsk, tsk!" Lena jerked back, dodging the hand that swung towards her. Jaffrey shot past her and rammed into the three soldiers. The soldiers held him back to stop him from attacking Lena again.

She glared at the Afande Commandant and his men.

"You shouldn't have held him," she shouted. "I am repeating this; whoever touches me will have to kill me first."

She waited for their response and got none.

The camp leader stepped forward, pushing her aside. "This one is just a child Afande Commandant," he said. "She has been away and does not know how to behave here just yet. I will talk to her right away." He trembled.

"No need for that, Muzee Olum," Afande Commandant said.

The crowd whimpered. Mothers grabbed their children's hands and hurried away to the safety of their huts. Lena looked on in desperation as the people cowered away. One thing disturbed her. If Muzee Olum still sent girls and women to Jaffrey's bunker, wasn't her sister Lilly already a victim? She hoped not.

"Get your people organised Muzee Olum," Afande Commandant said. "You are aware we have visitors from the UN coming to the camp soon." He repeatedly jabbed into the air with his right index finger. "They are coming with the army commander. Make sure the camp is clean. And all those who are a shame to this camp; the sick, the malnourished, the crippled and the loud ones like this girl should be kept away as usual."

Lena looked around. Women and children who were fleeing had paused. The youth resumed their game of cards. The elders nearby breathed loud sighs of relief. An elderly woman ran over to Lena and grabbed her hand. It was Maria, one of the camp elders. Maria had been a friend to her family when they still lived in the village.

"Child," she whispered to Lena. "We were all afraid that the Afande Commandant had come to punish you. Thank God he was only talking about the coming visit."

Lena smiled at her.

"Good Lord," Maria said, sweeping her calloused hands over Lena. "You are back my girl". She dangled a rosary in her left hand. "My child, we missed your jolly spirit that used to flash like moonbeams across this camp."

Lena embraced Maria in response.

"Thanks for the welcome, grandmother." She cringed as the tip of Maria's rosary pressed against her spine.

"I don't see my sister and brothers here. Are they okay?"

"All is well with them my child." Maria smiled at her.

Afande Commandant stared at Lena. She stared back. She had stood up against Jaffrey, whom even Afande Commandant feared to reprimand. Lena thought she noticed a smile on his face. She told herself he was smiling at her courage. But the smile was brief, like a wisp of cloud on the face of a hard, cold moon. As he ordered his men out of the camp, Lena let out a laugh. The loser was retreating. She had won the right to the turf.

She moved closer to Muzee Olum.

"Baba, you ought to defend your people better," she said.

His eyes had sunk deeper into their sockets, just as they had for many of the camp inhabitants. Starvation, she thought. His kinky hair was a dense forest of matted bristles. Lena wondered if a comb could find its way through that hair if one tried it. His oversized old checkered black coat concealed the rags that made for a shirt. His pants left one leg bare from the knee to the foot.

"Tell them. Tell the camp to get ready for the visitors," Lena said.

He turned away from Lena to the crowd. "You all heard what Afande Commandant said. Now, if the block leaders can meet me at my compound we will be able to do what Afande wants before the visitors come."

Lena picked her way deeper into the camp to find her hut, pausing occasionally to let Maria catch up with her. She asked about her old friends, and soon discovered who had married, who had been abducted by the LRA, who had escaped, who had died and who had left. Maria told her about the many girls who had escaped the poverty and gone to work in other places.

"Escaped poverty?" Lena halted abruptly and grabbed Maria's hand. "What do you mean escaped poverty? How?"

"Jesus child! They escaped the misery of this camp the same way you did."

"The same way, grandmother?" Lena prayed with all her heart that Maria's story would not have old Esther in it.

"You know Madam Esther, don't you? The same kind old lady who took you to Kampala."

Oh no. Not the old hag! Lena let go of Maria's hand and turned away. "Not her."

"Hmm! God protect us, child. Don't tell me you are jealous!" Maria laughed. "Thanks to her, our girls have found better options of life elsewhere. Haven't you met your sister Lilly there in Kampala?"

"No. Not Lilly!" Lena screamed and covered her mouth with her hand. "Not my Lilly." She turned and faced Maria. Her mouth felt dry as she whispered, "What exactly are you saying grandmother? Kindly repeat what you have just told me."

"Good Lord Ayugi! Child, are you all right?"

"Yes I am all right. What did you say about Lilly?"

"They said she works in the same place with you."

Lena turned and ran off in the direction of her hut.

She stared at the small hut that stood in the middle of the left flank of the camp. The mud-and-wattle walls erected by hers and her brother's hands after the fire in which their mother died, still stood thin and timid on the floor of cow dung. The roof had blackened with age and some layers of thatch had been eaten away in parts.

"Okulu," Lena called out. "Okulu!" She flung aside the thatched door and stooped to look for her siblings.

In a short while her eyes got used to the dimness inside the hut. No Okulu. No Lilly. No Okello. No Odoch. She inspected what little her siblings survived on. Except for the jagged rim of the empty cooking pot – broken perhaps by hands too young to handle heat – and the tattered sisal sacks that made for their beds, the children had tried to keep clean and orderly their meagre belongings; a few plates, saucepans and their mother's old clothes. A stream of light filtered in through a hole in the thatched roof. She immediately resolved to patch up the roof within the day.

"Okulu!" She rushed outside.

"Okulu went to look for firewood this morning." A woman came out of a hut next to Lena's. "Who wants him?"

"Mama Jen, I am Ayugi." Lena dashed towards her. "What about Lilly, what about Okello and Odoch?"

"Ayugi! Welcome home." Mama Jen held her in an embrace.

Maria inched forward, panting.

"Is our Ayugi all right? Child, why did you run away from me like that?"

"I have never seen Lilly since I left here. Did that witch tell you I was working in the same place with her?" Lena looked from Mama Jen to Maria.

"What is wrong? Ayugi, is Lilly in trouble?" Mama Jen asked.

"Mama Jen, you said Okulu went for firewood but what about Okello and Odoch, where are they?"

Mama Jen called one of the boys who were watching them from a distance. "Child, go to the edge of the camp and tell Okello and Odoch that Ayugi is here."

The boy dashed off in excitement.

"Do they still look after sheep and goats, at the camp's edge as before?"

"What else is there for anyone in this miserable confinement, child?" Maria sighed. "At least it keeps the boys busy with something honest."

Lena felt some of the weight in her heart ease out. It was a bit relieving to know that three of her siblings were alright. She sat down on the cowhide Mama Jen spread out for her.

"Come and sit with us, grandmother," Lena said.

She waited until Maria sat down before speaking again, "I haven't seen my sister. I wasn't working in the same place as her. Mama Jen. Grandmother. My sister is in trouble. All the girls that Esther took are in trouble."

"What are you saying, child?" Mama Jen took Lena's hand. "Madam Esther took many girls, including my daughter Jen." She turned to face Maria. "She took your granddaughters too, grandmother. Not so? I mean the twins."

"May heaven protect them." Maria waved her rosary towards Lena. "Tell me about my granddaughters? What kind of trouble are they in?"

Lena noticed the desperation with which the women tried to contain their anxiety.

"Well…" Lena wished she had good news to tell the desperate women. "All I can say for now is that if that Esther woman took your girls, then they are probably in trouble wherever they are. I know because when she took me, she handed me over to …untold slavery. I am only still alive because I dared to escape. And when I escaped, they caught me and threw me in prison."

"Ahhh! Good Lord." Mama Jen suppressed a scream and sat upright.

"Jesus, child! What are you saying Ayugi? My 12-year old twin granddaughters Apio and Acen are my only children. I want them back this minute." Maria stood up, tightened her wrapper again and turned to look around rapidly as though she was afraid of being caught conspiring. Then, beating her chest in grief, she cried.

"Calm down grandmother." Mama Jen implored. "Let us dig more into this before we conclude. Then we can see what to do about it." She helped Maria to sit down on the stiff cowhide.

"As a block leader, I should have done a little more to protect those children," Mama Jen mumbled, her hands cupping her cheeks.

"People trusted old Esther. Anyone could have taken her for granted," Lena said. "Besides, you are just responsible for thirty households. But girls were taken from other blocks as well."

"I hope you are wrong, child," Maria shook her head from side to side. "That woman took hundreds of girls from across the camp in a spate of just two years. Hmm! And, here I am, waiting for life-changing gifts that will never come."

"And to think that she was here only a fortnight ago, hmm!" Mama Jen said. "And, she took with her fifteen of our girls."

Lena felt a shiver shoot down her body. Old Esther was a curse. A curse that took her away from her family three years ago, forced her into sexual slavery, then into jail. Upon gaining her freedom, the curse still lived and haunted the camp.

A flurry of difficult questions crowded her mind. Who

was old Esther really? Why did she choose to come to their community? What had become of the girls? Were they being held in a brothel as she had been? Lena wished she could get answers to those questions. But answers or not, she would find her sister. She would not rest until Esther was arrested and Lilly brought back. She could start by working with Mama Jen and Maria to inform other leaders and parents about what was happening. Esther had to return all the girls.

"What exactly happened to you, Ayugi my child?" Mama Jen, now seated next to Maria, said. "I still don't understand when you say our girls are in trouble."

Lena remained silent. Opening up was expensive. Her story was dirty. Her story was stigmatising. Men and women would compose songs about her. Her siblings would walk around in shame.

"Ayugi?" Maria said, waving her rosary repeatedly at Lena. "Please tell us everything."

Lena sighed.

"You all saw me grow up in the village, saw me struggle in this camp and saw me leave three years ago," Lena began. "If you have just the slightest respect for the way I carried myself throughout the time you have known me, then trust in the little I have to share with you. For the sake of my father's name, I would rather not tell you the details of my enslavement."

Lena hoped that they knew her well. Back in their village, before they fled to the camp, she had been a pacesetter; the most sought after companion by girls who wanted to be in the good books of the village. Mothers praised her to their stubborn young daughters. They would say: 'I wish you could be like Ayugi. I wish you could be hard working like her.'

Back in those days, at the gathering of dusk, the women, youth and children in the camp would gather to listen to tales she retold of her sojourn as a student in Gulu University. They even found humour in the tales she told them about the deeds of Uncle Okello's wife. Many villagers confessed they had fallen victim to her uncle's wife when they visited Lira. At such times many listeners went back in time, recalling with nostalgia their old peacetime, everyday life.

"I don't even know what to say. My mind is so disturbed by the devil Esther."

"But child, what about the money she brought your brother every time she visited?" Maria asked.

"She has been bringing money to my brother? But why?" Lena's shock sent her on her feet.

"Good Lord, Child. You don't know?" Maria said. "Since she took Lilly with my granddaughters one month back, she has since paid one more visit. But before that, each time she visited, she brought some little money for your brothers in your name, and said you would one day visit when your job allowed."

Lena shook her head in disbelief. That Esther woman was very careful. Very cunning. How was it even possible to convince people that the woman was dangerous? A criminal?

"That woman is evil. She even continues to deceive my family like that? She takes us into slavery and uses money as a cover up."

"You are a brave girl, Ayugi. We believe you can find the words to explain to us what is going on. What happened with you?" Maria said. "You remember those years back when the twigs in the nearby woods dwindled, and girls, fearing the rebels and the leopards, stayed away from the deep of the forest? Uhm? Do you remember how you braved it all? How you pioneered fruitful trips into the forest, each time returning laden with beautiful loads of neatly arranged wood on your head? You always were a beautiful challenge to all girls."

"Grandmother, Mama Jen, I will tell you, but I think at this point I need to see my brothers first."

"I am sure they will be here soon," Mama Jen said.

"And, you know I only gave that woman… what's her name again, child?" Maria casually placed her hand on Lena's shoulder.

"Esther?" Lena said.

"Yes, that one. I gave her my granddaughters because I believed they were coming where you were."

"True. We all trusted that woman, grandmother," Mama Jen said.

"They are so dear to me. I am all they had ever since their father was killed and their mother abducted by the rebels. These dry breasts of mine nursed those two from infancy. May the good lord give Ajok everlasting peace in her grave. If it wasn't for her expert hands my grandchildren wouldn't have survived. If only the rebels had not killed her, she would still be here with us."

"Yes grandmother, I remember her too," Lena said. Who would ever forget that midwife, Ajok. And who wasn't aware of the twins' predicament? That was about twelve years ago when people still lived in their beloved villages. When their mother was abducted, the twins were a piteous sight for two days, crying for their milk. Her own sister Lilly was only a couple of months older. Lena had accompanied her mother to Maria's homestead. There, several old women had taken matters into their hands. These women had noticed the danger the twins were in and so they encouraged Maria to wet-nurse her grandchildren. Exhausted with grief, Maria had surrendered her old dry breasts to the village midwife.

Peeping over her mother's shoulder, Lena had muffled a scream as the midwife pulled out a razor blade from her bag and made double cuts into each of old Maria's aging breasts. A teeth-gritting sound had issued from Maria as the midwife went ahead to fill the wounds with a concoction of herbs.

'It will hurt a little so the milk can form,' the midwife had warned. When Lena visited Maria's compound three days later, Maria's tender breasts had started dripping milk into the hungry mouths of her grandbabies

"Those sweet twins, taken too. They are so young. Just like Lilly," Lena said.

"Jesus, my little survivors." Maria grunted and crossed herself. "May God help them survive again, wherever they are."

"Where do you think the girls could be now, Ayugi?" Mama Jen said. "And what can we do to bring them back?"

Lena adjusted to a kneeling position and cleared her throat. "The best guess I have is that your daughters are in Kampala; locked up in a house, and maybe performing terrible deeds you wouldn't want to know about. I think what we need to do now is to inform the camp leader immediately so that we can find that Esther woman. She will have to bring back our girls."

"Let's go now. Now." Mama Jen said, rising to her feet.

"I am afraid I cannot go with you just yet," Lena said. "I must stay right here and wait for my siblings."

"You are right, child," Maria said. "We will go talk to Muzee now."

As Mama Jen lifted her long wrapper and joined Maria to go find the Camp Leader, Lena saw her three brothers rush in from the opposite direction.

Okulu jumped and grabbed her in an embrace. Lena

staggered backwards as she held him. They held each other for a while after which they both let go and stared at each other. Lena was surprised at how grown her brothers were.

By the time she left the camp, Okulu was a quiet, skinny, fourteen-year-old-boy. Now he was taller than her. If he had been better nourished, he would be a sturdy young man. Heading a family of four had rubbed hard on him and his veins stood out thick and sinewy on his arms and forehead. His eyes dug into hers with a mature, thoughtful gaze. Lena dropped her own gaze as tears flowed on her cheeks. She capped her face in her hands before she once again flung herself towards her brother for that longed-for, warm embrace. Her other two brothers, Okello and Odoch, equally skinny and famished, at the ages of nine and seven, rushed in and lumped up the embrace.

"Lena, did you come with Lilly?" Okulu asked, suddenly freeing himself from the embrace.

Okello and Odoch let go of Lena and they all gazed at her as they waited for her answer.

"No. I left her in Kampala."

"How is Lilly?" Odoch said.

"Does she also have a good job? Do you stay with her?" Okello said.

"Ok ok, all of you stop asking questions," Okulu said. He moved closer to his beaming brothers and took their hands. "Lena is tired. And she must be hungry. Let's prepare her some porridge. Do you still like millet porridge, Lena?"

"Ayugi. Ayugi, he is here," Mama Jen said as she entered her compound. Maria and the camp leader came hurrying after her.

"Boys, Muzee Olum needs to speak to your sister now. We won't be long," Mama Jen said.

"We are going to make porridge for Lena," Okulu said.

Lena noticed Okulu's disappointed look and spoke to him. "It's okay, Okulu. Go prepare the porridge. I will come shortly. Make my porridge ve...ry thick. You remember how I always loved it." She wanted to sound playful to reassure her brothers that everything was all right. She had already noticed their confused looks as they stared at the panting women.

She watched Odoch and Okello hop their way to their hut as they chackled in excitement. Okulu remained standing where they left him. His gaze kept shifting from his sister to the two older women and the camp leader.

Lena sat down with Maria on Mama Jen's cowhide. Mama Jen hurried inside her hut and came out with a stool for Muzee Olum. She joined the women on the cowhide.

"Tell him, Ayugi," Mama Jen said. "He wants to hear everything from you."

Lena narrated the bits of her story she was comfortable with.

Muzee Olum stood up. He shook like a tree branch in the wind. "Esther? The Esther we all know? Is that what she has been doing to our children? God help us."

"That's it, Muzee. This child has been her victim, we can't doubt her," Maria said.

"God help us. God help our children. God make them safe wherever they are," Mama Jen said.

"I feel so tired." Muzee Olum dropped back onto his seat. "I am tired of this useless life, this helplessness, this weakness that has been brought upon us!"

"Enough!" Maria waved her rosary at Muzee Olum. "What sort of leader are you? First, you let our girls down, dishing them out to the soldiers in the name of keeping us safe. You almost surrendered this child Ayugi to that good for nothing soldier. And for what? Look how Esther just comes and deceives you until she has wiped the camp of our girls?"

"Grandmother is right," Mama Jen said. "You have to do something about that woman now. You have to do something about our missing girls."

Maria stood up and adjusted her wrapper. "What are we going to do about it, Muzee?"

"After the visitors leave I will inform the people to be careful about anyone asking to take their children away. I will tell them about that woman."

"Yes. But is that it? Will that help bring our daughters back? Is that all we are going to do?" Mama Jen said.

"And what if that woman hears the rumour and stays away from here forever? No. We need to get her arrested very soon," Lena said.

"Father in heaven protect our girls," Maria said.

Everyone looked at the camp leader, his torn shirt fluttering in the wind.

"Listen my mothers. These are strange times. We don't have police here in this camp like we had in our community those good days. The only choice we have is to take our case to Lira, which is miles away."

"This tough child here is a survivor." Mama Jen slipped her hand around Lena's. "She is evidence that can help us against the woman. If we work together we will find that woman and then find our girls."

"I agree," Lena said. She thought about Arthur and swore that if they didn't get help from the police she would turn to him. She could depend on him. "Let's inform the police."

"You are right, child," Muzee Olum said. "But we can't do that now. We have to wait until Monday when we can get transport."

"We can go now. I have some money which we can use," Lena said.

"He is right, Ayugi. We won't have any means until Monday.

On Monday morning, Lena went with some elders to the old market square to catch a ride from the trucks that plied between Lira and IDP camps beyond Acokara. She thought about Martina as she passed some money to the truck driver.

CHAPTER SEVEN

Arthur walked a client to the door of his double-roomed office on the first floor of Kampala House. He looked at his watch. It was approaching lunchtime. Several floors above him, a door banged and a couple of raised voices echoed down. They must be at it again; he shook his head, and smiled. The noisy duo had a reputation for virtually quarrelling over anything and everything: cases, the company car, books, and even women. They probably quarreled with each other in their sleep, Arthur mused.

A gust of wind whizzed past, raising a cloud of dust that twirled towards the office premises.

Arthur hurried back to his office. He had another client waiting, and an urgent trip to Kenya later in the afternoon. The client needed a human rights lawyer for a divorce case, not him. He reached for his phone from the desk crowded with papers and files. He made a call to another law firm and referred the case.

He longed for a cup of strong-brewed Star Coffee before embarking on the journey. He placed a cup on a saucer and prepared coffee. He stood sipping it in appreciation, inhaling the strong aroma of Ugandan coffee.

His phone rang and he received it with reluctance.

"Hello Arthur, it's Lena."

"Oh Lena!" In haste he cleared a spot on his desk where he placed the steaming cup.

"Arthur, I am calling from Lira."

"Ooh. Nice to hear from you. I am glad you reached safely.

How are your siblings?" Arthur said.

Silence.

"Lena, are you there?"

"My little sister Lilly is… that woman who took me…"

Arthur noticed the wobble in her voice. "Oh no! Don't tell me she… did that woman take her too?"

"She did. Arthur."

"I hear you."

"Yes, that woman took many more girls than you can imagine."

"That's so sad. Listen Lena, this is a serious case. But first, you need to report to police."

"We have just come out of the police station in Lira as I speak."

"That's a good start. I mean, reporting the case to police."

"We thought so, but it seems as if… Anyway, I am not sure it will help much. The first response we got from the Criminal Investigation Department here is not helpful at all."

"What did they say?"

"The officer said it is absolutely normal for young girls to be taken as domestic workers. The CID himself has two little girls working in his household. He told us it keeps them fed and housed."

"Unfortunate! Didn't you tell him about your experience? I mean, didn't you tell him the woman sold you into slavery?"

"No. He waved us away before we could even tell him about what happened to me. He was not helpful at all."

"That's absurd indeed. I still think you can talk to him again. Or to someone else he will listen to."

"We are poor people, Arthur. Few people invest their time

in our kind. But even if we are listened to, it is always the usual promise of 'it shall be investigated'. And that is why I need you to help me...help us, if you can, to find that woman."

Arthur kept quiet for several seconds. It was so absurd that these things took place in the open every day and no one bothered. Yes, there were a few laws in place that protected people from exploitation. But they were forgotten laws and law enforcers never took them seriously.

Arthur thought about the numerous prostitutes on the streets in Kampala; some of them had chosen to be there, others were there under duress – working for mafias just like Lena had been. Many times the police attempted a clean-up of prostitutes off the streets but hey never bothered to find out if the girls were willing offenders or victims of trafficking.

Arthur remembered his missing sister Molly.

"Listen Lena, I will need all details surrounding your sister's disappearance," Arthur said. "I will share it with some police officers who deal with such cases here in Kampala, and then we take it from there."

"My thinking is that if we find Esther, she will lead us to our girls. But we can't do anything without police help.Anyway I will let you know what comes up. But if we fail I will come over there and try searching for my sister."

"Ooh, ok. But I think it would be better for you to come when I am back. I have an urgent trip to Kenya this afternoon."

The phone went off abruptly. He tried calling back, several times but the line did not go through. He reached for his coffee.

CHAPTER EIGHT

Lena crossed to Mama Jen's compound along with her brothers. It was a day for receiving rations of posho and beans. As block leader, Mama Jen over saw the distribution of food items that the camp regularly received from World Food Programme. Lena was thankful to Mama Jen for keeping her siblings from starving while she was away. She wished someone had been there to protect Lilly and other children from the devil Esther.

Her efforts to find Esther were in vain. She and other women in the camp had contributed some money which they paid to a man who Muzee Olum said knew Esther's home back in Oyam. Muzee Olum had promised that the man had connections with police and that he would help in finding and arresting Esther. The month of April ended. May came and went, but Esther was yet to be located. The man informed them later that Esther's relatives in Oyam reported that they had not seen her in over ten years and that they didn't know her whereabouts.

Lena wanted to go back to Kampala and search for her sister, but she needed Arthur's help. And Arthur had not contacted her since the last time she talked to him. She had tried to raise him on his cellphone several times in vain. She hoped he had not simply changed his mind or changed his phone line.

She would wait for him. There was nothing she could do. She did not know where she could start the search for Lilly from. She thought about the brothel in Kawempe, where Esther's associates had held her. That obviously was the first place to look for Lilly.

But its owners had jailed her once. They were mighty people. She would just have to wait for Arthur.

When they got to Mama Jen's compound, crowds were already gathered, waiting for food.

"World Food has delivered the food already." Mama Jen announced to the gathering of thirty families that made up her block. "As usual, each family will be given two bags of posho and a bag of beans that should last until the next round in July. Make sure you do not sell them. I repeat, no selling of food."

"Owinyere, loud and clear!" Lena heard herself say as she joined the rest of the gathering amidst the clapping of hands.

Lena knew that Mama Jen was simply wasting words; more than half of the families often sold off their ration as soon as they received it. From the corner of her eyes she saw Rufino, a father of six children, happily cheering Mama Jen.

"Rufino." Mama Jen singled out the middle-aged man.

Lena turned to look at Rufino. His shirt exposed the bulge of his stomach. Rufino had the biggest stomach Lena had ever seen on a man.

"Rufino, please keep your hands off the rations of these families. You saw the consequences of your actions in the last three months. The families starved and some even lost their children."

"Who says I do that?" Rufino shouted and threw his arms wide, exposing the large sweat marks forming in the underarms of his grey shirt. "Ask them." He went on and laughed loud. "Hee, hee, hee!"

Lena did not like the hysterical high-pitched laugh. She fought the urge to block her ears with her hands, not so much to protect her eardrums but to shut out the haunting memories of her childhood. The man laughed like the hyenas that once ruled the nights of her village before the war. The animals would come in packs to enjoy the warmth of the deserted fireplaces as owners slept. She thought their laughter was devilish. They would go, "hee, hee, hee." She would shut out the wild giggles and cuddle closer to her siblings.

"Rufino, indeed you are no good," Maria said, vigorously pointing a stiff finger at the man. "Tell your trader friends that we have nothing to sell this time."

"Yes, yes," several voices chorused in agreement.

"But grandmother, did you sell your things to me? Did I sell your things? Hee, hee, hee!"

Again, Lena struggled to keep her hands away from her ears. Rufino was always the first to sell off his family's share to petty traders from Lira who somehow prowled the camp every time relief items were distributed. He was an aggressive 'middleman' who used his silver tongue to convince starving families to part with their rations.

"Look, Rufino," Mama Jen said. "You may think I am wasting time. But World Food has warned that it will no longer give rations to this camp if we continue selling the food."

"You see? Who will help us now? The rebels made sure we don't farm anymore. This World Food is the only hope we have," Maria said, waving her rosary towards Rufino. "You are no better than the rebels."

"Grandmother, World Food is only warning us," Lena said. "It is only if we ignore their warning that it will no longer give relief to our camp. The camp would then starve to death without them."

She thought about her family land back in the village. Close to fifteen acres, it had gone fallow since they left for the camp. But any attempt at going to farm resulted into death and abductions. The rebels still prowled the bushes.

"You hear, Rufino, you rascal?" Maria wagged a finger at the man. "I don't understand you children of today. Is it the war that changed you, or is it a curse? Can't you see the suffering of your people?"

"Grandmother, I am not anyone's keeper," Rufino said. "Okay, go ahead. Go on and eat posho and beans without salt. Don't yearn for sugar, or for abanjala. All these things need money. And to get money in this camp, you have to part with something that you have; posho and beans of course! Hee, hee, hee!"

"You all heard me," Mama Jen said. "I will blacklist whoever sells the next ration so that his or her family will not be given food next time."

Lena and her brothers hurried along with the rest of the families to the entrance of the camp. They joined the long queues of people watching volunteers offload food items from the WFP trucks. They waited for their share.

The mid-day sun scorched the ground.

"Lena. The ground is too hot now. May we wait by the veranda of Muzee Olum's hut?" Okello asked.

"Yes, go on. I will call you when it's our turn."

She waited for her name to be called out. "Okulu, you may also take a break on Muzee Olum's shade, if you wish."

"Yes." Okulu ran off to join his younger brothers.

"Ayugi Lena," a WFP official read out her name finally.

"Yes." She rushed forward to receive her family ration. Her brothers joined her.

"Okulu and Okello, carry the beans back home while I keep watch of the posho."

She watched her brothers giggle and dangle the 25-kilogram bag of beans between them. They were right to be happy, she smiled. Tonight they would go to bed with full stomachs.

But something was still missing...Lilly.

***

"Go get me salt." She nudged Okulu on the shoulder. Dusk was approaching. Her three brothers sat round the fireplace by the entrance of their hut, watching her stir the mixture of maize flour and hot water to make posho, the maize-meal cake. She had made another fire place upon which beans were boiling in a pot.

"Lena, we heard Orec gossiping about you while we were seated at Muzee Olum's veranda," Okulu said as he handed her the tin of salt she had requested.

"Which Orec?" She put the ladle down to receive the tin from him. She poured a scoop in her hands and added it to the bean soup. The meal was almost ready.

"There are only two Orecs in this camp. This particular one is Muzee Olum's son."

"Oh, the loud one. What was he saying?"

"He was talking bad about you." Okulu looked down at his feet.

"Let me tell her, let me tell her!" Okello jumped up. "He said you escaped from a prison in Kampala." He peered into her downcast eyes.

Lena turned away and looked at Odoch, her youngest brother. He was playing with the smoke as it rose up from his side of the fireplace. He seemed unconcerned about what his older brothers were saying.

"Come sit on my lap, Odoch." She beckoned to him.

She had expected that to happen. In their camp, news travelled fast. Nothing remained a secret for long. The camp leader must have confided in one of his wives, who must have found it hard to keep her mouth sealed. Or could it be Maria, or even Mama Jen? Those three were the only people in the camp who knew part of her story. It had to be Muzee Olum. After all, Orec was his son, the boy's mother was his favourite wife and she was a great gossip.

"Is it true you were in jail, Lena?" Okulu asked, his voice shaky with emotions.

Lena knew he was at the verge of crying. "Now listen," she said. "I have something to tell you, something that should only remain among us, no telling to your friends or anyone else. Promise?"

"We promise," they chorused.

She cleared her voice, uncertain how or where to start. "Does anyone remember old Esther?"

"You mean the nice old lady who took you and Lilly to Kampala?" Okulu asked.

"I like her, I like her!" Odoch said, tugging at the collar of Lena's dress. "She brings me bread." He smiled up at Lena.

"Oh, I am glad." Lena smiled down at him. "But listen, she is not a nice person at all."

"Really? But, she gave us bread," Okello said.

"And money," Okulu said.

"She gave you those things because she did not want you to know that she was a bad person," Lena said. "You see, she took me to Kampala and sold me to some really bad people. Those bad people locked me up in a house and made me work as a slave for months. I only escaped after burning down their house."

"Orec did not say that," Okulu said, his voice breaking.

"Yes, he only said you were in jail," Okello said and started crying.

"If you cry, people will know our secret. Some may make fun of us," she said. "That means I can't tell you the rest of the story now."

"Tell me, tell me." Odoch tugged at her collar. "Me, I won't cry."

"You know, I wasn't quick enough to leave the burning house. They caught me and took me to court. The court then said it was bad to burn down a house. For that, they put me in jail for some time."

"I hate the court!" Odoch again tugged at Lena's collar.

"Me too." Okello nodded. "But, won't they take you back?"

"No no no. No one will take me back."

"What about Lilly? Did Esther take her to bad people also?"

"I... no. Maybe she didn't take her to bad people."

"What if she took her to bad people, Lena?" Okulu heldback tears.

"Don't worry, I will find her," Lena said.

"Soon?"

"Soon."

***

Each morning, Lena woke up and stood at the entrance of their hut to wait for her sister. Sometimes she stood for hours, looking in the direction past Mama Jen's hut, waiting for old Esther to show up again. Because if she came, she would have to bring back Lilly. She would have to pay for all the misery that had happened in Lena's and Lilly's lives and in all the other girls' lives.

Every sunset, Lena stared in the horizon beyond the camp for Lilly and old Esther.

One rather wet and cold morning, Lena was standing at the entrance of her hut when she heard approaching footsteps. She hurried to the back of the hut, her heart opening up to receive Lilly, to love Lilly, to tell Lilly she would never ever leave her again.

It was Muzee Olum, hurrying his way into Lena's compound.

"Baba! You are almost out of breath. What is the problem?"

"Afande Commandant wants to see you," Muzee Olum said. "He says you have an urgent telephone call. He said it's from your friend, the lawyer. Who knows, he might be having some good news."

"An urgent phone call." Lena dashed past Muzee Olum.

Lena snatched the phone from Afande commandant. Her hand shook as she put the phone to her ear. "Hello."

"Hello, it's Arthur," the voice on the other side said.

Lena wept when she heard Arthur's voice.

"Lena."

"Arthur, where have you been? It was absolutely impossible to reach you."

"I mentioned to you that I had an assignment in Kenya. That resulted into another assignment in South Africa. Both assignments turned out really rigorous," Arthur said. "I tried to contact you but it was just not possible. I came back yesterday. I was lucky to have a friend working with World Food Programme here in Kampala. He helped me get the telephone contact of your commandant at the camp."

"Do you have any news about Lilly?" Lena said.

"No, Lena. I have no news about Lilly," Arthur said. "But something came up while I was away, and I need you here. Listen, do you think you can come to Kampala? Do you have transport fare on you?"

"Yes. I can come. In fact I wanted to come weeks ago."

"Do you have transport?"

"I have what I can use. Did you say something came up? About Lilly? Can I come now?"

"If it's possible, then come. Today is Monday – a busy day. But I will pick you from the bus terminal. Just give me a call when you get to Kampala."

CHAPTER NINE

Arthur was happy that he had made a good impression on Lena the last time they had met. He liked her because she reminded him of his sister Molly. Now that they shared something in common, he hoped they would work together and probably investigate the brothel businesses in Kampala. He would definitely help her look for her sister. But first, he needed to find her a place to stay.

He grabbed his cellphone from the office table and dialled the number again. It was busy. He waited a while and tried again. The line didn't go through. He considered having her stay in his apartment. She would sleep in the bedroom, and he would take the sitting room. But he wondered whether that would be appropriate and instead decided to book her into a hostel.

He called the owner of a hostel where he used to stay during the days of law school. The elderly man with whom they had developed a close friendship asked him to go over and check the available rooms.

The room he had visualised was occupied, but there were two other vacant rooms – one downstairs at the rear, and the other in the centre upstairs. He took his time scanning the interior of each and settled for the one downstairs; it had a single, wooden bed with a rather thick Royalfoam mattress. Arthur made a mental note to bring some extra pairs of fresh beddings to the hostel later in the day. A small wooden chair cushioned in bright red with a matching reading table were positioned in the corner. The room was quite modest. Arthur paid for one month and hoped Lena would like it. On his way home he entered a mini-supermarket and picked Vaseline, hair tonic and a small towel for her. He was about to get out when he saw a row of perfumes. He went over and picked one. One of his lawyer friends wore it and he loved the scent. He was not sure though of how she would react. He hoped she would not misinterprete his actions. 'I am only trying to make her life a bit more comfortable,' he thought as he handed over cash at the counter.

At six o'clock that evening, Arthur picked Lena from the bus terminal. He embraced her briefly before driving her to the hostel.

"Take a look around, and let's hear what you have in mind before we get something to eat." Arthur showed Lena around what would now be her home.

"You mean this is where I will be staying?" Lena said. She took a step back. "Arthur, for sure I never even at one point thought about the inconvenience I would cause you. I mean about accommodation."

"What?"

"Honestly I didn't mean to have you go through all the trouble. I should have looked for a place to stay first. But well, truth is I didn't even have anywhere to start from."

"Well, here you are."

Lena looked at the half-drawn, pink curtain. "Oh my God, that's a nice curtain." She admired the arrangement of bottles of cosmetics on the windowsill – hair tonic, Vaseline and a perfume. She picked the perfume bottle and smelt it.

"Prada?" She read on the bottle.

"Yes."

"It smells good. This is so nice of you. Thank you. You are

being too kind."

"Oh, it's nothing," Arthur said. He sat down on the red chair by the bed, and asked Lena to take a seat on the bed.

"Thank you, Arthur. Thank you so much."

"How was the journey?"

"Good. Even short, surprisingly. And yet I was looking forward to getting here. Arthur, Lilly was taken. Esther took my sister."

Arthur stared at her, unsure what to say or do. He thought she would cry, but she stared at him with the same desperate look he remembered so well. During the days of her trial, he had hoped to win the case and change that look in her eyes, but he lost it. And now he was not sure he wanted to commit and tell her he would help her find Lilly.

"So Lilly was taken," he said.

"What if she took her to the same people? What if she took her to pay for my sins? To compensate for the brothel I burnt down, Arthur. What kind of suffering is my baby sister going through? Can you even imagine?" Lena threw her hands wild in the air. "Look, old Esther ferried me to Kampala to them, and old wicked Esther took my little sister too. Arthur, where do you think my sister might be?" She shivered with emotions.

"Your sister is not paying for any sins, Lena. She is not.We must find that woman, Esther."

"We tried, Arthur. We tried. The woman is like a ghost. Remember when I called and told you we were at the police station? Well after that we tried to trace her roots, we paid someone to go to her home village in Oyam. Her family said they hadn't seen her in ten years. Ten full years. We didn't know how to proceed. And of course we didn't have the money to proceed; we didn't get any help from police. Arthur I don't even know what to say because some people in the camp chose not to believe me. Others just kept up hope that their daughters would return. But I know what I went through and I am sure it's what my sister is going through. But I will find her. If only you can help me."

Arthur reached forward and hugged her. She snuggled in the groove of his shoulder. He was glad he could comfort her.

"We are together in this," he said.

"I believe in you, Arthur. I do."

He let go of her, and then dipped his hand in his trouser pocket. He brought out a clean white handkerchief and passed it over to her. "I know how it feels to lose a sister like that."

"Yes. Just like that."

"So how long has she been missing?" He asked as he poured her a glass of water from the mineral water bottle he had brought with him.

Lena took a sip of the water. "Almost three months now."

"I have some friends in the police who could help beyond the usual laxity of the establishment. I am thinking, how about if they do a bit of checks here and there for us first?"

"Police? Well, maybe here in Kampala. But back home, people stopped trusting police."

"I understand. But I have some contacts I can trust," Arthur said.

"Well, if that is the case, then we can go for it. We should. And can they start by checking out the owners of that brothel? Old Esther might have sold my sister to them. And of course they must be having the information about her whereabouts."

"Of course, of course, that will be the first place to check out."

"I think it would be safer if those people did not spot our

familiar faces just yet, because if they do they may disappear perhaps."

"Those guys will do it, and then we will see how to proceed."

"But you could join those police friends of yours. I would trust you instead; I mean to get the right information because you know those brothel people are really bad. They can just buy off your friends."

"Oh no." He laughed. "Don't you remember the trial two years ago? I was your attorney. Remember? People saw me. They saw me go against them."

"Oh yes. You're right. But I am just wondering, how long do you think the police can take to get back to us?"

"Well, I can't answer that for now, but I will ask them to do it as soon as they possibly can. But again, we can't rush them. Let's wait and see what they can do."

"Okay. We will just pray that they are fast enough. It hurts to think that poor Lilly and those girls are going through what I went through. Probably worse. It's been months already. And you know, it really hurts me that many people in the camp didn't even believe me when I told them about Esther. Maybe if we were a bigger team we would have gotten somewhere."

"Hmm. I hear you."

"But let's do our best."

"Lena, tell me about that woman you shared your cell with. What was her name again?"

"Martina. Martina Maa."

"How was she like?"

"A pain. People didn't like her. She is a rich woman. Actually, very rich. So she thought that she ought to be treated special. So the guards hated her as well. She had rich visitors."

"You know what, while I was away, for some reason I remembered a trial and when I pieced information together I thought of that woman you had told me about. That trial was to do with abduction of a girl. There must have been major distractions in my private life at the time, otherwise how come I didn't follow up on such a case?"

"Yes. She told me she was in for abducting a child. But she said she was innocent."

"Well, abduction or not, did she also tell you about the source of her wealth? Did she tell you what she did for a living?"

"Yes. She mentioned a company called Zura Maids. She even offered me a job, which I refused to take."

"She offered you a job?"

"I just did not like the way she looked. For sure I thought she looked like Esther."

Arthur stared at her but his thoughts wondered off to the time of the trial of a woman for child abduction. The story ran in the papers for days. If he could find out the dates, he would start from there. But the question was, how come he did not do that then? How could such a case have slipped his mind? If he remembered well, rumours had it that the woman operated a child-trafficking business. Still the question was how come he did not follow up the case? Was he out of the country? Had he forgotten Molly? God forbid. He would never forget Molly. He would find Molly. One day. Perhaps it was that time when his mother was unwell.

"How I wish you had asked her what kind of job she was offering you. What kind of jobs do they have?"

"I was only thinking about seeing my family. I didn't pay attention to her job offer."

"Well, for now, get some rest." Arthur stood up. "I will come back very early tomorrow morning with someone who can take you around town for some clothes." He handed her some money from his wallet and a Nokia 3310 he had bought from a second-hand phone shop near the bus terminal. "In case of any emergencies, please call me."

"Thank you, but I will take only the phone. I still have some money."

"I am sure you will need the money." He placed the notes on her bed.

She turned the phone over in her palms. "This makes things a bit easier – like calling the numbers Martina gave me, just in case they go through. But if they are still off, I will go tell her now that I am here."

"Somehow you cared about her, I can see."

"I wouldn't call it 'caring'; truth is she gave me some money to pay for the calls. And I used that money."

"I think that is a good idea. When you go to see her, could you follow up and see if her job offer still stands?"

"I am not sure I can leave my brothers alone in the camp and come to work for Martina."

"Anyway, maybe I am just too quick to come to conclusions but already I am thinking that maybe she really was guilty of child abduction. And if she was, where was she taking the girl? How different is she from that Esther woman?" How different was she from that person, or those people who kidnapped Molly?"

"I don't think she does Esther's kind of work."

"And what if she does? Hmm? People in a similar trade will always know each other. What if we woke up in the morning, and found out that the two women know each other?"

"That is scary given that I stayed with her for all that

time. Anyway, she said she was innocent. Maybe she really was innocent."

"Listen, I have been thinking that Molly could have faced a similar situation like that girl your Martina abducted. Only that Molly didn't get as lucky."

"Hmm."

"It's getting late now. I should be going."

"Don't go yet. Let me first try calling these numbers again." Lena dug out Martina's list of contacts and dialled one at a time. Arthur had already activated the line. "Still off. All of them. I will try them again tomorrow. If they are still off, I think I will eventually go back and update Martina."

***

Refreshed and rested, Lena sat on the chair by the reading table. She thought of Arthur's quick restless feet and wondered how he still managed to plant them firmly on the ground. From his beautiful bony features and straight accent, she thought that he must be from far up north. The memory of his firm baritone voice assured her all would be well. For a moment, she wondered what his private life was like. What his family was like. And whether he had a wife?

She picked up her battered Bible and removed its precious cargo, her family. She lovingly traced each of their faces, pausing for a long time on Lilly's. She dusted the windowsill and placed the picture on it. "We will find you, Lilly."

She picked up the money and put it in her purse, then she slumped back on the bed. She thought about what Arthur had said about Martina. The possibility of Martina being in the same trade as Esther was scary, but it also gave her some hope that she and

Arthur might be close to finding out and exposing the businesses that enslaved girls. Finding Esther. Finding Lilly, finding Molly and the other girls.

She decided she would go back to Luzira the following day to see Martina, give her feedback, and then concentrate on her mission. She hoped she would find wardress Akurut on duty.

Wardress Akurut was the only friend she had made while in prison. She remembered her first few weeks of jail. She had continuously retched from the knowledge that their food was fetched in plastic basins, the kind they used for taking a bath back home. Her body had quickly wasted, her skin hurt from the slightest pressure. At first, she could not manage any hard work. The Katikiro of the ward suggested to senior Wardress Akurut that Lena be taken to the sick bay. After a week, Wardress Akurut made her a transporter. For weeks she hauled food from the kitchen to her ward in a yellow plastic basin. Her transporter role was a form of treatment – psychotherapeutically beneficial, enabling her get used to eating the food in basins. A couple of days later, her stomach could easily retain its contents. Indeed Akurut made her prison time bearable.

Lena closed her eyes and let her mind dwell on the guided shopping that Arthur had promised her. She had not said no. Surely, she needed a few nice outfits.

CHAPTER TEN

"My prayers have been answered," Lena said.

Senior Wardress Akurut lifted her eyes off the desk where she had been busy cleaning the only computer in the office. Her flabby mouth stayed fixed in a whistling pout as she stared at the visitor. "Lena!" She ran the cloth over the computer in two swipes, and then dropped it on the desk. "What are you doing here?"

"I prayed to God that you would be the one on duty."

"What a nice surprise! I am happy to see you." Officer Akurut smiled. She extended her coarse, thick, right palm to Lena.

Lena clasped Akurut's hand and lingered on it a while. "I am the lucky one to have found you, Afande."

"You look good." Akurut's smile widened. The girl was barely a few months out of prison and she already had a fresh look. A city-girl look; high-neck blue sweater complimented by a faded-blue skirt and a pair of Masai sandals. She even wore a perfume that smelt like flowers.

"Now tell me, do you prefer to come back to us?" Akurut led Lena to the rickety old bench for visitors. She loved such jokes. But sometimes she choked on these jokes because some ex-inmates with nowhere to go opted to remain in the facility. Akurut remembered the countless ex-convicts who confessed to committing crimes immediately after prison so they could be re-convicted and returned to prison.

"It's Martina. I need to see her."

Akurut stood back and glowered at Lena. Really? Lena was here to see the dearie Martina Maa? What did the two have in common? Martina was a violent, tired, demanding, upper-class old whore who, Akurut suspected, was probably sometimes high on drugs.

"You've come to see Martina," Akurut said, walking back behind the desk. She hoped Martina had not introduced Lena to drugs. She hoped Lena wasn't here to bring Martina some. It still puzzled her how the dearie old woman received the drugs. She often checked Martina's visitors. When she wasn't on duty, other staff did. So far no one had discovered anything suspicious.

"And what on earth might you want with that woman?"

"I left a valuable with her. Simply forgot to pick it when I left," Lena said.

Drugs, thought Akurut. With Lena in the picture, things might get easier. If Lena was a link, this was a chance to burst Martina's supply source. This could be a major stepping-stone to the top. "Okay. And what might that be?"

"Just some women stuff. My under garments." Lena was smiling.

Akurut laughed and wagged a finger at Lena, who laughed along.

"Ok. Lena, you will see her," Akurut said, promising herself to bait Lena with time.

***

Martina screamed when she saw Lena. Lena looked good and had come back to see her. The fruits of freedom were loud and clear with Lena's clothing. Prada, Martina's favourite spray, gave out a soft pleasant waft through the room. Her nostalgia for the free world deepened. "Come here, dearie." She reached for Lena and embraced her.

"Fifteen minutes on the dot. Mark that!" Akurut turned away and locked the two women in the room.

"Dearie, now tell me what you have been up to," Martina said. They had little time. She knew they needed to use it well.

"The list you gave me, remember?" Lena said.

"So I do, dearie. I haven't received a visit from them though. Perhaps you can explain?" Martina folded her arms and sat down by Lena.

"The telephone numbers are off, Martina," Lena said. "All of them."

"That can't be dearie. Let's have a look," Martina inched closer and grabbed the piece of paper from Lena.

"If I had a phone, we would try and call these numbers again," Lena said, almost to herself.

"I need a phone dearie; God knows I need a phone!" Martina grew distraught. Stress lines furrowed on her ageing forehead and drips of sweat ran down her face. She looked at Lena and tried to say something. But her mouth was dry and her tongue heavy. Seconds later, her hands went limp. She tried to hold onto the bench but gave up. She felt her body hit the cold, hard floor. Then darkness...

***

"Afande, Afande!" Lena screamed and repeatedly hit the door with her fist.

Akurut jerked her head and opened the door, fearing for Lena. She stared at the two women. The old dearie was lying helpless on the floor, Lena by her side. "Oh my God. What has happened now?"

"Help me, Afande," Lena said, her hands shaking. "Please help me. She just fell by herself. I didn't do anything to her. She just fell."

Akurut hurried to the two women and bent down to feel Martina's pulse. She had been leaning on the door with her ear to the keyhole. She made a quick scan of the room for any evidence of drugs.

"We were conversing, and she just fainted," Lena explained to Akurut.

"Just like that?"

"Just like that Afande. I think she is just ill. She needs to see the nurse. Don't you think?" Lena wiped sweat off her brows with the back of her right hand.

"I will just call for help so we can take her to the sick bay right away. Keep an eye on her," Akurut said. She hurried back to the office and returned with a cup of water. "Until help comes, let's have the miracle of cold water."

"Miracle of cold water?"

Akurut poured some water on Martina's forehead.

Martina turned her head from side to side, and then she opened her eyes. "Oh dearie!" She planted her hands on the floor as she struggled to get up.

"Martina, you are not well," Lena said.

"I am ok dearie. I am ok"

"Good. You can now walk by yourself to the sick bay." Akurut put away the water.

"No need, Afande, dearie," Martina said, leaning heavily on Lena and sitting upright. "I just had a slight fall – that was all."

Akurut studied Martina for a while. She turned to Lena and said, "Next time, try and minimize the noise. You almost unsettled the whole place with your bangs and screams, Lena."

"Sorry Afande."

Akurut turned to leave. "By the way, Lena, I am afraid your time is up."

"What?" Martina sat up. "But dearie, we have barely spoken. We still have five minutes of the time you gave us. Tell her dearie; tell Afande we have five more minutes left."

Disgust clouded Akurut's face. "No objections. It's an order."

"Please give us at least five minutes, Afande?" Lena requested.

"We must stick with the law, Lena," Akurut said. "If I add you five minutes, next time it will be ten, then thirty... Next, all other inmates will want more time." She looked at her wristwatch.

"Please Afande. Just this once." Lena raised her index finger in emphasis.

"Five minutes on the dot!" Akurut walked away and banged the steel door shut behind her.

***

"C'mon. Tell me. What do you make of this?" Martina said, edging closer to Lena. Martina noticed her fragrance again. Prada was an expensive perfume, and Lena, could not have prioritised it over other necessities only two months out of prison. Martina studied Lena through the corners of her eyes. Had the girl found her wretched managers? Had they lured her to join in their conspiracy to deprive her of her estate? Could dearie, dearie Lena be pretending?

Martina thought about many possibilities. Her anger mounted. She had built her empire from nothing. She had endured hardships. Now she had fifteen years behind bars in a dingy, filthy cell. And her damn managers were not helping. Instead, they had gone silent. No news, no visits, no updates about her firms. And here was Lena telling her that all their phones were off. She prayed they were not up to no good. They should know that she still lived, that she was still capable of hitting back if they dared stab her in the back.

"There is something wrong. I can feel it in my blood," Martina said. "My company managers have taken advantage of my confinement in prison and it seems I am losing everything. Damn them. Damn them all!"

Lena remained silent.

"Pretenders. You sweat all your life and even those you trust take advantage of your absence to grab your harvest," Martina said, her voice breaking. "Or else why would their phones be off? I am sure they have changed their phone numbers exactly for that reason. My fortune worth $20 million in the hands of savage thieves! You simply can't trust anyone. Anyone. Give me the contacts! I shouldn't have given them out in the first place." Martina grabbed the paper from Lena. "You see, I have always trusted people. But I get stabbed in the back."

Lena stared at Martina, a look of confusion on her face.

"Can I ask one more favour from you?" Martina said after a long silence.

"What?"

"Can I trust you?"

"Of course you can."

"Since the phone contacts are not helping. Can you help me find Mukwano or Tony at their homes?"

"I am not sure I can help with that, Martina."

"Please, Lena dearie. I have no one else."

"Martina, I don't think I will have the time. I am in Kampala to find my sister." Lena's eyes glistened with grief. "My sister Lilly fell in the same trap as me. I told you about that woman, Esther. She went back to Acokara three months ago and took away more girls. Including my sister."

"No, not your sister, my dearie!" Martina covered her mouth with the back of her right hand. She hoped the said Esther was not one of the suppliers of the Zura. But who knew? The Zura Maids business had a large network. She would try to find out – that is, if her managers ever showed up. She turned to face Lena. "I am sorry to hear that, dearie."

"God help me. I need to find my sister. I will find her whatever it takes." Lena jumped off the seat, unsuccessfully blinking back tears. "I should go, Martina. At least I have given you the feedback."

Martina hid a smile. At this point, she knew Lena would not turn her down. "You see, my dearie, I know Kampala quite a bit and I know lots of people as well. And so do my managers. It could take just a word from me and they would turn Kampala upside down to find your sister."

Lena sat back. "Really?"

"When my men come to me, I can assign them the job immediately. But that, dearie, is up to you. I mean if you can find them and tell them to come here."

"And where can I find them?"

"At their homes, my dearie. You won't fail to find them. Their homes are adjacent to each other. I mean Mukwano and Tony," Martina said. She quickly unfolded the paper Lena had given her and wrote down the directions to her manager's home. She gave the paper back to Lena. "There, directions to Mukwano's house. Tony's is just opposite Mukwano's."

Lena put the piece of paper in her bag.

Akurut unlocked the door. "Time's up."

"Your sister, Lilly, dearie" Martina ignored Officer Akurut's announcement. "Soon as my managers show up here, consider the job done – looking for her."

"Thank you Martina." Lena nodded several times and clasped her hands together. "And Martina, I am sorry I used some of the money you gave me to cover some personal expenses."

"What money, dearie?"

"The 50,000 shillings you gave me for the phone calls."

"Oh that. Just find Mukwano or Tony first." Martina waved her off. With her managers behaving suspiciously, she needed all the friendship she could get. Lena was her best bet for now. Maybe the girl could be trusted after all.

Martina watched Lena walk out of the room, leaving Akurut behind. She ignored Akurut and looked straight at the door. She didn't care what the dimwits did for a living. But this one, Akurut, was worse than any she had ever met. The woman always interfered in other people's business! Martina rose up. She had to calm down, she had to be tolerant. The dimwit could deny her any meetings with the managers if they come. She clenched her teeth and finally said, "My dear Afande, thank you for the extra time you gave Lena and I."

"Time is up lady," Akurut said. "I need to lock."

Martina glared at Akurut. Brushing against her by the door, she stormed out and made straight for her ward.

CHAPTER ELEVEN

Akurut woke up to the crowing of roosters in the neighbourhood. She felt for her mobile phone by the pillow. She pressed a button and blinked at the screen. It was a few minutes to six o'clock in the morning; Wednesday morning, another day for visitors to the facility. Inmates would have to clean up early enough so that they would not get in the way of visitors. She had forgotten to set her alarm for five thirty, and was now late.

She scrambled out of bed and shuffled around to freshen up and don her staff uniform. In the neighbourhood, other wardresses threw open windows and doors in readiness for the new day. Akurut was certain the noise could be heard across the prison compound. After all, a low wall of concrete was all that separated their line of tin huts from the prisoners' wards.

She slipped into her uniform and tied her belt just below the breastline. She smeared vaseline on her face, grabbed the red lipstick from her make-up container, and applied it without looking in the mirror. She picked the mirror and the eyebrow pencil, but put them back on the table and then rubbed off the lipstick with the back of her hand. She picked her batch of keys from the bedside table and stepped outside. She marvelled at the faint glow to the east, which along with the roosters gradually announced daybreak. Another day of exhausting routine.

She put on a shawl to protect herself from the chill of Lake Victoria, and hurried through the small gate in the low wall towards the prison wards. She touched her face. It was starting to go numb. She slapped both cheeks several times to wake them up.

The facility still slept.

Damn those wretched souls, she mumbled. She trudged to the old mango tree in the centre of the compound and flashed a torch to one of the lower branches. The old car steel wheel rim sat there, cold to the touch. A long thin rod, crooked with years of rough handling, nestled in its groove. With quick movements, she lifted the rod and repeatedly hammered it against the car rim.

Gong, gong, gong.

She rushed towards the wards, rod in hand. She rattled the chain lock on one of the doors before unlocking it.

"Up, up, up…up!" Akurut said, hitting the rod against the steel door of the ward. She walked along the corridor peering from left to right at the sleepy human forms dragging themselves from bed. One by one, they sat up.

She peered into their faces. She was disgusted at the smutty eyelids still heavy with sleep.

"Morning Afande…morning Afande." Each of the inmates waved.

Martina raised her head. The heavy sneer on her face unsettled Akurut. Lena's departure two months back had left Martina's ward with nine inmates. The old hag had placed Lena's mattress on top of hers and fitted them in a corner where she sat, her legs drawn up in a hunch. She cupped her face in the hollows of her palms, resting the weight of her elbows on her raised knees. She draped a black, mournful shawl on her back.

Akurut knew all the inmates. Somehow she found their tales entertaining. Listening to the stories of their past kept her going, kept her glued to one of the world's most trying jobs –

keeping criminals, learning to speak and laugh with criminals, and breaking up bloody fights and bloody plots. But the dearie old hag was a handful!

When Martina was still a fresh inmate, she had been full of herself. Unlike other inmates, she rarely sat on the floor of her ward. Her highness perhaps thought she was too good to sit on the bare floor. Instead, the dearie old hag loved pacing all over the ward, even during roll calls. She probably thought her type could never last a day, a week, a month, let alone a year in jail. She flouted herself all over the place, and set her own terms of jail routine.

Martina had a nasty temper, Akurut recalled. Whenever Akurut banged the ward door, Martina would stand on her toes and scream: 'Stop the noise, you lowlife! You pig... you shallow head.' Akurut had made it a point to memorise all the names Martina awarded her on such occasions; toad, frog, dog, monkey, donkey, thing, lost head, and mole.

Akurut felt unhappy that Martina had to share the ward with other inmates. The dearie old hag deserved misery and worse. If she were alone in a single room, Akurut would have loved to bang her door every morning and beat some sense into her head. But with all the other inmates, some as amiable as Lena, she restrained herself.

"Hey, you have an extra mattress?"Akurut asked.

"That was Lena's mattress," an inmate said.

"I see." Akurut nodded. "That means we have room for another inmate." It annoyed her that Martina enjoyed the luxury of space meant for two all by herself. Greed. Pure greed. Someone must take up Lena's space, Akurut swore. "I will add an inmate to this ward soon."

Akurut threw one more glance at the angry woman. She thought of the unrepentant bully, Arumo, who was on death row, and regretted that Martina was not qualified to share a room with a condemned tyrant. A horrible roommate would put Martina in her place. Akurut resolved to find one. She knew officer Ameri, the old jolly drunk from Lango, would help to identify suitable ones.

She moved on to the next ward. Of the thirty inmates, only three were still in their beds. The rest were already up and arranging their beds. As usual, she spared them the steely noise. They were a happy lot, and she enjoyed exchanging pleasantries with them. Meg, the scrawny middle-aged woman, yawned. Several other women did the same.

"Hey women! Are we okay today?" Akurut called out.

"All thirty of us are in, so no problem Afande," Meg said.

"Good." Akurut nodded and flipped open a file to begin the roll call. She had just finalised the roll call when she realised that there was a possibility of a missing person. "Katikiro," she called out. "Katikiro! You have a missing person and you have not reported!" Her heart was almost jumping out when Katikkiro responded.

"Afande. Sorry Afande, Grace is very ill. She has a bad stomach and is lying by the toilet over there."

"What?" Akurut hurried outside, the Katikkiro hurrying behind her. "What do you mean she is outside? How did she get out?"

"Just now, Afande. She rushed out just as you were entering. She was badly off."

"How did she pass by me? She better be by the toilet, Katikkiro."

"She is, Afande. She can't escape."

They rounded the corner of the ward and hurried towards the block of pit latrines behind the wards. They found the inmate on her side, teeth clenched and hands clutching her stomach. Akurut sighed, as her heart settled back in its place.

"She looks weak," Akurut said. "How long has she been sick?"

"She fell ill last night, Afande."

"Get some help and take her to the sick bay."

"Yes Afande."

Akurut watched the Katikiro and two other inmates carry the patient to the clinic. She had worked for eight years in this sprawling place of moles. It was trying, but she had given her whole life to the job, and she was proud of her achievement. Her superiors had already rewarded her hard work with a higher rank – from wardress to senior wardress. Not that she was in love with the job, but she needed it. Maybe with a better rank, she could even learn to love it.

Just like other staffers, she reported for duty twice every twenty-four hours for six-hour shifts. Every day, she followed mandatory routines; she ran up and down the narrow corridors of her block, banging on the heavy iron doors of the wards. She did it every morning at six and again at mid-day, just before handing over to other staffers. She was not friends with early morning routines, but she enjoyed the mid-day ones.

She walked away towards the reception. She felt her skin sticky with sweat. She chuckled. She had not realised how the missing-inmate moment had sent her sweating profusely. The weather was changing. She wondered whether it would rain soon. She loved tropical rains but not at an awkward hour when breakfast was waiting across the compound. Worse still, the humidity that preceded the rain was unbearable.

Akurut checked her watch. Visitors had the whole day. Some came in the morning, others preferred the afternoon. She knew that in two hours, the gates of the facility would be teaming with friends and relatives of inmates. She wondered if Martina's rich friends would turn up. She would watch out, as she always did, because who knew, the dearie old whore could get a supply of drugs. But the dearie's visitors hadn't been coming of late. They had missed several weeks already. She wondered whether Lena might return. She didn't want to believe that Lena could be in any way linked to Martina's drug issue – that was if Martina had any drug issue. Anything was possible. Akurut was ready to wait and see. She went to find Ameri.

"Officer Ameri, I am glad you are here already," Akurut said.

"What are you doing here at this time?"

"I need a favour," Akurut said. "A replacement for Lena."

"No new inmate yet, I am afraid."

"I would not mind one of the old ones," Akurut said. "Particularly, a bitchy one would do."

"That won't be a problem." Ameri laughed. "But I have an emergency at home, and no one to sit in for me."

"Again?" Akurut shook her head. "Only last week, I sat in for you twice." Everyone in the facility knew Ameri was a perpetual drunkard. Ameri would certainly race off to her favourite bar as soon as she left her desk.

"This is different, officer Akurut – you want a favour, I want a favour." Ameri nodded.

"Ok. Let's do it."

Akurut waited as Ameri scanned through the files and lingered a while on the name Meg. Akurut smiled. She was fond of Meg, a real talkative woman. Meg would keep the combative dearie old hag entertained till she dropped dead.

"Wise choice." Ameri laughed.

"Do it," Akurut said. "I will be back after lunch. Just make the transfer now."

CHAPTER TWELVE

Lena stood by the gate of house K15, waiting for someone to answer the bell. She frowned at the crooked reflection of her picture on the shiny black gate which stood tall and domineering. She thought it was almost twice her height. The gate and the perimeter wall hid what was inside from her curious eye. It was a posh, quiet neighbourhood separated from the slummy suburb of Kamuca by a golf course lined with eucalyptus trees.

Lena wondered how far Arthur had gone with the people who were to help them check with the Kawempe brothel. She had called and told him she was heading to the address Martina had given her. She had not told him that Martina had promised to help with Lilly. She didn't have enough telephone credit, and he hadn't called back. He was probably busy. She would update him later. She couldn't wait. Martina's proposal might help her find Lilly. The woman was wealthy, and wealthy people had connections. She prayed to God that Lilly and the other girls were somewhere safe.

The afternoon sun shone without mercy. She moved closer to the gate for the comfort of the small shadow the high gate had begun to throw. She had the piece of paper with Martina's description of the place: A kilometre after the Golf Course, look out for a big black shiny gate to your left. The only one that will reflect your image – you can't miss it.

She heard a dog bark from within the walls. The barks drew

closer. The barks turned into growls. Startled, Lena stepped away from the gate. She wanted to walk away, to stay safe from the dog. But what about Lilly? If Martina's men could help locate Lilly, she had to be brave and face the barking dog. She stepped back towards the gate hoping that the dog was on a leash. She was doing this for Lilly. She steeled herself to face the unknown.

The small gate grated on its hinges and let out a uniformed security guard.

"What you want, girl?" The guard asked.

Lena stared at the bulldog the guard restrained by a short chain fastened to its neck. She moved a step back as it restlessly leapt, and growled. "Please hold it back, sir," she said. Dogs had never been her favourite.

"I say what you want?" The guard shoved an index finger at her.

"I have a message for Mr. Mukwano."

The guard raised his hand to the cap on his head. He tipped it, moving it further back from his face. He gripped the dog chain tighter and sneered at Lena.

"You? Who you be?"

"I have a message for him. From Martina."

"Martina?" The guard held back the dog so Lena could enter. "You. Go wait me." He pointed to a set of lawn chairs neatly adorning a small cheerful garden by the gate. "I go tell him."

Lena smiled at his effort with English. She looked at the red-tiled, single-storied house, with a swimming pool on its left and a tennis court on the right. She was looking at money itself.

Seconds later, the guard rushed back, almost tripping over his feet. "You! Give message me!"

"It is verbal," Lena said.

"I take verbal."

She sensed Mukwano was too busy. Perhaps he didn't encourage random visitors. Maybe she could have made a prior appointment. Should she get out and go to Tony's house instead? She scratched her brain for a good reason that would perhaps make Mukwano want to see her. She couldn't find any.

"Tell him Martina is very ill," she said. "She wants to see him immediately for some business. Martina ill. Sick. Not well."

"I tell him."

A few minutes later, Lena saw a tall, burly, dark-skinned man appear from the house. A white sweatshirt and pair of shorts hugged his mahogany skin. She noticed he had a limp in the left leg. She wondered whether he got it from childhood or whether it had a nasty background. She jerked closer to the edge of her seat and sat straight.

A middle-aged woman with a white apron appeared from the left of the house, and lowered a tray with two glasses and a glass jug filled with juice.

"Thanks Ruta," Mukwano said and waved the lady off. He filled one glass for Lena.

"Now tell me, girl. In what capacity do you know Martina?" His tongue twisted words flawlessly. He had a strong deep voice. He sure looked like one who could know his way in finding her sister Lilly if Martina assigned him.

"I have been sharing a prison ward with her for some time," Lena said.

He made sudden quick shifts on his seat, leaning further back onto his chair. "So you are a criminal, girl?"

"No. I am not."

"I guess that's why you are out, because you are not?"

Lena affirmed his statement with a single nod.

"And, Martina sent you?" It was almost a grunt.

Lena sighed and straightened up to face him. "I came out of prison two months ago. Martina gave me your telephone contact."

"She had no right to give you my contact." He growled. "But tell me, you left prison two months ago. And you left her seriously ill, right?"

Lena feared she had gone too far with the tale of Martina's illness but she had to stick with it.

"Right," she said and then to her dismay, added: "She told me you were her confidante. I think she needs to dispose of some matters with you just in case her health worsens." Lena watched him cautiously. His features relaxed with this last statement. She hoped he would jump for the bait.

"You haven't answered my question. Has she been sick for two months?"

"She was well two months ago. But I saw her again this morning and found her ill." Lena swallowed. She hoped her lies wouldn't put her in any kind of trouble. "I am hoping that you can make it soon, sir."

"In that case girl, I will see her soon." He pushed back his chair. "Taxis hardly use this route. I can drop you off where you can find one. You can wait right here, I won't take long."

"Thank you sir." She was happy for a lift back to the city centre where she could catch a taxi. Walking from the last taxi stage of Kamuca had taken her nearly an hour. And if he chose to take the city centre route – she could take a taxi directly to her residence.

"City centre it will be." He grunted and made to leave. Pausing briefly, he said, "Did she send a similar message to any other person?"

Careful now, Lena thought. He could change his mind and send her to another of Martina's employees. She really didn't want to waste any more time. "She wanted you, sir. I was to contact the other workers only if I failed to get you."

"I see," he said and hurried away.

She went and asked the guard if she could use the toilet.

He pointed in the direction behind the house, where Lena saw a small banana plantation.

Lena hurried towards the toilet. As she passed a large window of the main house, she heard Mukwano's voice say, "Listen Ahmed, Martina is finally ill. I will go confirm this but if she defies that illness, you know what to do. Sick or not, I want her out of the picture. You hear me?"

Lena cupped her mouth with her hand. A pang of fear shot through her body. What had she got herself into? Her knees felt weak. She tiptoed away to the toilet but she just stood in there briefly and came out, heading for the gate. She wanted to get away before anything bad happened to her. The gate was locked. She hurried to where the guard was sitting.

"Mr. Mukwano offered me a lift to the city centre but I have to leave now because I have to meet someone soon," she told the guard.

"You, you wait," the guard said, throwing anxious glances towards the main house. "He, Boss…he not like it."

"No, no. You open the gate."

"I says no! Wait Boss!"

"I have to go now."

"I said wait Boss!" He hurried away.

For a moment she felt as if she was trapped. She almost shouted for help.

She thought about Mukwano's words and worried that Mukwano could harm Martina. Perhaps Mukwano was a dangerous man? Again she wondered about his limp.

She recalled ghastly prison tales that trickled in from old convicts. From the female section, Arumo, the burly fearless inmate on death row, had the same limp as Mukwano's. Arumo always rubbed everyone the wrong way. Even the wardresses did their best to avoid antagonising the woman lest she struck. Arumo could put bedbugs in people's soup, give them a punch or a kick, or even stick a pocketknife in their backs. Arumo was unlike other prisoners on death row who never lost time professing their faith to Pentecostal pastors every Sunday. Prison never had any impact on her.

Lena studied the blue sky. A school of pure white egrets glided their way south, running away from the unfriendly cold north. The birds were right. Better to leave early lest one got engulfed by the cold.

She heard a clatter and sat up. The guard was opening the garage gate. A sleek black right-hand drive BMW pulled out on to the driveway. Mukwano beckoned to Lena.

Lena hesitated. She did not want his lift any more.

"Come on," Mukwano said, waving at her.

Like a zombie she walked to the car. The heat of the day had intensified. Her grandmother, God rest her soul, had often reminded her that rain followed the heat as surely as night followed day. June was always a warm month, with intermittent rainfall.

The winds mourned.

***

Mukwano drove very fast. In the back seat, Lena fastened and unfastened her seatbelt. They approached the city centre and snaked through the dense traffic jam.

"Please drop me off at the petrol station just before the traffic lights," she said.

"Sure, girl," Mukwano threw Lena a glance of approval.

His mind raced to Martina. Things could never be better in a man's life, he thought. What was more appropriate than for a well deserving man to bask in the glory of a fangless rich old witch who was about to dispose of her $20 million worth of wealth? Not that it would change a lot of things really. The physical assets were already unofficially history to Martina. He and Martina's other associates led by Tony the lawyer had spent the last couple of months managing the estate. The ideal plan was for him to own up to 80% of the estate eventually. The remaining 20% would go to silencing Tony.

Mukwano judged Tony a fallen lawyer. Twice Tony had failed to defend his client, Martina, before the Courts of Law. The trial and the appeal had been a big flop. Mukwano smacked his lips. That alone had silenced the lawyer. Recently he had become rather distant. He had been absent from the VG company for close to four months. He would deal with Tony in his own time.

Now, Martina had sent for him and not Tony. Perhaps Martina still trusted him more than she trusted Tony. Unlike Tony, he had never failed her in any of his assignments. He had been her closest associate at the VG. He had worked hard for that. His was a rags-to-riches story. He had very little education – having dropped out in primary six. All of his shrewdness had been a matter of hard work and patience, he thought.

He still had no idea of his origins. The only home he knew was the Naguru Children's Home in Kampala. At the age of ten he had become restless, daily marching up to the administrator at the Home to find out if she had finally discovered his blood relations. When he failed to get an answer, at age thirteen, he ran away to the streets of Kampala. After a week of hunger and cold, he went looking for a job. A sympathetic man asked if he wanted to be a karaoke dancer at his bar.

"You have the body of a dancer," the man told him. That is how he became a karaoke dancer at a bar in Kawempe, a Kampala suburb. For two years, he danced for survival, though he never enjoyed it.

Mukwano still vividly remembered the couple that approached his employer. They had said they liked him, and wanted to give him a better chance at life. They offered the bar owner a small payment. The couple later sold him to the owner of an elite string of brothels in Kawempe.

At fifteen, already accumulating knots of stern muscles down his arms, he became a bouncer, serving the faithful patrons of the brothel. His life as a bouncer lasted twelve years. He had a sensitive job that forged him both friends and enemies. Clients comprised top government officials, diplomats and wealthy businessmen who, society considered, happily married. All he had to do was bury their secrets deep. At first, he was an ignorant, honest bouncer who played to the rules. For every twisted smile that came his way, seeking reassurance, he gratefully shot back a smooth one. His employer reminded him daily that these clients were the ones paying his bills. He had in his possession immeasurable secrets that could shock the world – lurid details of the brothel's clientele.

After a few years, a fellow bouncer opened his eyes. It was possible, this fellow had confided, to mint a neat heap of money from the same clients if they so wished. These clients would have to part with a little more fortune to have their secrets kept. Nothing came cheap, the fellow had advised.

Now and again, they experimented with a few choice clients. Using proxies outside the brothel, they would dangle the lurid details before an unsuspecting client. The client often had only one way out – to buy back his secrets at an exorbitant price. Those who failed to cooperate often found their stories on front pages of Uganda's leading tabloids the next day.

Sometimes Mukwano disagreed with his co-bouncer over which client to sabotage next. There was the Chief Executive Officer of a multi-billion dollar petroleum firm whom the co-bouncer had known was not to be touched. Mukwano often benefited from the CEO's generous tips when he visited the brothel. However, the CEO's wealth kept tempting the co-bouncer until he could no longer resist it.

The co-bouncer went behind Mukwano's back and worked with their underground contact to fleece the man. But the CEO had hired a hit man to provide cover as he delivered the money in the dead of the night. The bullet hit the underground contact in the neck, just as he grabbed the pile of cash. Before he died, he confessed that he had been taking the money to Mukwano's co-bouncer. The CEO then turned his full wrath on the co-bouncer, killing him that same night. That marked the end of the blackmailing business.

Mukwano remained friends with the CEO, but he lived in fear. He left his job, and used his savings to set up a small brothel in the slum of Katwe in Kampala. His own brothel.

He needed girls, cheap but beautiful girls who would bring in clients. He had frequented other brothels to learn and create necessary links. On one of his errands, he bumped into the CEO, who later introduced him to Martina. Most of Martina's girls were young, innocent and desperate for survival.

Mukwano chuckled and turned the wheels of his BMW as he recalled how Martina had desperately fought to secure his services. She wanted an extra pair of hands on deck to help build her business. The nature of her business did not allow her to bring just anyone she had explained.

Martina had learnt of his aggressive, fearless tactics and the energy he had invested in crafting a robust network of clientele. In less than a year his business was thriving. When he opened another house in Ntinda, one of Kampala's more progressive suburbs, closer to Martina's business premises, she pressed even harder. He learnt that she had no children, having lost her only child, a son, many years back; Martina had explained. And she had no known relations. A hard working and trusted employee like Mukwano would help fill the void.

He agreed to work for Martina.

He learnt a lot from a younger Martina then, and she relied heavily on him to protect her estate and interests. Now she was sixty-four. A sixty-four year-old African woman in an African jail for fifteen years was just as well written off. But that wasn't enough since he was not sure whether Martina would leave her business solely to him? He had his plans and they had to go his way.

Over twenty years back, before Martina hit it off with brothel business, she had stunk of absolute poverty, living a life of worthlessness in the Katwe slum with her seventeen-year-old son. She had failed to provide him decent treatment and he had died of malaria. Now was her turn to die, Mukwano hoped. Being the only ear to Martina's words would secure his plans better.

He dropped Lena off at the next stage.

***

Lena hopped out, and closed the door. She was happy to finally be out of Mukwano's car. Her ambitious morning had turned into a near nasty experience. Her body still pumped high levels of adrenaline. She hoped she was not over-reacting, but she needed to speak with Arthur and get his opinion. She needed to tell him that there was a possibility of Mukwano being an asset in looking for Lilly. But then, was Mukwano a good asset? Would he look for Lilly?

She decided to stop tormenting herself. She would wait for Arthur's opinion in all this. She had done what Martina had requested. Martina would get to see Mukwano. She would talk to him directly about her businesses and about Lilly. She wished she was part of their meeting, to listen in, to describe Lilly and give more information to Mukwano. But there was another worry. Mukwano could hurt Martina. She wondered whether she needed to alert her. But maybe she was wrong. Maybe she had miss-conceived the words she had heard him say as she walked by the window of his house?

She watched taxis squeeze through the thick traffic. Pedestrians streamed passed, jostling her from side to side. The heat of the day was unbearable. A whirlwind lifted dry leaves, dust and polythene bags above the cars. Lena held her skirt down and watched the dusty gust lose strength against the tall bank building a block away.

"Young woman," an elderly lady said, touching Lena. "I think a person in that car wishes to give you something," she said, pointing at the car.

Lena had not noticed that a few feet down the road Mukwano's car had stopped and his thick dark hand was waving something through the passenger window.

"Hey! That's my purse!" Lena sprinted towards the car.

"Careful!" The old lady raised her voice in disapproval.

"You young girls have got to be careful with men."

Lena saw her purse hit the pavement as Mukwano continued along with the traffic. She noticed Kampala's little street urchins close by as she ran for her purse. She picked it up just as three other quick pairs of little rough feet rushed over. "Damn him!" The man had barely given her time to jump out of his car. He had made her forget her purse. Her entire life was in that purse; her phone, cash, and keys.

The sidewalk was fast filling up with people. She walked to the taxi stage, and joined the waiting lot. Lena worried. What had two years in jail done to her? In jail, she had lived a life of scarcity, where most things one 'owned' were temporary and belonged to the state. It was simply pointless to look after one's few belongings. Nobody was interested in stealing them anyway.

She watched Mukwano continue at a snail's pace. The traffic jam was sickening. As she watched moving cars, her mind played over Mukwano's actions while she was in his car; he had acted quite strange; they never spoke but he had continuously gurgled like an amused baby. The smiles that kept flickering on his face had bothered her and even reminded her of the stupid grin of the terracotta Luzira head. Perhaps the man was not balanced in the head? She wouldn't want someone else's mess to complicate the search for her sister.

She recalled the expression he wore on his face moments before she hopped out of his car: an on-top-of-the-world look.

She decided once and for all, to call the front desk and ask to speak to Akurut. She would ask Akurut to let Martina know Mukwano was coming. She wasn't sure if he would change his mind and not see Martina, but she just had to warn them anyway. Perhaps she didn't even need him in her search for Lilly.

She walked into the safety of a bank building to make the call. There were security guards and so the street urchins wouldn't dare play their stuff under the watchful eyes of the mean men. She unzipped her purse to get Martina's piece of paper. It was an official paper from prisons for use by prisoners who wished to write letters. It bore the Prison's contact address with a landline telephone number. She would call and ask for Akurut, or Ameri. The other wardresses were not that generous to inmates.

CHAPTER THIRTEEN

"Awww!" Akurut yawned. "I hate the tears that always follow this jaw-jerking exercise. I hate the hunger. I hate the stale brown posho and beans. I hate this lowly place." She dabbed her face with an old handkerchief as she thought about Lena's call earlier. The call had been a pleasant shocker. It still puzzled her how Lena accessed her cellphone contact. She couldn't recall sharing it with any inmate or ex-inmate for that matter. Well, the important thing was the message. Lena had said that a potentially dangerous man was on his way to see Martina. Akurut had decided to stay in the vicinity in case the potentially dangerous man came.

Lena thought Martina could be hurt. But Akurut knew she would not tell the dearie old hag anything. Saying such things to prisoners was unethical and contrary to the prison's rules. Anything that caused prisoners to feel insecure was not acceptable. In any case security was the guards' business and she would handle it her own way.

Akurut wondered about the relationship Lena had with Martina. She couldn't put any pieces together to come to a good answer. But she would try and find out, somehow. She cast a weary look at her bare feet, and then at the pair of boots that stood by an old jacaranda trunk nearby. She hated the old boots. She hated everything. She even hated the tingly feeling on her feet as she kicked the dry leaves that had fallen from the line of jacaranda trees under which she stood. One day, she hoped to get a higher rank and enjoy the perks that came with being part of the higher authority: a real officer's bungalow, a fat salary, a good night's rest – and never again to catch the cold off the dawn of Lake Victoria.

She looked at the dish of beans and posho she had received from the kitchen staff and cursed. Prison food was unbearably messy. Today's meal was not any different. There were countless weevils floating on the watery soup. Akurut found that annoying but she thanked God that they had both beans and posho as meal. Sometimes posho got served several hours after the beans were long eaten and digested.

Akurut heard the prisoners' laughter. They were perhaps still celebrating the full meal. She was among the few staff members who shared the prison lunch. However, she hoped that a better pay would change that. Better pay would change many things.

Later, Akurut dragged her feet to the office, nodding greetings to inmates and colleagues she met along the way. At the office, her eyes caught the Luzira Head hanging askew on the wall. She thought that some staff must have dislodged it accidentally.

"You," she said to an inmate who sat on a waiting bench at the front office. "Adjust that Head immediately."

She pulled out a note of shilling and passed it to another inmate. "Go get me a bottle of mineral water from the canteen."

Dearie Martina? Could be hurt? Akurut mused. Well, why not? The woman was in jail for abducting a child. It's also possible she could have annoyed other people as well. Or might it be a quarrel to do with drugs? Could they have supplied her drugs and she failed to pay? Or could she have paid for drugs and they weren't delivered and so they would want to threaten her not to demand her money? But who is this 'they?' She hoped Lena would come another time so she could get more details from her.

Akurut leaned her heavy body against the reception door and watched activities on the compound. On visiting days, wardresses were deployed in large numbers. They milled about waiting to share prisoners' delicacies from visiting relatives and friends. Akurut was certain that some of them had shunned today's prison food in the hope of a better meal. Poor salaries had reduced wardresses to beggars!

The inmate she had sent to the canteen brought her bottle of chilled water. She knelt down and gave it to Akurut.

"Thank you." Akurut gulped down the water as she watched dark clouds hung over the lake. Moments later, drops of rain quickly gathered momentum, taming the steamy heat of the afternoon.

Akurut closed the door and walked back to the front desk where a youthful senior wardress sat.

"Hi. I am sitting in for Ameri," Akurut announced.

"Oh, ok, do you mind handling the register while I do the summons?"

"Let's make a deal, Officer Carol," Akurut said. "How about I handle male visitors while you handle the females?"

"New regulation?" Carol raised her eyebrows.

"Not that I know of," Akurut said. "Just negotiating. Remember I am simply doing old Ameri a favour," she added. Carol was being stubborn for no good reason. Everyone hated to pair up with the old drunk Ameri. "But it's still not too late for Ameri to come back though."

"Ok, ok!" Carol shrugged and pulled out another register book for herself. "You and I know that anything is better than sitting next to a brewery."

"Of course, of course!" Akurut laughed and moved to take

the empty chair at the other end of the counter.

"At least I will breathe freely this afternoon. Ah Ameri!" Carol sighed and shook her head.

A pair of mean looking newly arrived female convicts entered. The prison officer accompanying them shouted, "I hope you two won't continue with your stupidity." Then she turned to Akurut. "These two have been quarrelling throughout the journey."

"They had better stop if they are to survive in this place," Akurut said.

"Just wait and see," said one of the convicts. "My uncle is a senior officer in the army. He will get me out. In no time."

"In no time," her fellow convict nodded, a sneer on her face.

"And who might that mighty uncle be?" Akurut laughed.

"You just...just wait and see," the woman convict said.

"My dear fellows. As you will soon find out, we have inmates of great backgrounds here. And tell you what; they all wait upon the law. We have politicians, tycoons, even ministers serving this government. Who do you think you are?" Akurut said.

"Just wait and see!" The woman said unrepentantly and dropped to the bench.

"They both fought not to board the prison bus," a male prison officer who had accompanied the female guards said. "We had to force them."

Carol laughed and shook her head. She waved at Akurut: "Officer Akurut, your assignment I guess."

"I said visitors, Carol." Akurut laughed. This was proving a fun afternoon after all. "I said I wanted to handle visitors, male visitors. These male guards are simply helping deliver female convicts. Differentiate between visitors and guards, my dear."

Carol ignored her and continued smiling over her large book.

"Well, in any case," Akurut said, "Let's deal with these newcomers immediately. Then we can handle the visitation."

"That settles it," Carol said.

Akurut frowned as the rain started to pound the lake. She hurried to shut the reception door to stop rain from getting inside. Then she sat by the window and watched the jacaranda trees as they swayed about in the furious wind. Akurut pondered her private assignment. Visitors would be late today because of the heavy downpour. She wondered if Martina's visitor might change his plans and not come. If only he could come. If only she could catch him with drugs, haa! Catching a visitor bringing drugs to a convict could help her get a little recognition from her superiors. She would be the famous drug fighter.

It rained for close to thirty minutes, and then it stopped. Akurut threw open the reception door.

One by one, the visitors trickled in, pretending civility to her and Carol. She believed that outside the facility no one would notice her. Prison warders were looked down upon, undermined, ridiculed, and even rated as the lowest in civil service. Yet here these visitors were, hoping the wardresses could help them see their loved ones. Some visitors came in groups. There were priests and pastors with their Bibles tightly sandwiched in their armpits, aggrieved and disgruntled spouses, embarrassed and anxious parents and in-laws, teary and hollow-eyed kids; some of them visiting for the first time. This was her turf. She had the authority to allow visitors to see their jailed relatives.

She checked the clock on the wall. It was 3:20 pm. For the next twenty minutes, she registered ten male visitors and settled them with whomever they wished to see. She occasionally stole a glance at Carol who had a long line of female visitors to attend. The story remained the same every visiting day; majority of visitors were always women.

"Looks like we could do with an extra pair of hands, Akurut," Carol said. "Want to help here?"

Akurut joined the two junior wardresses helping Carol.

At 4:00 pm, a tall dark skinned man limped over to the counter. He had a thin green spring file with him, and wore a scowl on his face. He stood tall and domineering in front of Carol. Akurut peered at him. Officer Carol was busy handling an elderly couple who often visited their granddaughter who was on death row.

"Good afternoon sir. My colleague will attend to you." Carol made the referral.

Akurut watched the man limp towards her desk.

"It is Martina Maa I have come to see," the man said.

The face was not new, Akurut noted. He occasionally visited Martina. She nodded, and passed the man the visitation form to fill in. He had never been any threat to Martina, Akurut thought. But just in case Lena was right, she would keep close. She accepted the form the man passed back. On the form, he had signed the name Tony.

"This way please." She directed the man to a male warder for a thorough body and baggage check. She watched as the warder scanned the man, and then let him go. Tony was clean.

She beckoned him towards the facility's small rooms where there was more privacy and less opportunity for eavesdroppers. Most inmates often used spacious halls on the left wing.

Akurut picked the small room closest to the reception. It was still empty. She directed Tony to wait on one of the benches.

"How is she?" Tony asked.

"Who?"

"Martina. I am told she is very ill."

"Well, you will soon see her." Akurut rushed out wondering when Martina fell sick. Inmates always lied to get favours. She went back to the front desk, and delegated one of her two junior assistants to take over from her.

***

"Dearie, dearie me! Mukwano! They mentioned Tony," Martina exclaimed, bursting into the room. "Four months! What took you so long my dear Mukwano?"

Mukwano struggled to stabilise himself on his feet. Something was wrong. The woman was supposed to be very ill, at the brink of death. Mukwano felt dizzy. The room became too small for the two of them. He felt a gush of heat flow down his whole body. He wondered whether it was a set-up. Who was the girl who had come to tell him Martina was ill? Did she want to play games with him? Well... he dared her!

He asked Martina to sit next to him. He thought she looked strong, healthy, and very, very angry. "You are not ill, dear madam?"

"My dearie, why would I be ill?" She sat facing him.

Mukwano fidgeted with his file. Damn that girl, he thought. She had better keep out of his way.

"Now, tell me young man. What have you been doing with my firms?"

"Why, the estate is running good." Mukwano said. "Faruk is exporting another batch of three hundred within the month.

We are also expecting eighty from Lira this week. I personally sent Okello with twenty station wagons we ordered from Japan to South Sudan for the UN Mission. Other businesses remain the same. Our turnover last year was twice more than the previous year. I will submit the papers during my next visit."

***

Akurut leaned against the wall by the corridor an d listened to the whole conversation. She wondered why the mighty man called himself Tony, when his name was Mukwano. Was he an imposter? But why would he want to lie about his name to the prison authorities? Then he appeared to be the old dearie hag's right-hand man, or son? And the old dearie was certainly in command, from the way she ordered the man about. Akurut listened attentively, waiting for the moment when the old dearie would demand the drugs.

***

"Dearie me. Can you explain why all of my four contacts, you inclusive, have switched off their phones?"

"Our phones are on, madam." Mukwano sat forward. Prison or no prison, Martina always had untold levels of authority over him. That was something he needed to stop with immediate effect. He should be the top man and that is what he would fight for.

"Now look here, friend," Martina squinted her eyes at Mukwano. "You are not here to play cat-and-mouse with me, dearie. Why are all the phones dead? C'mon, I want straight answers."

Mukwano was amused by Martina's attitude. The jailbird was behaving as though it was business as usual. He could as well just walk out and ignore her entirely. But the danger in it would be other surrogates like Tony, whom he did not have under his grip yet. And then that new girl whose name he could not remember. He was ready to play along and see how things would turn out. Time was on his side. Fifteen years of jail term for Martina was not a short time.

"These days telephone networks are bogus. They over-subscribe customers but fail to upgrade thir systems. That's why we get frequent blackouts. And of course, sometimes the batteries are down."

"Dear, dear, dear! Bogus! Rubbish. Mukwano, I can see you are still the scheming, big thug that I tried to liberate years ago. And do you know what makes me so disappointed? You are not good at it! Not smart at all in coining up your lies."

Mukwano looked away. She was always right. She could tell what went on in his mind. She had hired him because he was good with business. She was even grooming him for next of kin. But he wasn't a man who took chances. Waiting for Martina to pass over her company to him would be waiting for the world to end. And now he suspected she wanted to change her mind about his being her next of kin. He would do everything possible to have the company in his control, with or without her will.

"Now listen good to me," Martina continued. "Dearie! This kind of skeletal information can never do. You know me well, Mukwano. I want a neat account of all my business transactions for the months I have been away. You have only a fortnight to get that done. And please, keep your lies to yourself."

"Within a fortnight madam. Same place, same time I

promise." Mukwano looked about him.

"Just remember: not a single minute past," Martina stressed. "I will want to see Tony along as well."

"Tony? Well, I think he is out of the country right now. I will submit the report as directed in a fortnight though."

"Did you say he was out of the country?"

"Not sure, madam. But all the same I will submit the report as directed in a fortnight."

"Without a question, my dearest Mukwano," Martina said. "By the way, did you receive any consignment from Lira about three months ago?"

"We receive consignments several times a month, madam." Mukwano etched his brows in surprise. "Why?"

"Just a dream I had about a dear little girl called Lilly." Martina looked away.

"Just a dream, Martina?" Mukwano laughed and moved closer.

"And, do you doubt that?" Martina peered at him. "Well... find out if you have her somewhere."

Mukwano cleared his throat. "I will find out about your dear little Lilly, Madam."

"Thank you!"

"And if I do, what do I do with her?"

"Ah?" Martina appeared surprised. "Dear me! Just bring her to me!"

Mukwano stood up. "I see. I think my time is up," he said. "Tony is away. We have a lot of work. I was thinking we could use an extra pair of hands to move things faster."

"See what you can do, Mukwano."

"The young woman you sent to find me. Who is she? Do you

think she is someone we can take on? I mean you already know her."

"Dearie young Lena?" Martina beamed. "Hire her immediately."

"Good." The girl dared lie to him. The girl dared prove smarter than he was. "Her contacts madam?"

"No idea, my dear Mukwano." Martina shook her head. "That would be your assignment, looking for her."

CHAPTER FOURTEEN

Lena stood waiting for her turn on the veranda of Nalongo's eatery to buy a meal. She had been there for almost a quarter of an hour. Customers, mostly university students, refused to line up and went straight to be served. She decided to wait a little while longer, after all, she wasn't in a hurry.

The temporary structure that housed the eatery was behind her hostel – just a stone throw away. It partly stood on a small patch of ground used as a waste dump. Fluttering polythene bags, household wastes and old car parts threatened to spill over to where she stood.

What passed for a motor garage sheltered the eatery on one side. Young men in their oil-stained overalls surrounded two cars – and were quickly dismantling the parts. In jail, she had been with two or three female convicts linked to stealing cars. The women even boasted about their deeds. How they were part of a racket that stole cars and dismantled them to be sold as spare parts, and how some were smuggled into the DRC and South Sudan. Lena thought the garage served for a den of cut-throats in the night. She would never dare pass that way even as early as dusk, she vowed.

Her stomach rumbled. Today she would do a take-home meal. The food vender had a simple 'first come, first served' policy carelessly scrawled in charcoal on the dirty wooden door. But the policy wasn't working in the muddied corridor. The rowdy students shoved and pushed to be served first.

The rich aroma of food always got to her whenever her

window stayed open. And now her mouth watered at the mixed aromas of just about everything – pilao, beef, chicken, oh just about everything. Her stomach felt like pins were pricking it. It rumbled continuously, like the thunder that rolled across Lake Victoria to Luzira in the rainy season.

Hunger reminded her of her siblings. She knew that back home, Okulu must be preparing beans and posho for supper. He was quite dependable. She could count on him to feed his young brothers the same way he he did when she was in prison. She thought about Lilly, wondering how she was. She thought about Arthur, hoping his busy schedule would allow him check with his police friends – the ones he said would help investigate the owners of the brothel she burnt down.

She thought briefly about Martina and Mukwano and wondered how their meeting had gone. She hoped it was alright for her to trust Martina, to confide in her about Lilly, about old Esther. Perhaps Mukwano was not really a bad man. Her mind raced. Perhaps she should have waited a bit to call Akurut to warn her about him.

For lack of alternatives, she had called the front desk hoping to speak to Akurut. That drunkard Ameri had answered the phone and informed her that Akurut was out, and then she gave her Akurut's cellphone contact. If that man Mukwano was really a bad man, then she hoped Akurut managed to pass the information to Martina in time. Lena knew that Akurut and Martina weren't friends, but she hoped Akurut would remember that it was her responsibility to keep inmates safe.

"Hey sister, your order?" An elderly lady interrupted her thoughts. "You have been standing here for a long time."

"Yes Nalongo." Lena moved closer to the doorway of the

eatery. Only a handful of students remained. A heavily built young man, dripping with sweat was attending to them. "Can I have steamed mushroom in peanut sauce?"

"What food?" Nalongo said.

"Aah. I think Matooke," Lena said.

Nalongo prepared her order quickly and handed her the container.

"Thank you." She received the container, placed it in a black polythene bag, and paid the bill to Nalongo.

In her room, Lena, unwrapped the banana leaves in which the peanut-mushroom sauce was wrapped. This was her favourite dish. Its distinctive aroma wafted over the room. She closed her eyes, threw her head back and took a lengthy deep breath, savouring the aroma. The luxury of such a delicacy reminded her of her mother's delicious dishes – the ngwen, the alaju, amola, agira – all the dishes they had enjoyed before her family was forced to flee into camp. She had missed that food most when she was in jail. Thinking about it made her miss home, miss her family, miss her mother.

She said a short prayer, and began eating. She was halfway through her meal when her cellphone rang. It was Akurut.

"Lena, Lena, is that you?" Akurut said.

"Yes, it's me. How did you get my number? Oh, I have remembered. I called your phone. How are you, Afande?"

"So you thought the man was potentially harmful to Martina? He didn't even touch her."

"I didn't. Well... I was just guessing."

"No problem anyway."

"So how did he react when he found she was not sick?"

"Listen, I am running short of airtime."

"Wait, Afande. Just a second. May I come over and see you, please?"

"Sure. Today?"

"Yes."

"I will be heading to Mama Rachelle's Restaurant to relax. It's five o'clock now. Let's say I will be there at six."

"Where is that?"

"Nakawa. Near the market. Take any taxi passing through Nakawa, and ask the conductor to drop you at Mama Rachelle's."

"I will be there."

CHAPTER FIFTEEN

"Damn glass! Out of my sight. Out of my sight!" Mukwano lashed out at four glass vases on the round marble platform in his parlour. He ignored the blood on his hands.

Ruta cringed and tiptoed backwards as the glasses crushed to the floor. The boss had called for a jar of drinking water.

"You! What are you doing here?" He turned his reddened eyes at her.

"You asked for a jar of iced water, Boss." Ruta rushed forward, then paused. Broken glass littered the floor. She lifted the jar and drained the water into the drinking glass she had brought along. Her hand shook as she handed the glass to boss. Blood oozed from the palm of his right hand and ran down the glass.

"I will wash and dress your hands, Boss," she said. She waited for a response, but there was silence.

She looked at the broken glasses. What a waste! The four beautiful flower vases from boss' last trip to Dubai were gone. Also strewn about the floor were cigar stumps.

Boss drank all the water.

"Now, get out!" Boss returned an empty glass to her and reached out for another cigar. He lit it, closed his eyes and let out plumes of smoke through his nostrils and mouth.

Ruta tiptoed to the centre of the parlour. Such a mood called for extra discipline within the house. She hovered by the doorway. Boss was really angry. She wondered whether it could be the girl who came and left with boss earlier in the day. Omadi had said she came from Martina. Perhaps the girl had annoyed boss?

"What did she do to you, Boss?"

"Get out of my sight, old woman," Mukwano roared. "Call the guard immediately."

Ruta withdrew from the parlour. She would clean up the mess when calmness returned. That was the norm of the household. Boss gets angry, messes up the house, all remain in place until the crisis is over and boss is happy again.

She peeped at him from the doorway and cringed as more cigar stubs hit the floor. Boss' eyes grew redder with each puff.

***

Mukwano stared at Ruta as she cleared away the broken glasses. He thought about Martina. She had made a very unfortunate move. "She thinks she can still boss me around? She thinks I can continue making millions for her when she sits doing nothing?" He mumbled. He would prove to Martina and all the others that the estate no longer belonged to her. The estate worth a whooping $20 million was already his. And nobody could do anything about it. Nobody had the right to. But first, he must get the land titles and company deeds. After pleading with that fool of a lawyer for a long time, he now knew what to do. He was fed up.

"I will take matters in my own hands," he mumbled. "I can't afford to make any silly mistakes. I will deal with Tony today. Right here. In the comfort of my lounge."

He reached for the telephone on the side table by the sofa, and placed a call to Tony.

He hated Tony. The lawyer was a huge stumbling block. Tony had all the legal papers to the estate. Worse still, he had solid loyalty to Martina. The fool remained stuck like a leech to the old ways of the world; feeble-minded, picking crumbs that dropped from dinner tables of the rich and powerful, working his hands coarse for a paltry reward. Disgusting, he thought. He, Mukwano, had tried all sane means to get the legal papers of the estate, but in vain. This time around, he had to get them, whatever it took. Tonight, he must lay his hands on those papers.

"Answer the call, you fool!" Mukwano said as he pressed the redial button.

"Hello there?" Tony's voice came down the line. It sounded fresh, even happier than Mukwano was used to in the ten years they had known each other.

"I am glad you could find time to eventually answer my call," Mukwano said through gritted teeth. The lawyer's voice irritated him. He would soon sort that out.

"What do you want, Mukwano?" Tony asked.

"Just remember you are speaking to the Managing Director of the VG."

"I will try my very best to remember, Mr. Managing Director," Tony said. "Now, what do you want with me?"

"Do you still remember your old Martina?"

"Mukwano. What is it this time?"

"Oh, simple! Looks like you and I will have to endure each other for a while. Your Martina has called for an immediate audit. Two weeks at most."

"You have finally agreed to an audit?" Tony said.

"Of course. I have no choice. I have put it off too long and she is getting angry."

"I am glad you finally care."

"I said I have no choice. Can you come over this evening and we sort out a few details?"

"We do not need to meet. Just avail all the financial accounts to Otuko Associates. That's all."

"No pal. You know your role in ensuring we do not clash with the law."

"Sorry I have another appointment this evening."

"Then you can let her know that you no longer have time for her."

"Not quite. Maybe I can come over right now then I return for my appointment. I bet ours will not take too long."

"That's perfect."

"Have you informed the finance manager? He cannot afford to have a similar Management letter like the one of the last audit," Tony said.

"That is why I need to meet you first."

"Then expect me within the hour."

"Come to my house," Mukwano said.

"Why not office?"

"I have already left office. I am calling from my house." He waited for Tony to hang up, then he threw the receiver against the wall.

***

Omadi waited by the door. "You asked me come sir," he mumbled.

"Next time anyone claims to know Martina, do not let them in. I do not know Martina, or anyone connected to her. Do you understand?"

"Yes sir." Omadi affirmed with a tight military salute. He remained in that state till Mukwano asked him to sit by his feet and help plan for a big night. When boss said big night, Omadi knew right away what that entailed. His job would be to clean up.

CHAPTER SIXTEEN

Tony was surprised to receive a call from Mukwano regarding financial audits. He slotted the phone receiver in place and walked to the window. He drew the curtain aside and stared at the long shadows of the trees in the compound. His gatekeeper was at his post, poring over some old newspapers. Faithful old man, Tony thought. He had kept the house safe and clean for months. He made a mental note to raise the guard's pay by half at the end of the month.

His eyes swept past the high roof of the gate to the compound across the road. The red-tiled roof towered above the trees – proud and showy like its owner, Mukwano. He and Mukwano were neighbours. In fact their houses faced each other, only separated by the road, but he did not remember when he had last visited Mukwano. Probably it had been a year ago during Martina's trial. He needed to put a strong defence for Martina, and each time there was a new development, Mukwano wanted a briefing in the cool confines of his house. The briefings stopped when it was clear that Martina had lost and would be convicted.

Later, Mukwano started hounding him for the legal papers of the VG. He badly wanted the land titles and the company deeds. With Martina in prison, he acted as if he was the bonafide owner of the group of companies. That marked the end of his visits to Mukwano's house. Since then, they only met at the VG offices, and occasionally at Luzira during visits to Martina.

But he would now go to Mukwano's house again since

Mukwano had finally agreed to an audit. He only hoped that Mukwano would as well agree to have Otuko Associates carry out the audit. The last time Tony had phoned him, Mukwano did not answer. And he did not call back. That was four months ago. Martina had ordered an audit of her estate. As the attorney, his assignment was to see a logical audit process take place and a final report submitted to Martina. Martina had appointed Otuko Associates, an audit firm she trusted. But Mukwano always insisted on Real Associates.

Real Associates were quacks who did not conform to the law. They were auditors, but Tony knew that they also ran rackets ranging from smuggling and trafficking to high profile assassinations, and had even worked their way into owning thousands of chunks of suspected 'petroleum rich' land in central Uganda. Three years earlier, RA had popped out of nowhere. Nobody knew exactly who the proprietor was.

RA had influential networks all over Kampala. The firm was 'untouchable.' They knew somebody influential in all places that mattered in government and in the private sector. Tony had heard they were capable of anything; they could twist records and systems to suit clients' needs. There were even rumours that they made big bucks selling frame-ups of otherwise innocent, successful citizens on behalf of rivals. In fact, Tony had long suspected RA's hand in Martina's going to jail. If their hands were clean, why then did they seem jubilant when the judge sentenced Martina to fifteen years in prison?

He had heard from his gatekeeper that they had gathered at Mukwano's house for a cocktail. Omadi had innocently asked Tony's gatekeeper if Tony wasn't turning up for the cocktail at Mukwano's house. Tony had wondered why Mukwano would be part of such a thing. He got his answer when Mukwano started calling himself the bonafide owner of the VG.

Tony knew that RA could stop at nothing, even silencing an opponent, to service its shady clients. Because of them, the accounts of the VG had not been audited as Martina had demanded. Mukwano had seen to it that if RA wouldn't have the contract, no one else could. He thus refused to avail the accounts to Otuko Associates.

When Mukwano rejected Otuko Associates for the audit, Tony almost involved Martina, the only person who could order Mukwano to cooperate. Then he got a lucrative legal deal in the Democratic Republic of Congo with the BELGO Mining Company and had to leave immediately. BELGO was still new in the DRC. The Belgium Company was eyeing the vast gold deposits in eastern DRC. He took the job, part-timing as their regional legal representative. Somehow, it had kept him busy, distracting him from Mukwano's sinister schemes at the VG.

He wondered what could have happened to cause Mukwano to accept the audit. Four months was a long time. Probably he had managed to convince Martina to hand over to him the VG ownership? He decided he would visit Martina before returning to the DRC.

He drew the curtain further and continued staring at the red roof opposite. It was not easy having a neighbour like Mukwano and his sneaky guard, Omadi. The telephone call confirmed Tony's suspicion about Omadi. The evening Tony arrived at his gate from the DRC, he honked only twice and as the gate was being opened, Mukwano's smaller gate also grated open and let out Omadi's frame. Omadi was a keen private eye for his boss. Mukwano himself used to joke about the information he received from Omadi. He would say, 'When will you finally settle with that beauty?' Or, 'those two men who visited you this morning, what were they up to?' In past months, he had even contemplated shifting house to some other location. But he stayed here on Martina's request. Now that she was away, he did not have to live here. He would make it a priority to shift before his next departure to the DRC, he promised himself.

He no longer trusted Mukwano. Mukwano had ordered Martina's portraits off all the walls of the VG offices. Besides, he kept pestering him for the company documents. Thinking about it sent a chill down his spine. Every day seemed an opportunity for Mukwano to reveal his ugly greedy side. He suspected that if Mukwano had the papers in his keep, Martina's life would be in grave danger. The old woman was not yet aware of it and he was not about to let her know. She was easily excitable, and such information would not be good for her in prison. Besides, he didn't have concrete evidence to support his suspicions.

He didn't like Mukwano's house as meeting ground, but his schedule in Kampala was tight with unfinished lawyerly business, which he planned to dispose off within the four days he would be in the country. Martina's audit was a necessary interruption he had to sacrifice time for before Mukwano changed his mind.

Tony walked into the kitchen and fixed himself a cup of tea.

Thirty minutes later, he walked into an adjoining room that served as his office. He pulled out a file bearing the Otuko Associates list of audit requirements and placed it in his brief case. It was almost six o'clock.

CHAPTER SEVENTEEN

"Hey, hey." Lena clutched her bag to her chest and shoved her way towards a taxi. She was in the middle of a sea of travellers desperate to get to their next destinations. This was her fifth attempt at struggling to enter a taxi. She watched with sadness as it crawled away. She pulled out her cellphone and checked the time. It was already six o'clock.

It had been a busy and exciting day for her. The day before, she had started the morning with a shopping spree in town, thanks to Arthur, then an adrenaline-filled morning with Martina in Luzira. Everything was happening so fast. This morning she had visited Mukwano's house, now she was off to see Akurut to find out what happened during Mukwano's visit to Martina.

She was eager to learn what had transpired during Mukwano's visit. Akurut was probably already at Mama Rachelle's Restaurant. Lena hoped Akurut would hold a table where the two of them could have a private conversation. She wondered whether Martina had told Mukwano about Lilly during their meeting. Could she really trust the man?

Lena became anxious, wondering how she would get to Nakawa in time. Akurut had told her that she would see Mama Rachelle's Restaurant signpost with a list of local dishes; Malakwang, boo, akeo, lakotokoto and goat ribs. She stared at the taxis that snaked passed, already filled with passengers. Crowds struggled to get into the next taxi. Her phone rang. She felt the vibration and dug into her bag as she struggled to find a seat in the taxi.

"Where are you Lena?" Arthur's anxious voice came through.

"In town, Arthur. On my way to meet Akurut."

"All the way to Luzira?"

"No. It's some joint called Mama Rachelle's at Nakawa," she said.

"Can't you push it to tomorrow?"

"Why?" Lena asked.

"It's a little late, don't you think?"

"It's important, Arthur. Besides, I am already on my way," Lena said. "And Akurut might be at that place, waiting for me. I will give you all the details soon. Have you heard from your friends yet?"

"No. But I have scheduled a meeting with an old police friend to try to speed up things a little bit."

"Oh. Ok. I hope that one can speed things up. When will you meet him?"

"Tomorrow evening, most likely."

"May I join you?"

"Listen. I was just checking on you. I have to go now. Will see you soon."

Her taxi passed crowds of people still waiting for their opportunity to get means of transport. Lena wondered whether she should try to find Lilly on her own. Arthur seemed really busy. She could start by checking with the brothel. But she knew her limitations. She told herself to calm down. To go see Akurut, and then meet Arthur as soon as he was free. She needed to believe in him. "You have every reason to believe in him," she mumbled.

Lena stopped the taxi at the signpost for Mama Rachelle's Restaurant. She paid the fare and jumped off. She checked the time on her cellphone. She was already late. She scanned the place for Akurut.

She liked the little square bamboo tables that decked the dimly lit square of the acacia garden. She could see Rachelle's was an average citizen's hideout. She smiled at the youthful couples drinking away the evening. Then her nose picked the aroma of pork and goat ribs sizzling on two high charcoal stoves on both sides of the garden. Lena looked again and saw Akurut bent over a plate of goat ribs. She was chewing away fast.

The corner table Akurut had picked was perfect. She sat facing the entrance, her back to the wall. She had a full view of the rest of Rachelle's. Akurut was a trained officer indeed, Lena thought.

***

Akurut looked up as Lena approached her table.

"Finally you are here."

"I am sorry I was delayed. It wasn't easy getting a taxi from the city centre," Lena said.

"Never mind," Akurut said in between mouthfuls. "Who doesn't know about Kampala's little headaches – the traffic jam, the noise, the beggars, the pickpockets? Order something."

"What?"

"Where I come from, it is rude to eat alone. Order something."

"You actually called when I was finishing my meal, late lunch. Early supper," Lena said. "But thank you, Afande."

"Don't afande me here, young woman," Akurut wagged a finger. "You have to get used to the fact that you are no longer a prisoner. You are free." She sunk her teeth into the meat and smiled at Lena.

"And, how is The Head?" Lena asked.

"The what?"

"That beloved thing of yours with its stupid grin?"

"Oh! The Luzira Head." Akurut laughed. "Still reigning over us." She walked to a nearby washbasin and washed her hands.

She returned and sat down. She dried her hands and lips using the paper napkins on the table, and then said, "The Head aside, I am surprised you know very little about your friend's life." She crossed her arms on her chest and stared at Lena. This was her chance at clearing her suspicions about the old dearie. About the possibility of the old hag using drugs. Could Lena be aware of this? She hoped Lena would not dare withhold any information from her. She wanted all the information that could help pin down Martina for drugs. Because if she, Akurut, got the opportunity to expose such a racket, she would be sure of a promotion.

"True. Very little," Lena said.

"But we all know that inmates who become friends often share a lot," Akurut said.

"She and I were not really friends," Lena said. "We just shared a ward."

"And some food brought in by her visitors, I could say." Akurut added with a laugh.

"Of course."

"Tell me Lena, besides food, what else would Martina receive from her visitors? She used to talk a lot. What did she tell you?"

"Why? Does it really matter?"

"I am just curious." Akurut nodded. "Maybe it can help me know her better."

"This is like an interrogation. But yes. Martina shared a lot of things with me. She told me about the places she had visited, the sights she had seen, the food she had savoured, the clothes she liked, the shoes and perfumes, but maybe not everything about her life. Whether she was a harlot, a thief, a superstar, even a business magnate, I really don't know. I only know what you probably already know. That she was imprisoned because of something to do with the abduction of a girl."

"That's all?"

"That's all."

"No drugs, perhaps? Martina never used to receive any drugs from visitors? She never used to do drugs?"

"Ah ha!" Lena jabbed a finger at her. "We always knew that you suspected some inmates were on drugs, Afande. Anyway, I never saw Martina with drugs. I never saw anyone with drugs."

"I thought we had agreed that Afande no longer applies between us," Akurut said.

"Ok. I don't even know what those drug things look like. But for all the time I spent with Martina in Luzira, I never heard her speak about drugs."

"But, how would you know if she was a user if you don't even know what it looks like?"

"At least I have seen people outside Luzira who are drug addicts," Lena said. "Even in Acokara camp, we have plenty of them. Always drunk. Some even mentally ill. Martina never looked like any of them."

"I was just asking. If you never saw anything, then perhaps she doesn't use drugs. But she was always quarrelling." Akurut shifted uncomfortably in her seat. "Well, I will continue watching her."

"Okay. And how did it go with Mukwano and Martina?" Lena asked. "What happened when Mukwano visited?"

"By the way, he never called himself Mukwano. He

registered as Tony."

"Tony? But why?"

"And at first I thought he was indeed Tony, until I heard the old hag call him 'Mukwano.'"

"Do you know what they spoke about? Please tell me." Lena sat straight on her chair.

"But Lena, how are you involved with these people? Martina's people? How do you know them?"

"Of course through Martina. She sent me to them when I was getting out. She wanted them to come and see her."

"When he came he asked about her health. Like he came to see a sick person. And when he saw her, he behaved like someone who had seen a ghost."

"I am to blame for that," Lena said. "I am the one who told him that Martina was very ill. I thought if I mentioned that Martina was ill, he would sympathise and agree to go see her."

"That explains it," Akurut said.

"Explains what?"

"Why he thought the dearie old hag was very ill."

Lena chuckled.

"The man almost failed to take a seat. He was in shock," Akurut said and laughed.

Lena laughed along.

"But I don't understand, Lena. You asked me to keep an eye on Martina. That Mukwano seemed to be potentially dangerous. What is going on, girl? I hope you are not involved with some gangs. I hope you don't get yourself involved with dangerous gangs out there."

"I am not, Akurut. For sure. Anyway, now I regret everything. The lying. The thinking he was dangerous," Lena said.

"Why would you think he was dangerous?"

"I am probably just guilty of lying about Martina's health. However, I also eavesdropped on his phone conversation and heard him say something which scared me, but maybe I misunderstood things. I think I am... I am confused a little. I need to settle down and recollect myself."

"Like I said, Lena, I hope you are not involved in anything dangerous out there."

"Nothing like that. I wouldn't risk my life. My siblings need me," Lena said. "Did they talk about business at all?"

"Oh, and by the way, the dearie old hag was sort of angry with him. She ordered that he deliver an audit report about her businesses to her within a fortnight."

"I see. In that case, now I know I have done my part, linked Martina to her managers. I admit I was wrong about him being a danger to Martina."

"And he wants you, Lena," Akurut said, raising her index finger at her.

"He wants me? Why would he want me?"

"He suggested to the dearie old hag that if she wanted the audit completed in time, then you were to be brought on board. And she told him to look for you."

Lena sat on the edge of her seat, her eyes almost popping out. "But he barely knows me." She shook her head. "Did you say he suggested it or was it Martina?"

"He mentioned you to Martina," Akurut said. "So if you need money, all you have to do is locate him rather than him finding you."

Lena placed both elbows on the bamboo table and held her head in her hands.

"But Lena, I think you probably are better off without anything to do with that dearie old hag and her people," Akurut said. "And from what I see, you are not doing bad financially."

"Oh, you mean these clothes. They are nothing but charity," Lena said.

"So you will take those people's offer."

"I have got siblings to raise Akurut. But I will keep your advice in mind."

Akurut scratched her neck. "Well, you are my friend, Lena, and I won't stop protecting you. By the way, the old dearie has resumed her nightmarish dreams."

"Resumed?" Lena laughed. "Had it stopped?"

"Inmates say they hadn't heard her since you left," Akurut chuckled. "Looks like you were the one triggering the dreams dearie, dearie Lena. I hear she doesn't scream in the night. Anyway, today she told that Mukwano guy that she dreamt about a Lilly."

Lena bent forward. "What else did she say about Lilly?"

"She told him to find her and bring her to visit."

"Please tell me everything."

"She asked him if he had received something from Lira."

Lena desperately tried to conceal her excitement. "Something from Lira? What something from Lira?"

"The mosquitos are forcing me to hate this place. They are not our jolly old lake flies which have no interest in human skin," Akurut said as she scratched her neck. "Lena. I hope you are not hiding your connections to Martina from me." She leaned across the table so that her head appeared closer to Lena's. "I insist. What is going on?"

"I really don't know now," Lena whispered. "I am also piecing together bits of information to understand more about Martina.

I told Martina about Lilly, and she promised to ask Mukwano to look for her. But if Martina asked Mukwano if they had received something from Lira then it cannot just be a coincidence that Martina talked about Lilly and Lira. What is that 'something' from Lira? Whatever it is, I am thinking it must be connected to Esther. And Esther is connected to Lilly."

Lena stood up.

Akurut held Lena back to her seat. "What is going on, Lena? Who is Lilly?"

"Martina is in prison for abducting a girl. Maybe she is indeed involved in such rackets?" Lena said and tried to stand up again. "Afande, I need to leave now."

"Why? Where are you going?" Akurut said, relaxing her grip on Lena's shoulders.

"I need to see Martina now!"

"No prison allows visitors at this time."

"Akurut, I am back to Kampala to look for my little sister, Lilly. The old woman who lured me to Kampala and made a slave of me has done the same to her."

"My God, Lena! And you haven't been telling me all this time?" Akurut moved over and wrapped her arms around Lena.

Lena hugged her back.

"Forgive me. I had no idea you harboured such a heart-wrenching story. Have you informed the police?"

"The police?"

"That woman should be arrested and charged."

"We already informed the police back home, but what did they do? Nothing. We tried to look for the woman on our own but we failed."

"But how does Martina know her? I mean your sister? Why

does she ask Mukwano to bring her?"

"I told her. But now I am thinking that Martina has a connection to the girls disappearing. And if I remember well, Arthur one time mentioned that during Martina's trial days, rumours spread that the woman had brothels. This is all confusing to me, Akurut."

"I've never liked the old hag. It's unfortunate, Lena, that you and other innocent people like you end up in prison with real hardcore criminals. Some of them are anything bad you can think of, I tell you."

Lena remained silent, staring at Akurut.

"So yes, it is possible that she has connections to those responsible for what you went through. You have to be careful. Don't take Martina's job. Stay away from them. Mukwano doesn't know where you stay. Just keep away."

"I understand. But I have to go back to Martina, and get more information from her."

CHAPTER EIGHTEEN

When Omadi got a job with Barakiya Security Ltd, a private local security firm, he was made to understand that it was a guard's duty to keep clients and their premises secure, as provided by Ugandan laws. That was the instruction Barakiya had given him during his training.

Boss was responsible for two payrolls that covered Omadi's services. He received 525,000 Uganda shillings per month from Ms. Barakiya Security Ltd. But he also was paid 350,000 shillings from a discreet account known only to him and his boss. To receive a total income of 875,000 shillings per month was a dream come true for him. Not many security guards in Uganda earned that kind of money.

Tonight, Boss needed his extra services. Omadi was ready. He was always ready. Boss took care of the hardest part, the killing. The last two victims were Boss' business associates; the Indian Rhamji, and Faruk. Their families were still looking for them, running announcements on radio and TV. Boss cleaned up really well. Omadi doubted the relatives would ever find out about their people.

All that Boss required of him was to be the undertaker. The first time he watched Boss kill, he almost ran away. But then he thought about his own security. Leaving would make Boss insecure and what would follow was clear. Boss would hunt him down. Omadi consoled himself with the money. With 350,000 extra shillings a month, he hoped he would accumulate enough to build a decent house in the village.

Omadi sat on the floor next to the sofa. He looked up at Boss' eyes. They were as fiery as goblets of charcoal in a burning stove. He wondered who Boss' next victim would be. But he dared not ask.

Boss took his time dubbing away the blood dripping from his hand with tissue paper. Shards of glass still littered the floor.

"Me call Ruta for removing glass?" Omadi looked up at boss.

"Omadi. I do the talking, you listen. Understood?" Boss roared.

"Yes sir." Omadi got on his feet and saluted.

"Now. Follow me." Boss got up and left the room.

Omadi followed. They went behind the servants' quarters to the banana plantation. Only two days back, he had weeded the garden and even thinned the stems. It looked neat and it held its secrets well.

"There." Mukwano pointed. "Next to that second hint of a mound. That is the spot you must dig out as soon as my guest settles down with me inside the house."

"Same size as last hole, sir?"

"Of course you idiot!"

Omadi nodded frantically and saluted.

"Now go and man your gate. And remember: Until we settle, no extra activities."

"Yes sir."

The bell rang. Omadi ran and opened the gate. He gaped in shock.

"Is he in?" Tony brushed passed him.

Omadi did not respond. His mouth was too dry and his tongue too heavy to say anything. Luckily, Tony did not wait for an answer.

***

Mukwano waited at the porch with two glasses of chilled beer. It was a long time since he had shared a drink with the pathetic lawyer. Still, he just did not feel like having one tonight. But he would do it if only to lighten the mood.

"Good evening," Tony said as he accepted the glass of beer.

"Hello."

Mukwano led the way into the parlour, briefly pausing by the door to ensure that Ruta had cleaned up the mess from his last tantrum. There was no trace of cigar stubs or broken glass anywhere. He smiled.

"You may take a seat anywhere you like," Mukwano said as he dropped on a chair.

"I am afraid I will be leaving for another meeting in a few minutes," Tony said and sat on a sofa.

"Tight schedule?" Mukwano beamed. "You are even plumper. And your dark suit is very smart. Where the hell have you been these past four months you geek?"

"On private matters, not exactly important for this meeting," Tony said. "Out of the country, if you must know."

"Globe-trotting all those months," Mukwano said and stood up. He began slowly pacing the floor, his hands neatly planted on either side of his enormous waist. He loved to take charge of situations.

Tony placed his empty glass on a coffee table nearby.

"I can see that your trips greatly deprived you of Ugandan beer. Want some more?"

"Mukwano, it's already coming to seven. I have approximately twenty-five minutes to leave this place. I told you I have a meeting elsewhere."

"Pretty busy." Mukwano laughed. "As usual, the Managing Director of the mighty VG continues to have no authority over the absence or presence of the VG lawyer. You are absconding from duty at the VG, pal."

Tony ignored Mukwano. He pulled out the list of audit requirements, stood up and began arranging them on the coffee table.

"A meeting in twenty minutes, huh? Where if I may ask?" Mukwano prodded. He wondered whether Tony was planning to visit Martina tonight. By law, Luzira was under lockdown past 5 o'clock. But who said this crooked lawyer wasn't capable of finding his way to the old wretch in the dead of the night? Stopping him here and now was timely.

Tony continued arranging the papers on the table in silence.

Mukwano felt a sliver of rage tear through his veins. He pointed a finger at Tony. "Answer me, Tony. You are in my house."

"Are you threatening me?"

"No. I am simply being a host. I need to know what kind of guest I am hosting."

Tony immediately stopped arranging the papers.

Mukwano glanced at the spread-out papers on the coffee table.

"Do not even waste your time with that."

They both resumed their seats.

"I am going to negotiate with you, Tony. But only because you have something I need from you."

"If it is about the legal administration of Martina's estate, I advise you negotiate with her directly." Tony rose and started putting together his papers.

Mukwano strode to the door, turned the key and pocketed it.

"What are you doing?" Tony stared in disbelief.

"You are being stubborn," Mukwano laughed and casually walked back to his seat. "Tell me. Who is Martina to you, anyway?"

"Why do you ask? She is my client, of course. I am her attorney."

"Tony Tony. I will offer you a deal. If you take it, we can forget about this incident."

"I already told you. Go negotiate with her."

"Not without the papers."

"I can squeeze my schedule and accompany you to Luzira tomorrow. We can have it sorted out. I would carry the documents with me."

"And, wouldn't it take ages to retrieve the papers from safe custody?"

"No, let's agree on tomorrow. I have them at my disposal and can avail them any time you need them." Tony bent down to pick his briefcase. His hands shook. He stuffed the papers in the briefcase and hastily fumbled with the lock.

Mukwano passed his hand beneath his own seat and retrieved his pistol. He had oiled it twice that month so it should offer no resistance. He smiled as he pointed the pistol at Tony.

"No, no! W-wait!" Tony dropped the briefcase and raised his hands up. "You can't do that to me."

"Give me one good damn reason why I shouldn't."

Tony stared in disbelief.

"I already promised to go with you to Martina."

"Not good enough, lawyer." Mukwano let out a wretched laugh.

Tony made quick successive strides for the door.

"Take your time. Are you looking for this?" Mukwano dangled the keys.

"Please, don't kill me." Tony was desperate. He went down on his knees. "You can take the papers if you want."

"And where are the papers?"

Tony hesitated.

"Where are the papers?"

"At my house," said Tony. "In a black polythene bag in the attic."

"Thank you, Tony. I believe you," Mukwano beamed. "You are now beginning to read me."

Tony slowly picked himself up, all the while looking at Mukwano. He grabbed his briefcase from the floor.

"Please open the door," Tony said, his voice quivering with fear, "I would now like to leave."

"No," Mukwano said and laughed. "You are not leaving my house, Tony." He held the pistol in one hand and caressed it with the other.

"But why? Why, Mukwano?" Tony said, his eyes wide in disbelief. His body shook. His hands went limp. The briefcase hit the floor and flew open scattering the papers stuffed inside.

Mukwano laughed. All his victims looked the same at this point. Wide eyes, quivering limbs. Mukwano enjoyed their empty stares of resignation, of lost hope, of surrender.

"Dead men don't talk. And I lack patience for pretenders who don't cooperate. I will send you within the minute to join Rhamji and Faruk. Your grave is being dug next to theirs. And, believe me; they have been gone for almost a month now. Nobody can find them. Nobody will find you either."

Tony grabbed the door. He rattled the knob, and heaved against the shutter. He glanced at the pistol and then quickly looked away. In a flash, he dashed to the window. The wind fluttered the curtains. With his bare hands, he tried to pry the burglar proofing wider so he could escape. "Help! Help!" Tony tried to shout but his voice was muffled in terror. He let go of the window, and dropped to his knees. His legs could no longer hold him. He licked his dry lips. He closed his eyes tight as Mukwano inched the muzzle to his temple.

***

Voices from the parlour filtered into the kitchen. Ruta made a sign of the cross. She kissed the cross of her rosary, and let herself down on the kitchen stool. She closed her eyes and listened to Tony beg for mercy. Boss was evil. There was nothing Tony could do to save himself.

She felt old and tired. A shiver of shame shot through her body as she rocked back and forth. She placed her rosary on the kitchen table. Maybe it was time for her to go back to her village in Rukungiri.

Ruta blocked her ears with her hands. Tony, of all Boss' associates, was the only one who ever bothered to ask after her health. She wondered why Boss had chosen Tony this time. A few minutes later, Mukwano yelled at her.

"Call that guard!"

***

Mukwano stared at the bloody mess. He was proud of his gun and its silencer. Nobody would know about Tony's death except himself, Omadi, and Ruta.

***

Ruta rushed to the garden.

"Omadi, it's Tony," she whispered.

She saw tears run down Omadi's cheeks. He sat on the ground, cupping both cheeks in his hands with his knees raised to support his elbows.

"I know."

"Stand up Omadi."

Omadi heaved in silence.

"Omadi!"

Boss yelled from the house.

Omadi wiped his face with the back of his hands and got up.

"Boss wants you now," Ruta said.

"The body…bury," Omadi said and rose.

"I will help you carry the body, then clean up afterwards." Ruta hurried after him to the house.

***

"We have more work waiting. Come to me within the minute," Mukwano said and walked away.

Omadi flattened the soil on Tony's grave. "Go to him when hands dirty, he screams." He mumbled as he hurried to wash his hands and legs. "And now Tony dead!"

Omadi almost collided with Ruta at the door of the parlour.

"Sorry. You me knock almost," he said. He stepped back to allow Ruta move away with her bag of spluttered brain and flesh. "Bad work, mine better," he whispered.

Ruta nodded.

Omadi knocked and entered the parlour. "You asked me,

Boss," he said and saluted.

"Let's go," Boss said, and picked the pistol from the coffee table Ruta had just cleaned. He placed it on his waistband and walked out. Omadi followed him. It was already dark.

"Fetch your gun," Boss said as he strode across the compound towards the gate. "Tell Ruta to come close the gate."

"Ruta, gate," Omadi said. He slung his gun on his back and ran back to his boss at the gate.

Ruta closed the gate.

Omadi and Mukwano crossed the road and stood in front of Tony's gate.

"Knock." Boss whispered to him.

Omadi made three raps on the gate.

Tony's guard opened.

"Get back inside and keep quiet." Boss pressed the nozzle of the pistol on the man's temple and pulled the trigger. The guard staggered backwards before his body slumped to the ground.

"You know what to do, gravedigger."

Omadi hesitated. "This man big. Me go call Ruta for carry."

"Lazy man. Go find a sack, put him in and drag him away. If anyone sees you, I will kill you."

"Boss mad…mad," Omadi mumbled as he rushed back across the road. He pressed the bell on the gate and Ruta opened.

"Mad, I say," Omadi said to Ruta.

"Who?"

"Boss killed Tony guard. Me bury now." He brushed past Ruta who covered her mouth in shock. He went to the store and picked a sisal sack for the body.

"Me bring body. Me bury near Tony."

"And Boss, where is he?"

"Tony house. Looking something."

"That will be the papers which Tony said were in the attic. And still he killed him," Ruta said. "Boss is unstoppable."

Omadi nodded and stepped outside the gate dragging the empty sack on the ground. The nozzle of his gun scrapped the back of his head as he moved.

CHAPTER NINETEEN

Arthur was happy with the report Lena had just given him. "With all this information, I should be able to work backwards and find out more about that Martina case," he said. "Fortunately, I have a few contacts who can help me gather information on brothels in Kampala. We will also involve some experts who will investigate that Esther woman. They will need to go to... is it Oyam?"

"Oyam. I hope they succeed. We failed completely."

"Experts, Lena. I am sure they will track her down. Believe me, we will find your sister. What is important at this point is not to take anything for granted."

It had been a busy day for him, but he had rushed to Lena's hostel when she phoned him to say she suspected Martina to be connected to Lilly's disappearance. He had found her perched at the edge of the bed, waiting for him. She looked sad and from the slight puffiness in her face, it seemed as if she had been crying. She had started narrating the events of the day before he even sat down.

"And you know, at first, I hadn't paid attention to her reaction that time I told her about Lilly. Now that I am connecting the dots, I think that woman reacted in a suspicious manner when I mentioned that Lilly had been taken by the same woman who took me. And since she is in for child abduction I think this woman maybe knowing or connected to old Esther's racket. They are all abductors."

"You need to visit her again," Arthur said.

"I thought about it too but..."

"But what? Listen, If you can get Martina to talk, to tell you a little more about her businesses, about Mukwano and maybe about what put her in jail, we might be able to find Lilly and other girls, don't you think?"

"What put her in jail? You know she is in for abduction."

"Of course, but we need to get her perspective of the whole matter – to talk to her, dig into her business and find out what it's all about."

"Oh. Ok," Lena said.

"But," Arthur said, wagging his index finger, "do not give her the impression that you suspect anything. Convince her to be open with you. Ask after her business. Ask about Mukwano, her other associates and what manner of business she runs. Tell her about your visit to Mukwano's house and the bait you used. Tell her he had refused to see her until you lied to him that she was sick. We need information to proceed. Remember we are not taking anything for granted."

"You are right. I think I will have to. But I will have to wait for the visiting day next Wednesday."

"We can work that out with Akurut, I guess. And you know what? I think I will come with you this time."

CHAPTER TWENTY

"My dearie, what a beautiful Thursday. Your worries are over!" Martina said and embraced Lena. "But who do we have here?" Martina pointed at Arthur.

"Oh, a friend of mine."

"Good morning, madam." Arthur gestured a greeting, withdrawing his hand when Martina ignored it.

"Dearie, I must thank you for getting Mukwano here finally."

"So he came?"

"Yes dearie," Martina said and smiled. She glanced at Arthur over Lena's shoulder.

"I am glad," Lena said.

"And, is he simply a Good Samaritan or your lover?" Martina nodded at Arthur.

"Ahh Martina!" Lena smiled. "Let's just say he is a gentleman and a great friend."

Martina peeked at Arthur. She thought he could make a good match for Lena. But she was not interested in the stranger. She wanted to convince Lena to work for her.

"You see my dearie, you need to get to Mukwano's house immediately. An important job awaits you in my company." She stole another look at Arthur. He had a book open and was bent over it.

"Sit down, Martina," Lena said and pointed at a bench. "If you don't want him, I can ask him to leave."

"As long as he continues reading his books dearie, I have no problem."

"Good. Now tell me. You want me to go to Mukwano's house?" Lena said.

"Oh yes dearie. And by the way, I asked him to try to help you look for your sister. He is happy to help."

"I really pray he finds her."

"For your information, Mukwano is very knowledgeable about Kampala," Martina said. "He has a solid network within the police force and other important people whom he can talk to," Martina said. "You need to meet him and give him details about your sister."

"I see." Lena nodded.

"And dearie, the job awaits you."

"I will think about it."

"But dearie, what's the matter?" Martina said. She was disappointed at the lack of interest Lena showed in the offer.

"I simply have a few questions on my mind, Martina. Did Mukwano perhaps tell you where they all have been in the last four months? Did he also explain why he was so unwelcoming to me until I mentioned that you were sick?"

Martina stared at Lena. "So he didn't want to come, dearie?"

"He didn't want to see me even though he had learnt that I was sent by you. He only came out when I told you were not well."

"Oh dearie me! So he came here because he was convinced I was ill? Oh dearie me!"

"And he didn't want me to reach any other person linked to you."

"I see. That worries me even more, dearie. Are you insinuating that my employees are stabbing me in the back? Do you know anything, dearie Lena?"

"No, Martina. I don't know your people at all."

"I don't know what to think, dearie." Martina sighed. "I only hope he will be here as promised, to bring me the audit report of my estate. He wouldn't dare fail me dearie, would he? He knows how much my estate is worth and that it is only me who can will away my wealth. So, if at all he is reluctant to comply, then at least he will play it safe with me. Now my dearest, will you take the job or will you not?"

"Yes Martina. I will take the job. But please tell me more about your business," Lena said.

"Sssh! You don't want to distract your friend who is really enjoying his book, dearie."

"Sorry."

"I will tell you, dearie. But what manner of business do you think I do, dearie?" Martina said. Just a few months of freedom had brought out a rare firmness and determination in Lena, she thought. Maybe it was the boy? Her suspicious eyes peered at Arthur.

"I do not know, Martina. I only want to understand the business so I can be more useful."

"So, you do not care about the kind of business I run?" Martina searched Lena's face.

"I don't care." Lena affirmed with several head nods. "Besides, I have siblings to feed back home."

Martina let out a low sigh. "I want you to promise me that you will take the job, dearie Lena. You see, I have to get someone, anyone, who can give me information about my firms. You have just revealed to me how Mukwano was reluctant to come. He could disappoint me. Besides, I still don't understand the sudden silence of the last four months."

"I already accepted, Martina. But I will be more effective if I have enough information."

"I will give you a brief, dearie. But you will be given most of the details when you start work."

Lena remained silent.

"Do you doubt me, dearie?"

"No Martina. But I need information so I can assess if I can really be of any use to you. I don't want to disappoint you once I am hired," she said.

"I know, dearie." Martina nodded and glanced at Arthur. She was happy he continued to read his book. She wondered how to disclose the nature of her business without any alarm. Lena had been a victim of her kind of business – lured into the trade with the promise of housekeeping. And yet housekeeping was what the Zura boasted of, at least on the surface. Martina shook her head. Would Lena still agree to associate with a 'housekeeping' establishment? All the same, she would try to convince her.

"You do understand that a housekeeping business is quite decent and distinct from brothel businesses, don't you dearie?"

"Why do you ask that, Martina?"

"Because, I don't want you to misunderstand me, Lena dearie." Martina stood up and held Lena by the shoulders. "If a genuine person offered you a housekeeping job with very good terms, would you take it up?"

***

Lena stiffened. She studied Martina's tense face. The woman was certainly hiding something. Housemaids business? Wasn't it the same excuse old Esther used? The fastest way of finding out was to get involved in Martina's affairs. Get into that business. That way she would get important information. Who knows, the Zura could even have links with that brothel place that had imprisoned her. She felt a wave of anger. Her dislike for Martina threatened to spill out. She struggled to keep calm. She stared into Martina's eyes and said, "Martina, I need to find my sister in addition to taking care of a desperate lot back home. I would gladly housekeep for a bit of money."

"Alright, Lena dearie. I will tell you about my businesses. But promise me one thing."

"What?"

"My businesses cannot be discussed with unauthorised persons." She threw a quick look at Arthur.

Lena was thankful Arthur still seemed to be absorbed in his reading.

"Who authorises?"

"Me."

"I understand."

"May I ask this Good Samaritan of yours to give us our privacy, dearie?" Martina looked at Arthur.

Akurut kept close by, entering and leaving the room several times – perhaps to catch a bit of their conversation while pretending to be checking on them.

"Let him go. You will not be eaten here, dearie." Martina laughed.

Lena asked him to leave.

"That's okay. I will see you later today, Lena." He waved at Lena and walked out of the room.

"Ok dearie. Where were we?" Martina said.

"You wanted to brief me about your businesses."

"Like I said dearie, you will get most of the details when you start work. Mukwano especially will tell you about it. You will also find others like Tony my lawyer, who will give you useful information."

"Is it the housekeeping business you mentioned earlier?"

"That is just one of them Lena, dearie. It is called Zura Maids. It simply connects young women who wish to work as housemaids to potential employers, but I also deal in salt mining in Western Uganda through my firm the Tastier Salt Ltd. You must have come across my products in sachets of 100gms and a kilogram..."

"You produce it? Tastier is quite popular in Acokara for its affordable pricing. I will be glad to make it even more popular when I visit my village."

"If you want, you can choose to work with Tastier directly."

"So you have the Zura and Tastier Salt?"

"Yes, dearie. I also import cars – both new and used – from Japan and sell them in Juba. So tell me. Are you still willing to take the job?"

"I think the Zura sounds good. What job would I be doing?"

"Private secretary, dearie. You will be my private secretary. You will be watching, listening and tracking important aspects of my businesses and reporting to me directly."

"It sounds like a nice job," Lena said in pretended gratitude. Now more than ever, she desperately wished to be part of the Zura establishment. It was one of the ways to find out about her sister's fate. "B-but I still will have to report to Mukwano since he is the Managing Director?"

"Dearest me. I am the owner of the Victoria Group. When I say you will report directly to me, I mean it. I will let him know about it. The rules are mine to make. That is why I have created the post of Private Secretary, the first of its kind in my group of companies."

Lena wondered what that entailed in role and scope. "I hope I will do it well."

"It's merely a title, dearie. But the roles won't be any different from what you may be familiar with. You will be watching financial transactions in my company, taking note of developments and relaying everything to me. You will then relay my thoughts back to them as if they were your own. You will watch the accountants without making it that obvious to firm managers. The managers actually report directly to Mukwano. As you know, he is my Managing Director now that I am here. He works hand in hand with Rhamji, Okello and Faruk. You will find that Rhamji, the Indian, is in charge of Tastier Salt Ltd. Okello is the manager of Tora Sales. And Faruk manages the Zura Maids. They are all hard-working people. You will be at the same rank with them, almost as though you were in charge of one of the VG firms."

"I see. But do you think they can easily accept me? I have no experience."

"I am the owner. They know that, dearie."

"Thank you, Martina." Lena stood up from the bench and stretched. The Zura sounded interesting for a start. She hoped the choice would enable her learn more about Martina and her gang of so-called friends. Maybe even stumble upon clues about her sister's whereabouts. She checked her watch. They had been seated for nearly thirty minutes since Arthur left. It was time to wind up her visit, she thought. She hoped Arthur was waiting outside.

***

"When do I start?" Lena asked. They were now standing outside the room. Akurut was standing nearby.

"Lower your voice, dearie. You can start immediately." But Martina knew she needed Lena more than Lena needed her. Lena would be to the company what her managers were not.

Martina was aware that the longer she stayed in jail, the more independent and powerful her managers became. Jail had made her toothless. With no known relations, the fate of her firms was in their hands. Tony, her lawyer, was the only one she still trusted fully. But she knew Tony was weak, and walked under the shadow of Mukwano. She was aware that her criminal record worsened the security of her estate. She needed to go slow, because any miscalculations on her part could turn her managers against her. The VG company could disappear in no time.

She would give Lena a good salary – more than enough for a decent home, full tummies and good education for her siblings. With time, Lena could gradually accept Zura in its entirety.

"Thank you, Martina," Lena said again and extended a hand in gratitude. "You know what? I sometimes wonder why you are in this place. You are very good to other people."

"Thank you, dearie." Martina beamed. "I myself had a terrible childhood. I became a complete orphan at birth, and an orphanage raised me until a Good Samaritan 'bought me' to be her own child. She turned out to be a drunk, and her drug-dealing boyfriend made a woman of me at age thirteen. I had a son as a result. Dearie, those were terrible terrible years I don't want to remember."

"Where is your son now?"

"Oh, oh! Didn't I tell you, dearie? I lost my poor boy because I couldn't afford malaria treatment. Two years after I buried him, I finally started making money." Martina wiped tears off her cheeks.

"I am sorry Martina." Lena waited for Martina to regain her composure, and then said, "Is it easy to find your office premises, Martina?"

"Yes. It's in Ntinda."

"Ntinda is fine with me. But where in Ntinda exactly?"

"I like your enthusiasm, dearie. You will go to Martina Arcade in Ntinda Township, one kilometer off Kisaasi road, adjacent to the Oval-shaped Church. On the second floor to the left wing you will see a green billboard of Zura Maids. A bodaboda can take you there."

"Ok, I will go there."

"But, don't you want to know the terms and conditions of your service, dearie, how much you will earn at least?"

"Oh. As a matter of fact, how much?"

"3,500,000 Uganda Shillings per month for a start. Will that be ok with you? Just for being my eye?"

"That's a dream for me. Unbelievable, Martina. Thank you so much!"

"You see, it is a win-win situation, dearie. Your phone, please, so I can immediately inform Mukwano about your new position," Martina said.

"No Martina. You know, phones are not allowed in here," Lena said. "But still, we have to deal with the issue of communication between you and me. I was thinking that we could make good use of Akurut to relay info."

"Of all people! I hate that rat! That's out of the question. We will find another way." Martina fumed.

The meeting was over.

***

Lena left Luzira prison alone. She felt unsure of herself. It was unfortunate that Arthur hadn't been able to stay longer. Sitting and listening to Martina talk about her businesses had drained her energy. She had confirmed that Martina recruited housemaids. She walked down the winding road thinking about Martina. How insensitive. How in the world could Martina think that Lena would trust the VG? The Zura? Recruiting housemaids? Hadn't old Esther used that very excuse to throw her into slavery? And Martina had been jailed for abducting a young girl. How could all that be coincidence?

As she made her way across the road to board a taxi, she decided to call Arthur. She needed to see him immediately, tell him everything before she forgot the important details.Arthur's number went through but he didn't pick. She dialled a number of times, until she gave up.

She was getting into a taxi when Akurut called.

"I heard everything the old hag said to you. Everything, Lena."

"Yeah. With your constant coming and going, I knew that's what you wanted."

"But you shouldn't. I mean, don't take the job. She is a witch."

"I am in a taxi right now. We can meet briefly if it's okay."

"Today?"

"Yes. My taxi will pass through Nakawa and I can hop off and be at Mama Rachelle's to wait for you."

"Good. Because I will not allow you to take that witch's job."

"It's more than the job, Akurut. But I can't conclude things on phone. Mama Rachelle's?"

"Yes. But Ameri just called to say she is held up somewhere. She will be relieving me in an hour's time. I can't leave my desk unattended to. Do you think you can wait?"

"Okay," Lena said. She would wait. After all, Arthur wasn't answering his phone. "I will wait."

"Once she comes, I will just board a bodaboda. See you soon," Akurut said.

The line went dead.

***

"Tell me Akurut. Last time, you were querying me so much about Martina. Now did you hear the businesses she talked about? You can see she is rich. She is so rich. She has a lot of money," Lena said the moment Akurut sat down at her table at Mama Rachelle's.

"Well, some people are rich with clean money, while others are rich with dirty money. But personally…didn't I tell you before? Personally, I still suspect some drug business somewhere. I really don't trust her."

"Guess what! I am now thinking about getting that job."

"Don't. Don't take the job. Stay away from them."

"I think they might have Lilly, for sure. If I take that job and get to know them from the inside, I might find her. I can spy on them, you see."

"Still, what if the job turns out to be a trap to re-enslave you? Of what use would it be to you and your sister? Maybe the woman already identified you and now she doesn't want you out there free? So she gives you a job, you go to work, and they capture you again. Maybe that's why she needed Mukwano."

"You are right. I can't just trust people like that. Not after what I have been through. But again, I don't think Martina would go for someone like me. I think such people target young, naïve girls."

"Would you like anything?" Akurut said, waving to a waitress to come over.

"Nothing for me, please. I am ok," Lena said.

"Bring me Mirinda fruity," Akurut said to the waitress.

"My mother taught me not to judge people by mere suspicion," Lena said.

"Your poor mother is probably angry about what you went through, and now Lilly," Akurut said. "Remember it's the same woman who took you away from your home who is also responsible for taking your sister away."

"But we can't be sure that old Esther is linked to Martina," Lena said. "We only suspect them."

"Let's face it, Lena. The woman is in for child abduction. Child abduction and human trafficking, aren't they connected?"

"Please don't."

"It's about your safety, Lena. Now that I am thinking about it, these things are actually happening everywhere so, so much. You probably didn't get to know this, but some time back – I guess it was last year – there were lots of stories on radio and TV about young girls being lured from their homes with promises of getting them housemaid jobs. Some were even taken to the Middle East for whatever reasons."

"All I want is to find my sister. There is a possibility she is connected to Martina."

"I understand, Lena. If you ask me, the old dearie is capable of anything. And by the way, those weren't just rumours. Women in Kampala marched in protest for those children who were being taken from upcountry and brought to Kampala to suffer, while others were sold abroad. Now if the old dearie is talking about a housemaids business, it's very possible that she is selling girls into slavery."

"We really need to find out the truth. Like you said yesterday, people who share interests tend to know about each other. If Martina is pretending to link girls to housemaid jobs when its actually sexual slavery, then she would know other people in the same business."

Akurut received the bottle of Mirinda fruity from the waitress. She inserted a straw and took a sip. "Yes we need to find out more. But how are we going to do this? Definitely not by you taking that job. You are not a trained investigator. And I am no better."

"Yes. We are just two insignificant people. An ex-convict and her little known ex-jailer. I should just take Martina's job, find my sister and forget the law," Lena said.

"You think it's going to be as easy as that? And do you think you will find her there?" Akurut said, spreading out her hands in frustration.

"Listen, I am thinking about something different. Now that I have the directions to the company building, what if I decline Martina's job offer and I instead go to the Zura as a different person seeking a housemaid's job? How about that?"

"Take a housemaid job? At the Zura? Are you quite mad? Now, I don't know what to say." Akurut stood up. Her lips quivered as though she still wanted to say more.

"Yes. I may take the chance. I am even more curious. Maybe this is my chance to save more girls like I did with the brothel."

"Rubbish. I never thought you were this dumb, Lena," Akurut said, and then beckoned the waiter once again. "I am thirsty."

"Okay. You tell me, how else can we learn what goes on in the Zura if we don't get in there?" Lena asked.

"Ah!" Akurut took her seat again. She asked the waitress, who had just arrived, for a bottle of water. "Some water, Lena?"

"Oh I forgot! I was supposed to call Arthur again. I called him earlier, but he didn't pick. I hope I get to him this time," Lena said and reached for her handbag for the cellphone.

"Ahaa! I am glad you mentioned him. He is a lawyer. He will know how to advise you. Talk to him first before you throw your life away."

"He is a very busy man. Besides, he is already helping out anyway," Lena said. "By the way, Akurut, Arthur has been so good to me. He helped me from the beginning. I don't know where I would be if it wasn't for him."

"Okay," Akurut said, and laughed. "Just keep in mind he is a man. Who knows what he sees in you? Who knows what he wants from you? Men are men."

"Arthur is just a good man, I tell you."

"Let's get him here then, and hope he will knock some sense into your head."

"He must be at work."

As she put her phone to her ear she noticed that the waitress was still waiting. She waved the waitress off, gesturing a no to Akurut's offer of water.

"No water for me either," Akurut said. "If she won't have I won't have."

The waitress hurried away.

***

"I hope I didn't keep you ladies waiting for too long," Arthur said as he pulled out a chair for himself. He sat down and dropped a small file on the bamboo table.

"Not really. I am glad you could come," Lena said. "This is officer Akurut."

"We've met before," Arthur said.

"Many times. You used to come visit her in Luzira,"Akurut said. "And of course this morning you came with her to see Martina."

He extended his hand in greeting. "I have heard quite a lot about you."

"Oh really? I hope Lena here hasn't been bad mouthing me." Akurut laughed.

"Just wait and hear. Really bad stuff," Lena said.

"Okay. I am really hungry, ladies. Have you had lunch yet?" Arthur rubbed his abdomen and stood up. He gestured to a waitress who had just served people at a nearby table. He remained standing until she came.

"What's the speciality today?" he asked her.

"It's only mulokony that is ready, sir."

"Mulokony?" Akurut said. "What on earth?"

"Cow hoof, madam," the waitress said.

"Oh, I like cow hoof," Akurut said, and laughed.

"I will have the same," Lena said.

"Same here," Arthur pressed a thumb to his chest. He sat down.

"Finally she accepts something," Akurut said. "You have the magic, Arthur. I hope you can also charm her into declining Martina's job offer."

Arthur stared at Lena. She stared back at him.

"She wants to take the job offer from the old woman," Akurut said. "A very bad move, I must say."

"But I said I won't. Instead, I will go to the Zura and offer myself as a housemaid."

"Oh! Ok," Arthur said.

"After my conversation with her, I now, more than ever, believe that she may be in the same rackets with old Esther. That's why I want to get in and investigate the business. Check if they have my sister. "

"Let me repeat myself here, Lena. You don't trust Martina. She runs a business of linking young women to housemaid jobs, and for all I know she is in jail for abducting a child. That job could be a trap to re-enslave you. And if you go in as a housemaid, there is almost no difference. If they want you, it won't matter if you went as an officer appointed by Martina or as a housemaid," Akurut said.

"Interesting," Arthur said, and bowed his head before Akurut.

"I think I need to explore all possibilities. We don't have any proof that her housemaid business could be selling girls into slavery. We are not even sure she knows Esther, or if her business has Lilly. Look, if I enter the Zura as a housemaid, and the Zura happens to be genuine, then I will be posted to a household. That could clear my suspicions."

"I think it's bigger than that, ladies. If you ask me, it's important that we don't ignore Martina. As she told you, her managers may know people who could help us find Lilly. But above all, if you took her job offer as it is, it's possible she could be tricking you. Look here, she knows you are looking for your sister. She also knows you were deceived and sold into slavery, and perhaps, that you don't trust her. If she is hiding something, she and her managers can use you to show that they run a genuine business. So that option may not really give us the big picture."

"How?" Lena drew her seat closer to the table.

"What if they are not genuine, but they know how to hide their dirt well – so well that one can't easily find out any dirt whatsoever?" Arthur said.

"I still think Lena should not go there at all,"Akurut said.

"Listen Akurut. I, too, am interested. I need as much information as I can on this business. And right now we can't afford to ignore any leads available." He turned to Lena. "By the way, I got a response from the police. That brothel in Kawempe is no more," Arthur said and pushed the file closer to Lena.

"What?" Lena said, ignoring the file.

"That's the report. But it doesn't help much," Arthur said. "Apparently the house was re-designed into a student's hostel after the fire. I believe we are back to square one with our search."

"I guess so. Well, that is out of the way now," Lena said.

"Yes. We can focus on looking for other leads. So, Akurut, as I was saying, we cannot afford to ignore Martina," Arthur said. "By the way, what didn't she want me to hear when she threw me out this morning?"

"Just a brief about her companies and what my job would be," Lena said. "And oh, she also said it was important for me to take up the job because it would put me in touch with her managers, who know a lot of people and possibly where to search for Lilly."

"Really?" Arthur bent forward.

Lena told him the details of what he missed during her meeting with Martina.

"So what do you feel about Martina now?" he asked. "Do you think she is the same person you thought she was? Old, harmless, in need of the sympathy she has recently been enjoying from you?"

"Arthur, please don't say those things," Lena said. "What I want now is to find out if my sister could be a victim of that woman's trade."

"I am glad you have found that you can't just trust anybody blindly. I have heard there are a number of brothels in almost all the Kampala suburbs – Ndeeba, Nateete and others. My contacts in police will check out all of them."

"Just before you came, Akurut here was talking about human trafficking, and trying to link it to Martina," Lena said. "Please explain to me in simple terms what exactly human trafficking is."

"Happy to," Arthur said. "Let's say what old Esther did to you is a typical example. She deceived you that there was a housemaid job waiting for you here in Kampala, then transported you and then before you knew it, she had handed you to some strange people who forced you into sexual slavery. However, unlike you, other victims may be killed for rituals, forced to work in factories, or to become beggars as we see with many children on Kampala streets."

"So you mean I am a victim of trafficking?" Lena said.

"I would call you a survivor not a victim. But Lilly is a victim. In fact, a lot of people think trafficking involves only crossing international borders; they forget that the child brought in from upcountry or from the village or from anywhere is also a victim of trafficking. It is a crime, but our country's legal and policy frameworks are still weak, and not as helpful as they should be in preventing such acts. But it is a global practice with intricate networks. People are reaping millions of dollars from it. Recent estimates suggest that 700,000 victims are trafficked internationally each year. The majority end up as slaves in Malaysia, the Middle East and parts of America and Western Europe. The figure could be larger than that, especially if we also consider trafficking on the African continent, where rings are smaller. Thousands of victims end up slaves within their own country."

"By the way, Lena, even the abduction of children in northern Uganda by Joseph Kony's Lord's Resistance Army was trafficking. Isn't that so, Arthur?" Akurut said.

"All that is human trafficking, of course."

"Imagine thousands of children who were abducted by the LRA. All those young lives destroyed like that." Akurut said. She stood and called out to a waitress tending to another table nearby. "Hey lady, our order is taking much too long."

"Indeed," Arthur said. "Much too long. My stomach is now grumbling."

The waitress approached. "What did you order for?"

"Sorry, I mistook you for your colleague. Your uniforms make you look similar," Akurut said. "We ordered cow hooves."

The waiter who had taken their orders rushed forward with a tray of steaming plates.

"Amen to that," Akurut said and left her seat for the washbasin a few feet away.

"You better do the same. This thing is good when still hot," Arthur said to Lena. "I will watch the table and handbags."

Arthur waited for Akurut and Lena to return before he, too, left for the washbasin.

They started eating.

"But from what I have heard, the Zura Maids doesn't abduct girls. Instead, the girls go there to look for jobs, not so, Lena? So these girls are to blame as well," Akurut said, turning a bone around to suck out the marrow.

"What?" Lena exclaimed. "Akurut, you don't know what you are talking about. Do you think anyone would choose to put themselves in danger? Do you think I chose to end up in slavery? No. I was deceived. The girls are deceived. Besides, it's because they are desperate for jobs."

"Of course those people have many recruitment tactics," Arthur said. "They use manipulative techniques to coerce, deceive and force the girls to enlist with them."

"I feel I have already busted them," Lena said. "I feel I already know all the details of their dirty work. I can't wait to start the mission, Arthur. I just want to penetrate the Zura now."

"Calm down Lena. Remember we have to be extremely careful. Let me tell you something. If we are to prove that the Zura deals in human merchandise, we have to look for evidence. We will have to ask and answer many questions: Does Zura or its associates run deceptive ads locally and abroad in newspapers? What manner of agreement is reached between the Zura and the victim and her family members? What nature of work do they advertise to those seeking to be housemaids? We need to also take note of patterns of recruitment, who actually links up the victims to the Zura? We could also try to identify any girl who is locally employed through the Zura. Or even better, one who deserted work."

"Why would we? That is certainly police work and we would do well to involve them from the start," Akurut said. "Because if our suspicions are true, these may be dangerous people, gangs, in fact. If you ask me, everything sounds really complicated."

"I know our police," Arthur said. "They would immediately launch a raid, maybe find nothing and later, when we need them most, lose interest in following up. Let's do our part: Get the real truth, and then we can involve them later. What if we are wrong? What if it's a genuine business?"

Arthur was more than enthusiastic to extend the traditional boundaries of pro bono services to the rescue of girls enslaved by the Zura. All they needed was to find inside details of the Zura establishment. If they could get in touch with girls who have been recruited as housemaids, or even lay hands on the Zura documents, the rest would be left to the police. But he was uncomfortable about Lena getting into the Zura. He knew it would not be safe for her. They would have to be very careful.

Arthur finished his meal and pushed his plate aside. He went to wash his hands, followed by Akurut. They both returned to their seats.

"Officer, I am glad we have you on board. You will keep a close eye on Martina. Remember she asked Mukwano to take Lilly to her. So, keep watch," Arthur said.

"I am more than glad to be on board," Akurut said and extended a firm handshake to Arthur.

Lena pushed her plate aside and went to wash her hands.

Arthur took note of key names and positions in the VG; Mukwano, Tony, Faruk, Rhamji and Okello. They agreed that Lena minimise her movement as much as possible. Arthur offered to go downtown and purchase a simple black hair wig, one black bulky jumper and a toe-length makeba skirt from the second-hand heaps at St. Balikudembe Market.

"When do you think you can present yourself at the Zura, Lena?" Arthur said.

"Ah. Immediately. Even now," Lena said.

"Let me see." Arthur pulled his cellphone from a coat pocket and flicked through the dates. "Mmmm. Let's see...Friday, tomorrow is not good. I will be in court on Monday. Tuesday next week. Let's get you into the Zura on Tuesday next week."

"As Martina's secretary or as a potential housemaid?" Akurut said.

"As a potential housemaid," Lena said.

"That's settled then," Arthur said. "Luckily I have some free time on my hands during that week. I will look up Martina's case to see if I can find something valuable."

CHAPTER TWENTY-ONE

"Good morning madam," Lena said.

The receptionist looked at Lena's dress, laughed and shook her head.

"How may I help you?"

"My name is Maggie," Lena said. "I am looking for a job as a housemaid."

"It's on a first come, first served basis. Interview fee is five thousand shillings. Pay here first, and then fill in this form."

Lena noticed the doubtful stare. She was not aware of the fee. She feared she could be turned away. She rummaged inside her bag, and retrieved a five thousand shilling note, thanks to Arthur's generosity.

Without a care, the middle-aged receptionist grabbed it and handed her the form, a one-pager.

"Fill it in."

Lena felt strange referring to herself as 'Maggie'. Arthur had suggested the name. The receptionist had plucked the form from a long, thick pink book. Each leaf, ripped off, left a stub almost like a cheque book. The receptionist recorded the amount on that stub. Maggie noticed no such provision on her form. She almost asked for a receipt but remembered she was supposed to be ignorant, poor and desperate for the job.

She had on an old makeba skirt that threatened to tear at the seams, again thanks to Arthur who had bought it. The black of her bulky jumper had turned dirty brown in parts and was threadbare at the elbows. The black Afro wig was her near salvation, except the fabric remained unkempt, and it jutted out uneven ends in all directions. Her feet had on bathroom sandals that Arthur had remembered to pick at the last minute.

"Atyang Maggie is your name. It is amazing what clothes can do to a person,"Arthur had announced. "From now on, Lena does not exist."

When she looked at herself in the mirror, she wept. She was all ragged like a lunatic. She looked pathetic. Arthur had simply waved off her protest and said her life and Lilly's were more important than her appearance during the mission. He told her he was ready to change his appearance too. He had to penetrate the Zura as someone else. He continued to tell her the details of his own plan, after which they held hands and prayed for success.

"And remember, in case you see Lilly," Arthur had said, "Do not, for anything in the world reveal that you know her."

"You keep on saying that, Arthur," Lena said. "But Lilly, God protect her, might see me and fall all over me!"

"If that happens, just feign mistaken identity. Remember your name is Maggie."

"Atyang Maggie. That's a pretty name," Lena said. "I will take it."

"Remember, no silly mistakes. Be focused. I will not be far from you."

Before she left the hostel, she used a headscarf to hide the matted wig, and wore a wrapper around her to conceal the rags. A few meters from Martina Arcade, Lena entered a public toilet where she paid the attendant two hundred shillings. She used a couple of minutes to stuff her headscarf and wrapper into her faded handbag.

Lena studied the form. It was a brief checklist where she needed to fill in her particulars. It was the usual; name, sex, age, marital status, tribe, physical address, next of kin, religious affiliation, education, languages spoken, any contagious diseases. She filled it in and handed it back to the receptionist.

"Wait over there." The receptionist pointed to a bench.

Three teenage girls clad in old oversized, dirty rags and looking scrawny sat waiting for their own turns. Lena thought she rivalled their desperate looks. The one on the left sat with her hand propped on the knee, her face resting in her palm. Lena sat next to her.

"Hello. My name is Maggie. You?" Lena said.

"Mine is Betty. Have you also come for a job here?"

"Hey! You don't talk unless you are asked to." The receptionist growled at them.

The girls waited.

When it was Lena's turn, the receptionist directed her to a door marked 'Admissions.' Almost like a school, thought Lena. Or a hospital. She dreaded meeting Mukwano, and hoped to God that somebody else was in-charge of the admissions process. If only she could get the admission, get enlisted and join the girls. She would then search for information and disappear as soon as she got it. She would avoid any contact with Mukwano.

She closed the door behind her and faced a woman. She was a plump woman with skin yellowed from what Lena thought was careless application of bleaching agents. Lena almost hugged her for not being Mukwano.

She sat on a wooden chair in front of the woman's desk. Sounds of hearty laughter floated from the reception area and Lena wondered who on earth made the mean receptionist laugh.

The woman at the desk studied Lena. Lena got worried. Were her disguises adequate?

"You are Atyang Maggie?"

Lena heard the woman say.

"Yes, madam. That's me."

"I can see you dropped out of school in senior three. Why didn't you finish your O-level? Tell me your story. Why do you want us to employ you?"

Lena had not prepared for this part. She had to say something quick. Anything that could fall in favour with this woman. "I am from Oyam district. My parents were killed during a rebel attack on our village. At the moment, my four siblings depend on me. We live in an IDP camp. I cannot provide for my siblings. That is why I need the job."

The woman kept quiet.

"Please." Lena said. She worried that the woman had perhaps heard similar stories from desperate girls before and was therefore not moved anymore. What if the woman rejected her? She wondered whether it was not a mistake to refuse Martina's job offer. Then she would need no funny disguises, no interview, no rejection. And she would have a good salary.

"How did you find this place, Maggie?"

"Oh," Lena fumbled. "A woman from our village whose husband works in Kampala needed a housemaid. She brought me with her three months ago. She promised that she would pay me. But she did not pay me. Now, my siblings need to eat and be in school. I need money." Lena paused. The woman was busy scribbling away on her notepad. It seemed the woman believed her story. She continued: "I talked to someone about my misery and she directed me here. She is also a housemaid who the Zura employed. She told me she is happy where you placed her."

"You see? We are good! We are the best in this country." The woman beamed. "Now, who is that good ambassador of the Zura?"

"I do not know her name. She never told me." Lena hoped to God the woman would not probe any further.

"Hmm," the woman nodded. "Any diseases Maggie?"

"What?"

"Your health is important for such a job. Any history of infections and sicknesses?"

"None."

"Any criminal records?"

"None," Lena wondered who in their right senses would reveal such records anyway.

"Any relative working in a government position, Maggie? We would need their help in case of a problem."

"None, madam."

"Good! When would you be available for placement?"

"I can even start tomorrow if you hire me."

"You will be hired as soon as we get calls for placement from clients. For now, you will report for training next week, on the 1st of July. We will house you as we train you for the job."

"Thank you, madam. How long does the training take?"

"Between two to four weeks. Depends on the demand."

Lena smiled. She was glad that the interview was over.

"Be sure to report here with your belongings on July 1st," she said. "That is a week from now."

"Thank you, madam," Lena said. She turned and exited the room, the Zura, the VG.

She mumbled as she sat in a taxi back home, "That was easy. I am beginning to enjoy the game!"

CHAPTER TWENTY-TWO

Arthur urgently needed to carry out quick data retrieval from the Judiciary of Uganda website. He had agreed with Lena he would be at the Zura Maids the same morning to seek a job. A placement with the VG could enable him to get important information, and at the same time follow up on Lena's welfare if she was given a job in the Zura establishment.

He hurried to the Makerere University Library for its high speed Internet. He gave himself a few minutes within the University facilities to log on and search relevant information on Martina's abduction with intent to murder case. A click sent him to the Uganda Judiciary site. He paused to glance at the mission: 'To dispense justice to all people in Uganda, through timely adjudication of disputes without discrimination.' Arthur wondered what that meant in a monetised system where more than half the population lived below the poverty line and in the hands of their often powerful, more economically abled exploiters. The word 'without discrimination' angered him.

A drop down menu; Law Reporting sent him to the data bank of the entire judiciary reports of Uganda dating from the 1970s. Martina had been indicted by the High Court and immediately sent to prison in 2007. He scrolled down to High Court 2007.

He was on Martina's chronicled case within a minute: It was Government of Uganda vs. Martina Maa (criminal session case No. 2001 of 2007) before Justice Fiona Mukyala.

Arthur thought Justice Fiona Mukyala was the most revered disciplinarian in the nation's Judiciary. As a law student, Arthur had been a great admirer of Justice Fiona Mukyala and her no-nonsense attitude. She publicly shamed people who tried to bribe her to pass judgement in their favour. She defended suspects with poorly prepared lawyers, often interrupting her own court to ask a client to get a better lawyer. Unprepared lawyers with cases before her shook like leaves in the wind. Her name would go down among the great African women.

He ordered a printout of the record and logged out.

"How much do I pay?" he asked the Librarian.

"Three thousand shillings."

Arthur paid the money and took the printout.

He folded up the papers and safely stowed them within the folders of his plastic file. He hurried out of the Library, off Makerere campus. He hopped onto a bodaboda and dashed to Nasser Road in downtown Kampala. Nasser Road was renowned for its mastery at forgery. Winding in and out of traffic, he spotted the scrawled words: Key Cutter and IDs. In normal times, Arthur thought, he would love to go after such a guy, squeezing life out of him every day in court. But today, he needed the man desperately.

He hopped off the bike. He felt very conspicuous as he made his way up the dark, narrow flight of stairs. It was unbelievable that he, a lawyer with a name to protect, was heading for forgery. What if he met someone he knew? But it was okay. Everyone has his days, he thought. The stairs led him to a short, fat man. They shared a greasy handshake; the man had been busy re-installing a faulty printer.

Arthur cleared his throat. "I lost my ID," he said. "Could you make one for me immediately?"

"Precisely." The businessman happily extended a piece of paper and a pen. "Put your particulars down here."

Arthur threw a few quick glances over his shoulders, to the amusement of the man. This was a case of using a thief to catch another thief, he comforted himself. If he were to present himself to the VG as a school dropout he would need new identity. He chose the name Jesse Kigulu, a former student of Makerere College School. He scribbled his wishes down.

"Want a transcript to go with it?" The businessman beamed in expectation.

"Yes."

Twenty minutes later, Arthur dashed out with his new identity card and an Advanced level transcript. He headed to MAX's, a unisex saloon in Wandegeya.

"Shaolin," he said to the barber, and then took a seat.

"That will be five thousand shillings," the barber said.

A few minutes later, Arthur peered into the mirror and saw a bald-headed man. Never in his working life had he ever shaved off all his hair. But this was a precaution he couldn't avoid. He was running late for the Zura. He paid the barber and dashed out. He headed straight for a roadside kiosk that had sunglasses displayed on a rack against the wall. They were of different shades and styles. Arthur grabbed a simple clear pair and put them on.

He hired a bodaboda and headed for Ntinda, to the VG.

***

"Can I help you?" The receptionist asked laughing.

Arthur noticed two poorly-dressed teenage girls waiting on the bench. He felt awkward. He hoped the Zura recruited male workers as well.

"I am Jesse. Here for a job. I mean, not the housemaids job though," he said to the receptionist.

The receptionist burst into laughter. The third door on the left of the narrow corridor opened, and a mahogany skinned giant of a man came out. Arthur knew this was Mukwano because of the noticeable left limp Lena had described to him.

"Sorry, I mean, I thought you considered men as well." Arthur silently cursed, wondering where Lena was. He didn't know whether to stay or just dash out.

The receptionist immediately got busy re-organising an already neat desk, and in the process scattering her items instead.

"What is the noise all about?" Mukwano shouted at the receptionist.

"I am sorry, sir. It is this young man here, sir. He is looking for a vacancy, sir," the receptionist said.

Mukwano ran his eyes up and down the entire length of Arthur.

"I am looking for a job, sir," Arthur said. "N-not as a housemaid though. I am sorry for bothering you, sir. But I am desperate. I can do any job."

"And who told you we are giving out jobs at this time?"

"I am just moving to any office, sir. This is the third place I have visited this morning and I hope you can give me a chance."

"Leave your contacts. If we need you, she will contact you. Now if you will excuse us, we have business to attend to," Mukwano said and turned to leave the room.

"Please, sir."

"You heard me right," Mukwano said, waving Arthur off. He then disappeared through the door he had earlier emerged from.

Arthur swallowed hard. If he failed to get a place in the VG, then his plan would totally fail. He needed information. Besides, Lena needed someone close by. And if the VG turned out rotten and she did any silly mistake, she could easily be caught.

He pulled out a handkerchief from his trouser pocket, dabbed the sweat that had formed on his brows and turned to the receptionist. "Madam, I really do need a job. Any job. I can sweep, clean toilets, be a messenger, anything."

"Young man, all those places are full. Now please excuse me. I have other people to attend to."

One of the girls seated on a bench giggled her way to the receptionist. Arthur knew he was supposed to step away, but he did not move. He felt transfixed to the spot. Somehow, he had to convince these people.

"Madam," he said.

"Look young man, why don't you leave your number behind?" The receptionist said. "As Boss said, if anything comes up I will call you."

CHAPTER TWENTY-THREE

Arthur knocked on the door.

"Who is there?" Lena said.

"It's Arthur."

"You look...oh my God, you look different, Arthur," Lena said as she held the door to her room wide open. "Please come in."

Arthur walked past Lena.

"What happened to your hair?"

"I know. I look like dirt," Arthur said. "And so did you this morning, remember?"

They both laughed.

Arthur couldn't sit down on the chair. Somehow he didn't want to tell Lena that he had not gotten the job. This was something he would have to work out privately; he had to do all he could to penetrate the Zura. He gazed at Lena wondering why he had thought it would be easy for him to get a job at the VG just like that? How could he have believed in that plan?

"Why are you looking at me with such sadness?" Lena asked.

"Am I?"

"I have never seen you this sad," she said. "Coffee or tea?"

"Coffee, strong," he said, and then sat down in the chair. "Any news from Akurut?"

"Nothing," she said. "So, did you find time to visit the VG today?"

"Sure."

"How did it go? Were you accepted?" She pulled out a kettle

from under the table, filled it with water from a small jerry can, and then lit the stove. She placed the kettle on the stove.

"Everyone laughed when I said I was looking for a job."

"But why? Was it your hairless head?" She laughed.

"No. Something much more serious. The Zura is a housemaid's bureau you know, and the receptionist thought I wanted a housemaid's job. It even brought your Mukwano out of his lair."

"So your awkward situation at the reception was the cause of the laughter I heard while I was in the interview room?" Lena said.

"Oh. Were you in the interview room by then? That means Jesse and Maggie almost bumped into each other."

She laughed.

Arthur looked at the file he had been carrying, and thought about the fake certificates it contained. It felt heavy in his hand. He placed it on the table. Even for a good cause like this one, he felt terrible that he had supported the dirty schemers in downtown Nasser Road. He kept it to himself though. It was a dark secret he would reveal only to security operatives once the case was over. He hoped that this might also be the beginning of ridding Kampala of forgers and con artists.

"Coffee," Lena said. She placed a steaming cup on the small table.

"Oh thank you," he said and reached for the cup. He took a sip. He loved it. "They said they would call me as soon as possible," he lied. It was better not to dwell too much on the VG for now. He would find a way into the VG, somehow.

"I am to report in a week's time for training," Lena said and sat back on her bed. "I am glad to be back here though. That place was somehow stressful."

"And who knows what rot might really be in there?" Arthur said. "Anyway, I looked up Martina's case this morning."

"What did you find?" She sat straight and gazed at him.

"Quite a lot," Arthur said. "Martina Maa was indicted for abducting a girl called Lucky Mukama. She was from Entebbe. It was said Martina intended to murder the girl."

"So she's a murderer as well? Did they say how she got the girl? Please tell me everything – everything," Lena said, drawing closer to the edge of the bed.

"Most obliged, madam." Arthur said, smiling. "You see, the government lawyers stated that in the early afternoon of 15 December 2006, thirteen-year-old Lucky Mukama was discovered heavily drugged and unconscious outside the gate of Martina Maa's home in Kololo."

"Thirteen. That's almost Lilly's age."

"Yes," Arthur said and felt for his phone. "Excuse me, this could be a client."

"Hello," he said. "Can I be of help?"

"Hello. Is this Mr. Jesse Kigulu?" a female voice said.

"I am," he said.

"You were at the Zura this morning. You are lucky you left your contact with us. My boss wants to see you."

"To see me." Arthur felt stupid repeating this. But he couldn't believe what the lady was saying and found it necessary to say something. "Now?"

He realized he needed to pull himself together fast.

"No. Tomorrow at 9am."

"Thank you, madam. I will be there at 9 am." He flicked his phone off and stared at Lena.

"That is good news?"

Arthur smiled. "It appears the VG Boss has a job for me. I will go to see him tomorrow morning."

"But Arthur, somehow I am worried. If that man gives you a job, will you be safe with him? He seemed cruel."

"I think if I do my job really well, I should be out of the VG within a few days. You should also do your best in the shortest time possible," Arthur said.

"If you ask me, the little time I spent in there was hell already," Lena said.

"No doubt about that," Arthur said. "But where were we with the story behind Martina's jail term?"

"Oh yes," she said. "Please tell me everything."

"Where were we?"

"The girl was drugged and left at Martina's gate," Lena said.

"Yes." Arthur nodded. "You know, the girl came from a fairly wealthy family, and they searched for her aggressively. A witness told the police that she had seen a silver grey truck with dark tinted windows parked opposite the girl's home. Kampala Regional Police took over the case from the Entebbe Police. They traced the truck to Martina Maa's compound. A blind raid on Martina's residence was immediately ordered by the Criminal Investigations Department and they found the girl dumped in front of Martina's gate, unconscious. Martina was in her house. They arrested her for abduction with intent to murder."

"Just like that?" Lena asked.

"Unfortunately for Martina, this was a time when the country was experiencing a serious wave of child sacrifice. But matters became worse when the girl pointed at Martina as her abductor."

"Maybe the girl was as sure about Martina as I am of old Esther?"

"According to the doctors who treated the girl, she was drugged with sedatives."

"The drug bit reminds me of Akurut's suspicions about Martina." Lena chuckled. "Maybe she knew about that story, that's why she suspected Martina to be involved with drugs."

"The girl stated that there were two men in the said truck who lured her by saying that her mother, who worked with Housing Finance Bank in Kampala, had sent them to pick her for early Christmas shopping. In the car, one of the men gave her sweets, and after eating them she became drowsy. But she remembered that they took her to a house. In that house, an elderly woman and another man looked at her and constantly shook their heads as though they disagreed on something. She couldn't make out what they were saying because she was drowsy from eating the sweets. Later, she woke up in a small room all by herself. The door was locked from the outside. She called for help, and a man with a big syringe rushed in and stuck it in her right arm without saying anything to her. The next thing she remembered was waking up in hospital with a severe headache and her parents by her side. Later, when the girl was well enough, the police paraded Martina and other people before her. She identified Martina immediately."

"Oh my God! And Martina? What did she say?" Lena asked, her eyes and mouth wide open.

"Martina did not deny that the girl was in her house," Arthur said. "But she said she had nothing to do with her presence there."

"But I don't understand the way the law works. Other people abducted the girl, but it was Martina taken as the abductor?"

"The law provides that all persons indirectly or directly involved in the disappearance of a person are liable."

"Maybe Martina was trying to enrol this girl in the housemaid's bureau. But again, why would they leave her outside her gate?"

"But Martina claimed that it was easy for anyone to find her home because she was a well-known businesswoman," Arthur said. "She claimed that on that day, a man called her house, and said he had a stranded girl who could benefit from her bureau's help. She instructed the man to take the girl to the bureau for assessment, but instead the man said he was in a hurry. He insisted on dropping the girl at Martina's. She agreed to see the girl along with her employee, Mukwano, who had dropped by for a quick briefing. When the girl was taken to Martina's house, Martina noticed her drunken state. The girl was drowsy and couldn't talk. Martina immediately realized that the stranger who had taken the girl to her house was hiding something. She refused to take in the girl and ordered the man to take her to the nearest hospital and inform the police. The next day, however, police descended on her house and arrested her. That was Martina's side of the story."

"Eeh! And yet the first day she joined me in my ward she said she was innocent. Now I see that she could be guilty. But I may still be wrong," Lena said.

"The Judge is the best we have in the country. She is known for doing a thorough job on her cases, my dear. I believe she based her conclusions and sentence on the strength of the evidence before her. Your Martina had a weak defence. Apart from saying she was innocent, did she ever discuss this case with you?"

"Yes and no. All she told me was that she would be in for fifteen years on child abduction. By the way, I think it can also be possible that she was set up. Maybe they drugged the girl half way so she would still be able to see Martina and identify her later. Why else would they then go ahead to completely drug her before dumping her strategically by Martina's gate? Arthur, I am actually asking myself: Why Martina's residence? Why didn't they drug the girl and then dump her at the VG headquarters or somewhere else?"

"I would need to borrow your brain to help me with a few of my clients, your honour. I am impressed with your take. Unfortunately Martina did not report the case and she did not say who the strange man was."

"Anyway, I am not defending Martina."

"I hope we will be lucky enough to confirm our suspicions of the Zura. Will they link you to a household, right away?"

"The woman said I will first undergo some form of training for about two weeks or more."

"I hope this training will take place at the VG, because that would be a good opportunity for you to spy."

"They said they will have me housed and fed during the training until I get an employer. They didn't mention where the training would be."

"Anyway, wherever it will be, eavesdrop on conversations, sneak into any files if a chance comes up, befriend an employee. But also, keep in mind that the Zura may be a legitimate business."

"Sure. As soon as I find out that they are legitimate, I will leave."

"Remember your objective for going into the Zura is not for a job, but for information. And, it won't matter whether the firm turns out to be clean. You will leave as soon as you have relevant information."

"When you went to the VG, did you see any other managers besides Mukwano? Martina talked of... was it three? Tony and two others."

"I wouldn't know them if I saw them. Anyway I didn't meet any other male employee of the VG apart from Mukwano. I recognised him because of that famous limp you talked about."

"I didn't meet any males there either. And I am really not looking forward to meeting any. If you ask me, Mukwano is already more than enough!"

"Listen Lena, I am thinking, what if I met Tony. He is the VG lawyer, isn't he?"

"Yes he is."

"You have his contacts, don't you?"

"I have his cellphone number which, by the way, never goes through," Lena said and opened her handbag. "But I also know his house. It's just opposite Mukwano's." She pulled out the wrinkled piece of paper from the bag. "Why do you want to see Tony?"

"I would love to talk to him about Martina, about her case. Perhaps I would even befriend him. With him, I might tap into the VG network of friends. Who knows where that could lead us?"

"Here is the contact. The paper is all worn out. Let's copy the numbers on clean paper."

Arthur accepted the paper and looked at it.

"On second thought though, meeting him or the other managers could later blow my cover if Mukwano offers me a job tomorrow." He folded the paper and put it in his shirt pocket.

"Maybe you can speak to Tony at the VG when you start working," Lena said.

"Yeah. Though that too presents a problem of its own."

"A problem? What problem?"

"At the VG I will be a senior-six drop-out."

Lena laughed.

"Yes. A sweeper, tea boy, some lowly position that would allow me access to any office. Now imagine a tea boy or a sweeper chatting with a lawyer. Anyway, leave that to me." He consulted his watch, and then stood up.

"Are you leaving already? You said you were taking a break from work."

"Yes I did take the break. I just have a few errands to take care of before I bury myself completely in the Zura come tomorrow morning."

"Oh. Okay."

"Listen, Lena. I think you should go see Martina again."

"Really? Do I have to tell her if I won't take her job offer? No way, I don't owe her that much."

"I thought it would work to our advantage if we got her side of the story. Remember, Lena, I am trying to get answers to some of the questions I have about Molly as well. I can't take any opportunity for granted."

"If it's important to you, of course I will do it."

"I am itching to learn more about that woman."

"We may have to wait for the official visiting day then. I don't want to put Akurut in trouble. She has already done a lot for me."

"Don't forget, I am a lawyer. I could present myself as Martina's lawyer. Lawyers are allowed to see their clients any day from Monday to Friday. We will go tomorrow after I have met Mukwano."

"The guards know me, Arthur. They still remember me."

"It doesn't matter. What you are or what you do when outside prison doesn't concern them. You will be my assistant."

"Would you like to speak to Martina? Wait a minute, I am losing track of time. Today is Tuesday, right? Yes. Visitation day is Wednesday."

"Perfect. And yes, I want to speak to her. But remember what happened the last time we visited together?"

"She threw you out."

"I will need you to convince her to let me stay. Tell her I am a lawyer and I want to re-open her case."

CHAPTER TWENTY-FOUR

Twilight found Mukwano alone, enjoying the serenity of his beautiful garden. It had been a wonderful day. He now and again replenished a glass of red wine to celebrate. What more could one want if all one's dreams were turning into reality? All of his plans were falling into place. In no time, he would be the sole owner of the lucrative VG group. He downed some more wine and savoured its goodness. He nodded in his honour. Fate had finally turned the tables on his archenemies. He had been too fast for them.

He was such a lucky man to have such workers as Ruta, the faithful house servant who could murder for him; Omadi the faithful fool who could slit his own throat for him. And the good Real Associates partners who could stake their own lives for him.

And then Jesse Kigulu, the stupid, desperate young thing walks into the VG looking for a job just when he needed a new messenger. Mukwano hoped he could make a good student out of Kigulu. He would let him start as a messenger all right. The boy was desperate. He could have suggested a noose man's job, and the boy would have gladly accepted. He would keep him on a tight leash – maybe let the RA guys mentor him a bit.

Mukwano liked the tactic, short circuit, which the Zura used to tame human merchandise. At the experimental stage ten years earlier, Martina had protested against the short circuit tactics yet their clients were complaining about the 'big headedness' of the girls. In the end, she had no alternative. She endorsed it to save the Zura from folding. Zura Maids had survived because of short circuit.

It was an unspoken rule within the VG establishment that short circuit was exclusively meant for the girl merchandise. But Mukwano would break that tradition. He would be the first to employ the tactics on staff. What he needed was his staff. He needed to hold the keys to their brains, lips and breath. He needed chains on their legs. And VG's short circuit technique would undoubtedly deliver both key and chain to him. He would then, as the owner, have unquestionable control of the establishment.

Kigulu would be his first target for the short circuit. He only had to wait for a week or so to employ it. What a way to start a new month, he laughed. He discarded the wine glass on the lawn, and instead celebrated his brilliance from a large wine bottle. It was a triumphant day.

So far, he had spent the entire morning raising hell about the disappearance of his deceased 'friends'. From the VG headquarters in Ntinda, Mukwano had demanded information concerning the 'theft' of US$1,600,000 by the three fools. He ordered the return of Tora Sales manager, Okello, from Juba, South Sudan. The RA partners had executed all his orders all right.

Already, Tony's unexplained disappearance was on every staff member's lips. Word had exploded among Kampala's VG network and immediately travelled along a telephone line back to Mukwano. In fact, the informer had noted that Tony had not been seen for close to four months. VG's money had disappeared within the same time. Everyone found it difficult to exonerate Tony from having taken part in the alleged theft.

The VG networks were at a loss.

Mukwano had gone an extra mile to harass the friends and families of the three men. The families had only a day to produce their men and the missing money; otherwise they would face justice for involvement in the theft.

Three loud honks outside the gate interrupted his thoughts.

***

From the corner of the garden, Omadi wondered what fool would dare visit their den of hell. Perhaps Boss had invited a friend and forgot to instruct him? Boss had few friends. Omadi could count them on his fingertips. Ahmed and Alug of the Real Associates were the two remaining friends who had not crossed Boss's path yet, thought Omadi.

The second round of honking rushed Omadi to Boss.

"Someone knocking, sir."

"I am expecting Ahmed and Alug tonight. Go check if they are the ones and let them in."

Omadi immediately let in Ahmed and Alug. They loved Boss but rarely came to his house unless there were important business discussions.

***

In the privacy of his luxurious parlour, Mukwano uncorked a large bottle of champagne and the three celebrated the goodness of life.

"We made sure we came immediately," Ahmed said. He loved Mukwano like an elder brother and would do anything to give him his dreams. Mukwano was their seed funder. He had secretly dipped his fingers into the bottomless vault of the VG three years earlier to give the RA its first breathe of life. Mukwano never hesitated to link them to all lucrative deals in South Sudan and in the VG itself. The seed fund had been non-refundable, of course, and for that they remained forever indebted to their friend.

"I hope this is just a stunt that you have pulled. Or, is it what I think with the three dudes?" Ahmed said. He immediately realised that his spoken thoughts had soured the champagne.

"And what would you be thinking in your peanut head, pal?" Mukwano said, dropping down on the nearest sofa.

"Those men disappear for more than a month, moreover with a whooping US$1,600,000 and you are just telling us today?" Ahmed rubbed in. He was of hotter blood than Alug. He liked picking manageable fights with Mukwano – fights that Mukwano, being their seed funder, often won. Tonight, however, Ahmed worried about Mukwano's drinking. Mukwano was already drunk, and a little argument could turn ugly.

"What do you think, Alug?" Mukwano said, ignoring Ahmed.

Ahmed refilled his glass with champagne. Mukwano aimed for smaller fish, his partner Alug, the humbler one.

"You want me to tell you the truth boys? Huh? That they are dead and buried? Is that what you want to hear?"

Ahmed exchanged a quick, worried glance with Alug. The confession greatly shocked him. The VG 'renegades' were Mukwano's friends. He immediately sat down next to Alug on a two-seat sofa facing Mukwano.

"Are you trying to make a man out of yourself, Ahmed boy?" Mukwano laughed. A series of hiccups escaped his chest.

The two partners remained still. There definitely was something wrong with their good friend tonight.

"You know we are always at your service, sir," Alug said.

Mukwano peeked at his friends. A drunken hiccup escaped his chest again. "You know why I called you here, boys?"

"Not at all," they answered in unison.

"Now listen carefully. Carefully. I have two urgent assignments for you tonight. One: I want you to study VG's financial system for the last year to the last details. Then, quickly apply your trademark astuteness to establish clever gaps revealing a combined $1,600,000 missing from the Zura and Tastier Salts."

The two men continuously nodded in respect to their host's instructions. Even intoxicated with alcohol, Mukwano still commanded their respect.

"The work has practically been done for you already." Mukwano burped. He fumbled for something in his wallet. In between burps and hiccups, he managed to bring out three flash disks. He passed them to Ahmed, "Everything you need to do a neat job is there. And two: prepare to run around and involve the police in all this by nine o'clock tomorrow morning. Like the good old buddies that you are, you will pick up from where I will stop.

"Basically my job is simple. On behalf of the VG, I will officially complain to the police about the embezzlement, and the disappearance of our three staff. The usual interrogation stuff should be wrapped up by midday tomorrow. I normally wouldn't stand such irritation, but this sacrifice is worth it, pals. I will expect you to handle the interrogation process. Make certain the three are implicated at all costs. A little bit of discomfort to family and close friends of these thieves would produce the right effect. And then, make sure you handle the publicising yourselves. These media rogues can be mean sometimes when there is no early worm to pick. Make them happy so that we grab prime space. You will find pictures, good ones I must say, in the files at the VG. Ask my secretary for them. When that is done, I have another urgent assignment for you." Mukwano staggered to his feet.

Ahmed uncorked another bottle of champagne, and the three had a toast to seal the scheme.

CHAPTER TWENTY-FIVE

Bad things seem to happen to me on Wednesdays, Lena thought. My mother died on a Wednesday. That old hag Esther brought me to Kampala on a Wednesday, and it changed my life for the worse. My two years in jail started rolling on a Wednesday. "Huh! I hope this particular one will be good to me," she mumbled as she hurried across the road, dodging the muddy puddles from the previous night's downpour. She arrived at the facility alongside Arthur.

"I should have parked the car closer to the gate," Arthur said as they walked the rest of the short distance to the prison's main gate.

Inside the prison enclosure Lena took in a deep breath, filling up her lungs with the fresh breeze of Lake Victoria. Mid-morning had been her favourite time of day for the two years she spent in prison. As far as she was concerned, lake breezes were a class apart. She did not have to rack her mind comparing this with downtown Kampala's dusty, carbon-filled skies, courtesy of thousands of old hand-me-down Japanese vehicles. She remembered that time during her six-month trial when she made endless travels from Luzira Prison to the Buganda road court in the city centre. She always felt sorry for the city people who had to endure such pollution daily. Lena loved Lake Victoria's fresh breezes.

She was relieved to find Akurut waiting on the front porch of the reception. She had called her earlier, and told her to do as

Arthur had requested – to register him as Martina's attorney and Lena as his assistant. And if possible, could they have one of the private visitors' rooms?

Lena walked with Arthur to the visiting room, to one of the benches. They waited for Martina.

Martina walked into the room escorted by a guard. Lena thought Martina looked confused, until she saw Lena and then her face brightened. The guard left the room.

"Oh dearie Lena." Martina walked forward and embraced Lena.

"This Head up here with its stupid grin," Lena said.

"Yes dearie. The Head will always be there, watching. You came with him again?"

"Arthur?"

"What does he want here?" Martina asked.

"He gave me a lift here. I am able to see you today because of him."

"So tell me, dearie. Did you speak to Mukwano about your new job?"

"No Martina. I am sorry, I can't take the job just yet."

"But, but dearie. Why? Why are you doing this when you know you need the job, and I need you?"

"In good faith, Martina," Lena said.

"What good faith, dearie? My estate is collapsing and you tell me about faith?" Martina said, starting to pace the room.

"Martina. I am going to be very frank with you. I am actually afraid of Mukwano because I lied to him as I told you," she said. "So he may be thinking of me as a liar. He may not even like working with me."

"No, my dearest. He can't do that. I know he needs an extra

hand in the office."

"How come he suggested me of all people? He doesn't know me. He only met me that day. And I even told him I had been in prison until recently."

"And dearie, what does it matter? What does it matter?"

"Believe me Martina, this has nothing to do with your own judgment. You actually have only me to pick from, unlike Mukwano who is out there in the world with countless better options. Look at it this way Martina. You told me the VG is a big business. So you must have qualified people working for you. I mean, I understand that you want me to do some special work for you. But if Mukwano also says he wants me to help him in the office, I can say, without shame, that I will disappoint him. I don't have the skills he may need."

"Maybe he just needs you for the simple part – like helping with identifying files that the auditors might need, anything."

"But doesn't Zura already have people who could do that?"

"Dearie, he told me Tony was out of the country. Faruk and Rhamji were too busy. Okello is based in Juba. At Zura, some work remains special. And you dearie, you keep on saying you don't have the skills. What did you study?" Martina said.

"I have a degree in Economics."

Martina jumped up in surprise. "And pray dearie, what were you doing trying to fit in a housekeeping job three years ago?"

"What was I doing? I am one of the hundreds of thousands of unemployed Ugandan graduates, Martina. And I happened to be looking to put food on table for my siblings."

"Yeah." Martina lowered herself slowly onto the bench and smiled. "Like they say, money doesn't stink, dearie."

Lena nodded. Martina's smile annoyed her. "Only that, in

my case, it stunk. I suffered deception almost similar to what that little girl from Entebbe went through. I think her name was Lucky Mukama. Unfortunately for me, the judge who handled my case thought different."

Martina gaped at her.

"Oh yes. Probably if my case had been taken up by Justice Fiona Mukyala, maybe I wouldn't have been handed a jail term. But I got some other magistrate, so the tables turned on me even though I was the victim. We shared a ward, Martina. The rest, as you know, is history." Lena wiped drops of tears off her cheeks.

"Dearie, dearie me! You know about the case?" Martina found her voice.

"It's in the data bank of the High Court."

Martina wagged a finger at Lena. "Tell me, dearie, what is it that you are doing? Why are you digging into my past?"

The two women stared at each other. Lena thought she had to assert herself here. She was not sure this was the right way to make Martina talk, but she decided to go for it.

"You've been good to me, Martina. You offered me a job and a good pay. I just wanted to get to know you better. In fact, that's why I haven't taken the job yet. Because I want to first understand you better. That's way I will be comfortable carrying out my job. Tell me your story Martina," Lena said. She hoped she had asserted herself well. This was her opportunity to do something for Arthur who needed to know more about Martina.

Martina sighed. She walked to the only window in the room and stared out across the compound.

Lena waited, wondering if she had gone too far. She glanced at Arthur, who was watching Martina.

"Nobody believed me, Lena dearie. Even my own trusted

one, Mukwano, accused me of being a fool. He didn't believe me, and it still hurts. But why would I want to talk about it now? It's too late, dearie."

"Listen, Martina. It's important for both of us. And guess what, my lawyer here wants to help. Well, last time I only told you that he was my friend. The truth is, he is the lawyer I always told you about. I told him all about you, and he says that the case can be re-opened. I told him you have been good to me, and he thinks he can help."

"You spoke to another person about this?" Martina glanced at Arthur.

"Your case was all over the Internet for anyone to see, Martina. So he read about you and got more curious."

"Tell me, dearie, what do they say about me on the Internet? Do they mention my businesses? What do they say?"

"The VG was barely mentioned," Lena said.

"Nothing?" Martina asked. "Nothing at all?" She left the window and returned to her seat. She looked exhausted.

"Dearie, I am glad the VG was not smeared by my trial. I don't want anything to touch my company. You see, the VG is my life. My family. Even after I leave this prison, I will have no one to return to, but the VG. Dearie, dearie me. Right now, I just can't help worrying about what is happening there in my absence. If you work for me, Lena, it will help me a lot, you see. It may help me decide who to trust and who not to."

"You know, Martina. If you feel that the VG may not be safe, then you have to do more. The VG seems to be big and you definitely cannot rely only on someone like me to keep it safe."

"I am desperate Lena dear. There are people out there, but I do not know who to trust. I mean ever since I was accused of abducting that child…"

"I trust that Arthur can be a big help."

"What can he do that my lawyer Tony couldn't do?"

"He can help re-open your case. If he can't have you released, maybe your sentence can be reduced, Martina."

"Fifteen years," Martin said. She reached for Lena's hand and pressed it hard. "That would be a big help. But I already appealed, and nothing good came out of it."

"Maybe you should talk to Arthur directly. He would be able to advise you."

"Maybe. Oh, how great it would be to get out of this choking place. This rot." Martina now gazed at Arthur. "I think I will speak to him now, and see if he has the backbone to take up my case. When you are in prison, dearie, anything that brings hope for freedom can be welcome. Oh how I would love to be free again!

***

Arthur adjusted his position as he felt the piercing stare from Martina.

"I actually know many lawyers in town. Big lawyers whom I can talk to," Martina said. "But this dear, dear girl, Lena. I want to make her happy. She says you can revisit my sentence. Can you?" She winked and bent her head slightly so that her eyes were levelled with Arthur's.

"Yes, I can revisit your case."

"Dearie." Martina laughed. "I am told my story is all over the Internet. What exactly do you wish to know?"

"The Internet may not always be right," Arthur said. "Tell me everything. Tell me what you feel you should share with me so I can be able to say if I can take the case or not."

"Let's see, dearie. First, I will tell you as clearly as I remember the story of my indictment," Martina said. "I still remember very well that fateful month of December. You probably dug that out already. I was in my house in the company of my manager, Mukwano, when this strange fellow entered with a thirteen-year-old girl. Earlier, he had insisted on bringing the girl to my house. I stupidly allowed it even though it was against my wish. But I intended to help the girl out through the Zura Maids bureau."

Arthur pulled out a notebook from his folder to scribble on. "I hope you are okay if I take a few notes from our conversation."

"Write whatever you like, dearie."

"So, you intended to enrol a thirteen-year old as a domestic servant?" Arthur said.

"Tell me, dearie. Wouldn't it be better than having the child roam the streets and face the wilderness all alone? If my Zura firm was not doing that already, our streets would be swamped with thousands of thirteen-year-olds by now."

"Yeah, I have heard about the Zura and its work," Arthur said and fought the urge to ask Martina for details about it. That could wait, he thought.

"When the stranger entered with the girl, Mukwano did not agree to see the child. So I met the stranger and the girl by myself. I was, however, shocked to find a seemingly well brought up child. Well brought up in the sense that her appearance told of plenty. My dearie, I had expected the usual stuff, a pauper in rags, begging me to liberate her. My curiosity instead sent me asking for her background. Unfortunately, she was drowsy and unable to speak back. Because the stranger never asked for any money, I thought he was innocent. I thought the stranger had simply rescued a spoilt rich youth from the street. Young people, mostly from wealthy homes, are doing a lot of drugs these days. I thought the kid perhaps fell in that category and had lost her way home. And so, dearie I advised the man to extend his goodness and drop the girl at the nearest hospital for treatment. The girl would wake up and trace her way back home."

"You say the stranger never asked for any money? So would you sometimes pay people who bring you such girls?"

"Oh dearie, dearie. A good turn deserves another. So they say. But this man never asked for any money."

"Aha."

"But dearie, I got the shock of my life the following morning when police descended upon my home and arrested me for what did not make sense then. They accused me of abducting and drugging a young girl, that I had the intention to use her as a human sacrifice. Ha! They then charged me in court, as you know. I should have listened to Mukwano."

"Mukwano?"

"Yes, he is my General Manager. Dearie Lena has met him already, and will be working with him if she agrees."

"Oh, good for you," Arthur said and winked at Lena. It was better to feign ignorance. "What about Mukwano?"

"Oh dearie, he had advised me earlier not to see the girl. He never saw the girl himself."

"Mukwano may have been right about that," Arthur said. "The girl was allegedly found unconscious early in the morning at your gate. Do you think the case would have taken a different turn, if you had completely refused to see her even when she was dumped at your gate?"

"I can't tell, dearie. But the girl wouldn't have identified me because she would not have seen me. However, there is little comfort in that now."

"I see." Arthur nodded.

"What I know is that there were escape routes I should have exploited but I didn't. For the past months since I was convicted, two clear options I should have explored have haunted me constantly: Why on earth didn't I hold the man and his charge and hand them over to the police? I knew the girl was not well and that she was with a stranger. A stranger who did not take her to hospital. The other option, even a fool would have taken. I keep thinking I should have waited for the girl to sober up in the presence of the stranger, and then interviewed her. I should have perhaps done something to wake her up: poured cold water on her, anything. But I just did not. Instead I asked him to take her to hospital alone."

She paused to look at Lena. Then back at Arthur. "And dearie, Mukwano thought whoever did it wanted to bring my VG down."

"What about your domestic servants? Did any of them witness the meeting?"

"Only the gateman who ran away after my arrest."

"Do you have his details?"

"Musa Adoma. An elderly guard Mukwano had hired for me from Barakiya Security Ltd. I sometimes thought he would have been my saviour in Court. But he deserted his work and company immediately after my arrest. Ms. Barakiya failed to trace him. Satisfied, dearie?"

"For now." Arthur closed his book. Something definitely did not add up.

"But, do you trust everyone within the VG? Take Mukwano for example. Was it always routine for him to visit your house at the time he did?" Arthur said.

"Why do you ask that? I was like a mother to all of them, especially Mukwano."

"Because it beats my understanding why Mukwano did not meet the strangers with you. At least he should have been with you as an elder and a boss to him. What if the stranger had turned against you?

"Arthur, dearie, are you insinuating that Mukwano could have been behind the whole thing?" Martina probed.

"I have no conclusion yet."

"You had better not dare!" Martina said. "And if you are interested in my case dearie, you must know I have conditions."

"I understand."

"You will not touch my VG."

"Lawyers follow their clients' instructions. Whatever you wish, Martina." Arthur smiled.

"The VG is my life. Lena here knows it. Don't you, dearie?"

Lena nodded.

"And Lena, dearie, I really hope you find your sister soon," Martina said.

"I hope so too. And I hope that things will turn out for the better for you," Lena said and stood up following Arthur. "I wish we still had more time, but we were only given 30 minutes here."

"The damn rules. Listen, dearie. Like I said, I am expecting Mukwano to be here with my audits. But I want to rely on you in case he doesn't show up."

"I am sure we will be back soon, not so Arthur?"

Arthur nodded in agreement.

CHAPTER TWENTY-SIX

For the third time, Arthur pressed the bell at the gate of house number K13. The gate remained unanswered. He wondered if he was waking up Tony's household. Seven in the morning was not that early.

He constantly threw uneasy glances over his shoulder at the opposite gate. It, too, remained closed. He prayed that Mukwano's gate remained closed until he finished his mission at Tony's. He tried a light push at the smaller gate. It opened. Arthur quickly stepped inside the compound and quietly closed the gate behind him. Not a single living thing in sight. A dirty, blue Benz was parked in the driveway.

"Hello! Anyone in?" He repeated this all the way to the front door of the house. He tried the bell at the door. It sent a hollow shrill through the house. Arthur studied the front windows of the house. The curtains remained tightly drawn. Everything remained still. He wondered whether Tony lived here all by himself. After about three minutes on the doorsteps, he decided to leave.

A few steps from the gate, Arthur noticed what looked like clots of blood in the grass. He stepped back and looked again. He immediately knew someone had been fatally hurt on Tony's premises. Perhaps Tony had travelled, and thugs broke into his premises and hurt whoever was care-taking? Maybe whoever it was managed to take himself to hospital? No cause for alarm yet. Arthur thought this could be a crime scene. He felt stiff with fear and decided to leave immediately.

He contemplated informing the police, but that could curtail his plans for the day. The police would see him as a suspect and hold him, and he could take a whole day at the police writing statements. No, he would not go to the police. But he would make an anonymous call.

He was running late for the VG. A few steps from the gate, he stopped and quickly dashed back to the front porch, where he wiped the bell clean with his pocket-handkerchief. It didn't deter him that Uganda's police was ill equipped to investigate thoroughly and take fingerprints. This was not an ordinary house. It belonged to a rich company's lawyer. He imagined the company could afford a few more shillings to hire private investigators to help the police in their investigations if they so desired. That had happened before with one of the rich mobile-telephone companies in the country. It could happen with the VG. He also wiped the small gate and the gatebell clean.

Opposite, a gate grated shut as he turned to walk away from Tony's home. It was definitely Mukwano's gate. It could have been a servant minding his own business, he thought, and waved it off. He wondered if it would be helpful to try to get hold of a servant or gateman from Mukwano's. He walked near the gate and raised his knuckles to knock. Then he remembered he had accepted a job from Mukwano, and lowered his hand. What if Mukwano was at home and recognised him? Going to Mukwano to talk about the blood in Tony's empty home was tatamount to going to the police, he thought. What excuse would he give for having gone into Tony's house? He would definitely be blowing his cover.

He walked until he reached the main road where he finally hopped onto a town-bound taxi and stopped at the first telephone booth he saw. He called 999.

"I am reporting a suspicious crime scene at No. K13, Kiira village in Kamuca. The house belongs to a lawyer called Tony. The house is empty but there is blood in the compound, nearest the gate."

Police wanted to know the caller.

"Charles, a friend of Tony's." He hung up.

CHAPTER TWENTY-SEVEN

"A beautiful morning. How many new girls do we have today?" The lady from the interview room beamed at the receptionist.

She is just as cheerful as last week, Lena thought.

"A great morning, Madam Nancy," the receptionist said with a smile. "They become big headed once they are admitted and start off late. We have got thirty from Karamoja, fifteen from last week's headquarter admissions, and now this late comer makes the sixteenth."

Lena was in her pauper clothes. She stood waiting at the desk, dangling a worn-out bag in her hands. In the bag, she had stuffed an extra, equally worn-out, set of clothing. Arthur had convinced her to leave her cellphone with him in case she would have to undergo a body or baggage check. She had painfully parted from her handset, her surest link to him.

"Why are you late, Maggie?" Madam Nancy turned and looked at Lena. "Was it tough leaving your old job?"

"You know them, Madam Nancy," interjected the receptionist. "Once they are taken on, they move from home to home to spread the news around and feel big. She probably celebrated the whole of last week until this morning."

Madam Nancy looked at the receptionist and smiled.

"Maggie, follow me."

They went out of the reception area and followed a corridor before turning east to the back of the building.

"Do you occupy the whole building?" Lena couldn't help herself.

"The whole second floor houses the VG Company. West Wing hosts the VG headquarters and the East Wing belongs to us, Zura Maids. It is a respectable company, Maggie. And it is a pleasure to have you pass through our hands."

"Is this the East Wing?"

"Isn't it nice and spacious?" Madam Nancy turned and smiled at Lena. "You wouldn't know anyway, being new and all."

Madam Nancy loved her job, Lena concluded. She began to doubt her earlier suspicions about the Zura. What if Martina was running a legitimate maid's bureau? What if the Zura had absolutely nothing to do with her sister? Where would she turn to next? Well, first things first. She needed to rule out the Zura first, and then move on to other options.

They hurried along the East Wing, passing several locked doors bearing different labels. Lena wondered whether the staff were busy doing VG business already and didn't want any distractions.

"Let's follow this corridor, Maggie."

They turned southwards and descended a winding set of stairs, almost as though they were going underground.

"Are we leaving the second floor?" Lena asked in a shaky voice.

"Relax. Offices are on the second floor. Training and accommodation for only a few days are in the basement." Madam Nancy explained in a rather sombre voice.

Lena inched her way alongside Madam Nancy. The clock at the reception had read eight-thirty in the morning but the stairway grew darker with each step. She wanted to turn back but a voice from within kept her hopeful that this route would take her to Lilly. Madam Nancy took the lead, and Lena followed. Lena cursed to herself in fear, expecting her head to go rolling off her shoulder any moment.

She sighed in relief as they finally hit the basement and stopped before a heavy metal door in semi-darkness. Madam Nancy hit the shutter thrice with her fist and immediately inserted a small card in the lock. The heavy door pulled inwards. She followed Madam Nancy inside. Lena blinked several times. The lighting inside was not any better than that along the stairway. A single, old, energy-saver bulb emitted dim rays from the centre of a large hall.

Her eyes slowly adjusted to the lighting. She immediately noticed many girls lined up naked against the wall and staring at her. What was this? Another brothel? Her eyes left the girls and immediately scanned the room for an exit, any exit. Behind her was the door she had come through. One needed a key to get in or out. Before her were three or four other metallic doors. She wondered where they led. Untold hell perhaps, she thought.

Her bag dropped from her limp hand. Her breath quickened. Could Lilly be among them? She wondered. Her eyes ran over one girl after the other, trying to look for Lilly. She quickly counted about forty-five girls. But none of them looked like Lilly. She looked at Madam Nancy to seek an answer – any answer.

"This is where you will be moulded into something marketable," Madam Nancy said and flashed her trademark smile that was barely visible in the semi-darkness.

"Marketable." Lena whispered in disbelief, her fears confirmed. Goodness! She was back to zero. She was trapped. So this was Martina's business. So Martina was another devil just like old Esther. Damn you, Martina. May you rot in hell, she whispered.

"Madam, where are we? Why are the girls naked?"

"No questions!" Madam Nancy said.

"But I am here for the job of a housemaid." Lena choked on her tears.

The girls appeared to be sad, frightened and helpless. Their hands clutched their naked bodies. Could any of them be Lilly? She peered at them in the dim light. None looked like Lilly. She was in danger. And there was no Lilly! Tears flowed down her cheeks.

She trembled as she said, "It's okay. I don't need the job anymore."

"What?" Madam Nancy said.

"I want to leave. I don't want the job anymore."

"Ha ha ha!" Madam Nancy laughed. "Don't be silly. Once we admit you, you are bound to the Zura. Huh? It's only us who can say whether you leave or not."

Lena tried to lick her lips, but her tongue was heavy and dry. It was a pity for her to be imprisoned when her sister was elsewhere. This was the third time she was being locked up. First she was in the brothel, then in Luzira prison, and now this dungeon? Her throat felt dry. She worried that they were going to treat her like they did in the brothel; lock her up, take away her clothes, and maybe starve her and beat her up if she refused to comply. What had she gotten herself into? Again, she looked longingly at the metallic exit door behind her.

"When will I start work?"

"No questions." A cruel female voice rang out.

Lena trembled. She couldn't see who was speaking. Then one

of the numerous doors in the hall's walls squeaked on its hinges and a woman stepped into the room.

"Hello, Warden. A new girl for Grade 'A' category," Madam Nancy said.

Lena noticed that the Warden was drenched in sweat even though it was still early morning. She was a short, middle-aged woman with large biceps. The right side of her face was badly scarred and heavy with loose skin. Whatever had hurt her face had barely spared the skin of her eye socket. It almost took away her right eye too. With such endowments, her face had a mask-like appearance. It promised hell, Lena thought.

Lena moved closer to Madam Nancy.

"Please don't leave me here, please," she said as the Warden drew closer to where she stood.

"I will do anything you ask. But please you can't leave me here."

The Warden turned and glared at Lena.

"Nonsense," she said and kicked the bag that Lena had dropped.

"Pick that up if it's yours. Madam Nancy, don't worry about her. You may take your leave now. We take over from here."

She immediately pulled in the heavy door shutter to let Madam Nancy out.

Lena tried to follow Madam Nancy, but the Warden gripped her hand.

Lena watched the door bang shut. Her heart pounded in her chest. She knew Arthur had reported to the VG to take up his job. She looked from the door to the Warden, a voice inside telling her to scream. A scream that would penetrate the metallic door, the concrete walls and maybe reach Arthur's ears somewhere in the building. She wondered if she would ever pass through that door again a free woman.

"Empty the contents of your bag on the floor for inspection. And do not let me repeat a single statement," the Warden ordered, her scar quivering.

Lena stooped down and retrieved her fallen bag. She unzipped and spread the meagre contents on the floor.

"A real pauper." The Warden used her right foot to further scatter Lena's few humble items. She kicked the wrap and headscarf to one side. She then pointed to the remaining items and ordered them disposed of, pointing to a large metallic waste bucket in the corner of the hall.

Calm down, Lena told herself. She was now afraid of drawing undue attention to herself if she continued resisting. She scooped her condemned items and threw them into the bucket. She walked back, put the wrap and scarf in her bag and waited for further instructions. She noticed that a man in a white coat had moved to the line of naked girls. Another mean looking woman stood watch over them. Lena's skin crawled with extreme fear.

The man in the white coat grabbed the first girl on the line by her jaws. He forced her mouth open and shone a small torch into it, turning her head side to side and frowning as he did so. Next, he ran the light over her naked body, from head down to her chest, pausing briefly to ogle her sharp, pointed breasts. He did the same to her buttocks and legs. He then shone the light into the girl's eyes, ears and nose, each time dipping what looked like a pair of forceps into a dish of liquid then using it to prod his way around.

He reminded Lena of a movie she once saw, about a slave on sale. Resigned to his fate, the slave opened his mouth and exposed his teeth to be checked, bunched his biceps to show he was strong enough for whatever manual labour awaited – did everything to make his seller and buyer happy.

The man was prodding the next girl. The girl was tall, skinny and light-skinned. She raised her head and held her back straight. Lena thought the girl's face looked familiar. She looked like a girl from the camp. As Lena's eyes grew accustomed to the dim light, she recognised the girl. It was Awino, daughter of Mr Oculi, the head catechist of Acokara Chapel. Once or twice Awino had joined Lena's expeditions into Alyec Otoo forest for firewood. She wondered if the girl was also Esther's victim. She would find out, talk to her later. She hoped the girl would not recognise her just yet. She worried that any mention of her true identity would mean danger. She would try to avoid Awino's attention until they were alone.

"Undress immediately and join the other girls!" Madam Warden barked at Lena.

The doctor checked her last. The rest of the girls, already humiliated, remained standing along the wall. They avoided looking at each other's bodies. Lena endured the prods and pokes on her body without making a sound. She closed her eyes through it all until a pair of pincers prodded her eyelids open. The physician needed to check for eye infections. She wondered what he found. Then she remembered the scars on her back. She didn't know what to expect once the doctor saw the scars. But the doctor didn't ask her to turn around.

"To the shower room!" The Warden threw open one of the four doors.

"In fours," the second woman who had stood by the white-coated man said, and then disappeared into the room.

The line of naked girls broke as each girl tried not to be the first to enter the shower.

"You heard the Assistant Warden," the Warden said. "Go to her in fours!"

Lena watched one group of girls after another file into the shower room, as others walked out naked and shivering.

"Next!" the Assistant Warden said.

Lena's group was the last. They filed in as the previous girls made their way out, shivering.

The Assistant Warden turned the tap on and raised a hosepipe at Lena and the three girls. The gush of water pushed them to the wall. It was ice cold. Lena bit her teeth and tried to hold her breath. In Acokara, she dared not dip her body in such cold water. Instead, she would get her body used to the water gradually, bathing her legs first, then arms, chest and abdomen before sending water down her back.

"Out!" The Assistant Warden said. "Next!"

Lena and the girls in her group filed out quietly. She crossed her arms over her chest to conceal her breasts.

"I said next!" The Assistant Warden shouted, and then walked to the door and scanned the hall.

"You are done with all of them," the Warden said. She then turned to address the girls.

"Back to the wall. Line up!"

They stood in a single file again, their bodies glistening with drops of water that soon formed small pools beneath their feet. Lena was mourning. Each girl's face reminded her of Lilly. They all had the same needs; respect and protection. Lena remembered the brothel she set on fire almost three years back. She prayed for an opportunity to do something that would rescue all these girls.

Lena noticed that all the girls were younger than she was. Half of them looked to be under sixteen years. A quarter of them looked to be about thirteen. Awino was not more than fifteen. Lena promised to seize an opportunity to talk to her. She had to. Some of the girls sobbed continuously but the wardens seemed unbothered by their tears.

"Here," the Assistant Warden said, and began tossing out clothes to the girls.

Lena raised her hands to catch a cheap, simple pinafore. The other girls did the same. Size didn't matter. The girls all lined up in pinafores of varying lengths. Some hems touched the floor, others settled just below the knee. Lena's pinafore hung like a mini dress.

CHAPTER TWENTY-EIGHT

"It is your first day of work and you are three minutes late, Kigulu?" Mukwano said, and continued reading from a file on his wide, mahogany desk.

"I am sorry, sir. It won't happen again," Arthur said.

The office was spacious and well organised. A potted plant stood in the centre. Several large portraits of Mukwano lined the wall. Two large glass windows with long heavy curtains held at the sides, let in fresh air. A huge bookshelf bearing several box files stood along the left wall. Arthur gazed at the bookshelf and prayed for a moment his eyes would land on the contents of those beckoning files.

Mukwano nodded several times before he lifted his eyes off the file to look at Arthur.

"You may sit."

Arthur sat in the chair opposite Mukwano.

"Welcome to the VG," Mukwano said and slid a sheet of paper across his desk. "Here, read through this carefully and ask if there's anything you do not understand. It's your contract. You are our new office messenger. I hope you can do better than the fool you have replaced."

Arthur received the document and ran his eyes over it.

"By the way, I am expecting a team of detectives from the police shortly," Mukwano said.

Arthur found it hard to concentrate. He kept loosing track of the text he was reading. He wondered why the detectives were coming, why Mukwano was telling him about it. He hoped it had nothing to do with him or Lena, and hoped it would be police officers who were not familiar with him. But he needed a 'Plan B' just in case. He quickly searched his mind. If any of the police officers recognised him, he would deny knowing them. Better still, he might just excuse himself and disappear. He mustn't compromise his cover.

"Are you okay?" Mukwano studied him.

"Yes sir."

Arthur adjusted his spectacles and looked at the text of his contract. His mind was engrossed on what Mukwano had just said about detectives. And what he would do if the officers came in.

Mukwano adjusted his chair.

"I am afraid I have to welcome you on your first day with us with such disturbing news, Kigulu. You see, we ran into a small inconvenience caused by a few misplaced individuals in the company these past few months. That means you will mostly be on your feet today. Lots of errands to run. Meanwhile, I want you to ask my secretary over there for the basic induction files. Make sure you go through all those carefully. They have almost all the basic information concerning your roles and responsibilities here. We will discuss them later. And in case the detectives ask you any question, tell them you are new here."

"Yes sir," Arthur said.

***

Mukwano's eyes followed Arthur. He was happy that the background check he had done on him had revealed nothing to worry about. He was used to that. Poor people lived lives too insignificant to go past their shadows. His thoughts were interrupted by the door opening.

"Police is here, sir," an elderly woman said, peeping through the doorway.

"Let them in Banya," Mukwano said.

***

Arthur took a chair in the secretary's office.

"You are a very lucky man, Mr Kigulu."

"Why madam?"

"Why? Because you got this job just like that." She snapped her fingers, and then opened a drawer and retrieved documents. She gave them to Arthur. "It doesn't happen like that here. Boss scrutinises employees as if he is inspecting food. Well, you are a lucky man. Just believe me when I say that. Soon you will get to know Boss, and you will understand what I mean."

"Well, I think you are right. I am a lucky man. I was so desperate for a job. So desperate. I am glad I got hired," Arthur said. "And I intend to give it all my attention."

"You better. If you do, Boss may even offer you a better job in no time."

"Those men who just entered Boss' office, are they detectives?" he asked.

"Yes," the secretary said. She sat back on her chair and started typing. "How did you know?"

"Boss told me we were expecting detectives shortly," he said. "He complained about some people. But he didn't tell me who and what they did. Who are they?"

"He must have meant Tony and the other two managers who

have disappeared," she said. "But they will be found. Boss will know what to do."

Arthur threw a cautious but surprised look at the secretary.

"Who is Tony?"

"Our Company lawyer who is on the run for stealing company cash." She walked to her filing cabinet.

"Oh!" Arthur said. He remembered the empty house and the blood clots. So Tony stole company money and disappeared? What about the blood on his lawn? Does he even know about the blood at his house?

"By the way, that's still in-office information. But of course this afternoon Boss will hold a press conference here on the VG premises."

The secretary was, no doubt, proud of her boss, Arthur thought.

"Eeh eh. I thought lawyers don't deal with finances. I thought they only deal with court stuff," he said.

"That's what I also don't understand. But maybe he was in the deal with the others."

"There were also other people?" Arthur couldn't stifle his curiosity.

"The managers Rhamji and Faruk."

"Maybe they were all together in the deal," Arthur said.

"But I can assure you the police will soon catch them."

"That explains police presence here then," Arthur said.

The secretary yanked out several green-labelled files from a small shelf behind her desk. "We lost money. A lot of money from Tastier salts and the Zura. The managers are now on the run along with Tony."

Arthur watched as she selected four thin folders and placed

them before him. She then put the rest into the cabinet. This
secretary was a blabbermouth. Arthur seized the opportunity to
ask all the questions he could think of.

"I hope they find them and all the money," Arthur said.

"They have been gone for... it's more than a month now, but
the theft has just been discovered. As for Tony, he's been away for
four months now. Nobody can find them. Boss should have known
better when they absconded from duty for several days without
communicating to the office. He tried to locate them in vain. Even
their families refused to say where they are. That is why Boss got
suspicious and studied the businesses they were entrusted with.
He found a large amount of money missing."

"It must have been a hard time for Boss."

"Yes. Boss was wild last week. We all had to keep out of his
way. In fact, Boss fired our office messenger for delivering some
letters late."

"Hmm."

"Yes. Otherwise this job wouldn't have been available for
you."

This was news indeed, Arthur mused. So he was replacing
someone. How he wished he could find that person who had been
fired. He wanted to ask her about him but he decided not to. He
needed to go slow. His mind went to Lena. He wondered how she
was fairing. He was starting to get worried about her. He shook
his head to brush off the disturbing thoughts.

"Shall I ask a few more questions, madam, if you don't mind?"

"You will learn a lot from those files, Mr. Kigulu. They are
human-resource files," the secretary said.

"I prefer you call me Jesse." Arthur smiled.

"Oh?" The secretary glared at Arthur. "But that is the culture at the VG. I will stick to Mr. Kigulu, thank you," she said.

Arthur sat through a ten-minute lecture on the VG and its three arms – Tastier Salts LTD, Tora Sales and the mighty Zura Maids. This was nothing he didn't know already, Arthur thought. The secretary spoke, giving the impression that everyone was proud of the Zura. When she stopped talking, he decided to make a move for the Zura. He opened the file. He wanted to find out what could be happening with Lena.

It was material carefully designed to give legitimate form and substance to the establishment. The Zura was a legally registered Uganda labour-sourcing firm with a limited liability. It's managers envisioned contributing to Uganda's development. Their priority was to make unemployment among youths history. For the last sixteen years, the Zura annually pulled 6,000 youth out of poverty. They mostly targeted underpriviledged youths from the countryside. The Zura contributed significantly to the country's tax base. It hauled in close to two million US dollars in profits annually.

"I can see that the Zura is doing very well."

"Definitely." The secretary typed away.

"Tell me about it, madam."

She told him. In between taps on the keyboard, she mentioned basics he already knew from Lena and what he had read from the folder. It was a waste of time. But he played along. He hoped she would say something new.

"Do they train the girls here?"

"I am sorry but I need to proceed with my work. Please read the files," she said. "Besides, Boss is the right person to clarify most of the things you need to know for your kind of work."

Arthur turned to the files. He needed more information.

***

At exactly eleven o'clock, the detectives moved out of Mukwano's office. Mukwano called out for Arthur.

"Young man, please ask the secretary to put the RA guys on line."

Arthur informed the secretary's office and was back immediately. "Have you finished reading the files?" Mukwano said.

"Yes, sir."

"Good." He smiled. "This is, all of a sudden, a very busy week, friend. I will ask the secretary to show you where you will sit, and then I will personally walk you around and introduce you to the rest of the VG staff. The Zura management will see you this afternoon. As a messenger, they all need to know you. Besides I have been seated the whole morning."

"Thank you sir."

Arthur wondered why Boss wanted to take him around himself. Such assignments were always delegated to secretaries. But he did not dare mention that.

CHAPTER TWENTY-NINE

Shortly after their hosepipe bath that morning, Lena, along with three other girls, had gone through one of the metallic doors to the kitchen. A large charcoal stove sat in the middle of the room. At the back of the room was a metallic table with stacks of plastic plates. The Assistant Warden walked to a corner and sat on a stool next to sacks of some kind of flour, probably maize flour. In another corner stood bags of charcoal. Two large chimneys protruded from the stove, disappearing into the ceiling.

"What are you waiting for?" The Assistant Warden called out. "Make the fire and use that large pan over there to make porridge."

Lena had hoped to talk to the three girls, to ask them how they came to join the Zura, if they actually knew what awaited them out there. But the closeness of the Assistant Warden denied her that opportunity. She longed to talk to Oculi's daughter, Awino, as well.

It was lunch time now. All the girls were fed on very light food – two ladles of watery gruel per plate.

"Two ladles are good for you. To keep you beautiful and nourished," the Assistant Warden said.

Even after the light meal, Lena still felt hungry and, like other girls, scooped every bit of porridge off her plate. Lena missed the beans and posho of World Food.

After the meal, the girls took their positions against the wall again. "You have all been brought here because you are very special," the Warden began. "As you know, and that must have been why you chose us, the Zura is a very reputable, global firm. We've got strong networks across the globe. How many of you have ever heard of Italy?"

Most hands went up.

Lena did not raise her hand. Today, she would have been marking her fourth month of freedom if Lilly had not been taken away.

"New York?"

Again the same hands went up. Lena sighed. She was beginning to be sure that the Zura was a scam.

"London?"

The same hands rose once again. Madam Warden glared at Lena. One by one, all the remaining pairs of eyes in the dungeon stared at Lena.

The Warden walked towards Lena.

"Do you think a creature from dust, a beast of ash that can be blown off the palm of my hand like powder, should be helped?"

Lena nearly collapsed from fright. The statement sounded familiar, she thought. It reminded her of Luzira, of bits of verses from her old Bible.

"Do you?"

Lena shivered. "Forgive me, madam. My mind had wandered. Please."

She sighed as the angry Warden turned away from her and faced the rest of the girls.

"Listen all of you. You are specially being trained to get international jobs," the Warden said, and walked around, pausing to look each girl in the eye.

"Thank you so much," some girls chorused. "Thank you, Warden," Lena said. She decided to play along. She knew that if she kept resisting, she might draw attention and blow her cover.

Madam Warden and her assistant smiled.

"We will prepare you for a good life in Britain, Italy, Malaysia, Saudi Arabia and America. But a good life means really hard work and submission." The Warden turned to her assistant.

"And endurance!" The Assistant said. "And just for your information, every year Zura identifies more than ten thousand of you. Of course, the international vacancies are meant for a chosen few. We send only up to four thousand girls out of the ten thousand. So consider yourselves lucky."

Lena watched as the girls smiled. For a moment, they looked like they had forgotten the humiliation and harassment they had suffered with the doctor in the white coat. She felt bad that these women were playing with the girls' minds, promising them heaven when hell awaited them.

"You are very lucky," the Warden said.

The girls giggled.

Lena felt a nudge at her shoulder and looked to her left. It was the girl from Acokara.

"Smile," the girl whispered, all the while smiling in the direction of the Assistant Warden. Lena realised what she meant and flashed a smile at the Assistant Warden. It was safe to be part of the lot, to pretend all was well and obey every command.

"Thank you," Lena murmured and hoped the girl heard.

"Did you hear that? Hmm? Did you hear me well? You are the lucky ones." Madam Warden took charge. "Even this training ground is special. It is only for chosen ones like you. It is meant for international business only. The local market gets them raw. No need to undo a people's culture when they would be sucked right back into it."

As Lena watched the Warden speak, she wondered which market claimed Lilly. She hoped it was the local market. At least there would be some hope of escaping, of finding one's way out. She hoped Lilly was somewhere in Uganda. She believed that Arthur was doing his best to find answers that could lead him to Lilly, to her and to all the other girls. From what she had discovered, she was already in unimaginable danger. Her hope of getting out of Zura was as small as a millet grain.

"Our training will take about two to four weeks," the Assistant said.

Lena stiffened. How were they going to spend two weeks holed up in the poorly lit, poorly aerated dungeon? Two weeks without knowing how Arthur was progressing, without knowing if she would ever get out, without knowing if she would ever find Lilly, was going to be hell. Perhaps she was already in hell.

"We will drill you with survival skills. It is at the heart of job security. Being submissive is an international standard for your kind of job. We will spend a good time working on that." The Warden smiled.

Lena shuddered and looked away. It was the cruelest smile she had ever seen. It mocked her. It mocked the girls, she thought. Lena felt drained of life. She looked at the girls she had foolishly thought she could rescue by enrolling as one of them. Now she too was trapped, like every one of them. Unfortunately for her, she knew the truth: they were destined for the world of sex slavery abroad.

"And oh, there is something else," the Assistant Warden

said. "You are all beautiful, slender, and skinny; very important attributes for international success. And so, we intend to watch your diet here so you can at least maintain that size."

"But downsizing your current weight would even be the best way to go," the Warden said, pointing at the girls. "That is why we will be modest with the meals you take. Our dietician recommends gruel, twice a day."

"You will discover that cleanliness is at the heart of your survival. Your hair, your face, your skin and your nails will have to be tamed to standard. And if there is more time, we will work on your English as well," the Assistant Warden said.

Lena noticed a few girls raising their hands close to their eyes to check the nails. Others patted their heads as if to ascertain that they actually still had hair. She wondered what good skin could survive on just a meal of gruel, what beauty could be groomed in a suffocating dungeon. She wondered why the girls could not realise that the dungeon was a criminal hideout.

"Shall we make the preliminaries now, mate?" the Warden smiled and turned to her assistant.

"Of course!" The Assistant said.

Lena noticed they never referred to each other by name. These were experts. They had done this not once, not twice. They had years of experience, turning thousands of helpless humans into commodities for Zura Maids' foreign markets. How clever, she thought.

"Now, we want to hear about you," the Assistant Warden said. "Tell us your name, how old you are, where you come from, your tribe and, if you went to school, how far you went."

"We will start with you." The Warden pointed at the girl who stood at the head of the line, just before Lena. It was the girl from

Acokara. Lena had fixed herself next to her so she could try to catch her attention. Like all the others, the girl stood there in her short pinafore, her hands hugging her chest to keep warm though visible mild tremors shook her body now and again. Lena didn't know if it was from the cold bath she had just had, from sickness or from fear.

"I... me I am Awino. 15 years old. I am stay in Acokara parish of Oyam district. Is Lango. I am not study. Primary five only and then rebel come for my village," the girl said.

"Good," the Warden said. "Some English to learn still."

"Next!" The Assistant Warden called.

The Warden and her assistant sat on low stools listening to the girls. The Assistant held a note pad in which she scribbled as the girls gave their particulars.

Lena wished she could talk to Awino. She had many questions she wanted to ask her, but she just didn't have the chance. Not yet. She thought about Lilly and wondered if she and Awino had come together. She wanted to ask if it was old Esther who brought the girl? When? Was she brought with Lilly and other girls? Was she sold to the Zura? Did she know anything about Lilly's whereabouts? Lena trembled with excitement. She vowed to find time away from the prying eyes of the wardens and speak to Awino.

All the girls spoke. Lena said that she was 18 years. If she had mentioned her actual age of twenty three, she would have been the oldest. The youngest, who had since forgotten the morning ordeal and was still visibly excited about international prospects, was merely twelve years of age. She is just a baby, Lena mourned, recalling her sister's own plight. She wondered whether the girl's nomad parents would ever know what happened to their daughter.

"Good! Our first lesson today will focus on what you have just told us," the Warden began.

"Do you know that we have just heard first class deception from the very depth of evil itself, issuing from each of your mouths?" She said to the girls.

The girls looked at each other in utter confusion. Nobody answered the Warden.

"I will show you what I mean," the Warden continued. "Come join me." She beckoned her assistant, who obeyed immediately.

"We are going to introduce ourselves to you. You must pay particular attention: I am the warden in charge of poor earthlings looking for placements around the world. I was born of poor parents some years back in a small village. My parents died of hunger and the Zura rescued me. I owe the Zura my earthly life."

"I am an assistant warden," said the Assistant. "I grew up on the streets of Kampala until the Zura rescued me, trained me, fed me and housed me. I owe the Zura my life."

The Warden continued: "Above all, never ever forget that Zura Maids is meant solely to relieve poor people from unending want of food, shelter and clothing. Poor people are hopeless people. Hopeless people are lesser people. Housemaids are lesser people. They are nameless, faceless and without roots. They are meant to serve, serve and serve. They do not know unless they are told. They do not feel unless they are asked, they do not understand unless they are made to. They neither ask nor say unless they are commanded to," the Warden said. "They do what they are told."

"In short, they survive because they submit unconditionally to those who feed them," the Assistant added. She then passed out a sheet of paper to each of the girls.

Lena strained her eyes against the dim light. The creed of the poor. Such a sad heading. She did not want to read the contents. She detested the wardens. They are the bosses of the dungeon; their mission is to break our spirits, make us desperate and regret being human, she thought.

"From now and possibly forever, forget about who you were before you came here. By the time we finish this session, that identity will be a thing of the past. It is evil. It is responsible for your current misfortune. And that is what the Zura is going to change. You will be new people with new prospects internationally. You will be out of poverty and misery. You will be earning big, friends! 001 to 046. That should be your identity and it's what you must use even while you are still here. When you complete your course you will have new names. In fact we are already processing passports with your new identities," the Warden chuckled.

The Assistant handed to each girl a small card with a blue label. "Pin that to your pinafo," she said indicating the chest above the left breast.

Lena's was number 040. Her hands trembled as she pinned it on her pinafore. She struggled to hold back tears. There would be no freedom, not for her, not for any of the girls. Lilly was lost forever. Her brothers would suffer with no one to take care of them in that camp. Martina herself was another devil. But she should have accepted that devil's offer. As Martina's personal secretary she would have been safe. She would have gotten the information she wanted without putting herself in danger. Tears escaped her eyes but she quickly dried her face with the back of her hand. Prison all over again, she thought. She closed her eyes. It was not so long ago when she wore No. UG50 in Luzira. Now it was No. 040. Back to captivity.

"I want a straight line," the Warden ordered. The girls moved back against the wall.

"Each of you, look at us," the Warden added and beckoned to her assistant to join her, and together the dungeon bosses studied the girls.

"You! 040! Come forth, you wild little earthling!" The Warden pointed at Lena.

Lena pulled out of the line and walked to the Warden.

"Turn around!" The Warden said.

Lena turned a full 360 degrees and faced the Warden again.

"Fool!" The Warden placed her hands on Lena's shoulder and made her face the rest of the girls. She heard what sounded like a giggle from the girls.

"Silence!" The Assistant Warden said. The girls fell silent.

"Read out what is on that paper! Now!" The Warden said and perched on a nearby stool. Her assistant did the same.

Lena lowered her eyes against the dim light and began to read, her voice low and melancholic. It was a recitation extracted from the Holy Bible. Lena, the owner of a battered Bible that had faithfully kept her company for two years, could not mistake its source. The Zura wisely used the book of Job, Chapter 4, Verses 4 to 21 to confuse and cause fear. In this recitation, the Zura was God, and the girls, the biblical Job.

The Creed of the Poor

Call out, helpless maid. See if anyone answers. Is there any
angel to whom you can turn?
To worry yourself to death with resentment would be a
foolish, senseless thing to do.
Evil does not grow in the soil, nor does trouble grow out of

the ground,

No indeed! People bring trouble on themselves, as surely as
sparks fly up from a fire
Happy is the person who accepts correction
Do not resent it when you are rebuked
The Zura bandages the wounds it makes; its hand hurts you,
and its hand heals.
Time after time it will save you from harm;
When you are hungry, the Zura will keep you alive and
protected from death.
The Zura will rescue you from slander; she will save you
when destruction comes.
You will laugh at violence and hunger and not be afraid of
death.
The fields you plough will be free of rocks;
Nobody will ever attack you.
Then you will live at peace all your life.
It is true, so now accept it.

Lena read it slowly. Some of the girls fought back tears.
Others, who did not understand English, looked on. The bosses of
the dungeon smiled in contentment.

"Good!" The Warden said at the end of the reading.

"Now, move back to the line."

Lena resumed her position against the wall.

The Assistant ordered the girls to identify the kind of
sufferings that a poor earthling was entitled to based on the
recitation: poverty, hunger, disaster, evil, death, destruction and
physical afflictions.

"Are you poor little earthlings?" The Warden said.

"Yes, madam," they chorused.

The younger girls sobbed.

"Good."

"What is expected of you, then?"

The girls were silent. Lena wondered if most of them really understood what she had read, if they even understood the Warden's question.

"As poor little earthlings, what is it you must do if you want a better life?" the Warden asked. Then she pointed at a tall girl from Teso who had introduced herself as Amoding, 19 years old, a senior six certificate holder.

"I will not resent or bring trouble upon myself. I will always accept to be corrected."

"Good! Do you agree with those remedies?"

"Yes," they chorused.

"Now girls, that takes us to our second session. We will help you to understand our creed further in the next two weeks," the Warden said.

Lena heard the sound of a zip opening. She looked beyond the Warden and saw the Assistant digging her hands into a large black bag, then pulling out a large bottle of something. She tried to make out what the bottle contained. But the light was too dim.

"And we will also give you treatment for whatever disease might be afflicting you," the Assistant Warden said as she approached the girls. She held a bottle in her hands and moved to the end of the line.

Oh no. Drugs, Lena thought. She decided she would not take them.

The Assistant gave three pea-sized green tablets to each girl. "Chew the de-worming tablets. They are good for your health.

They work properly when you lie down, which is what you are going to do next."

The girls accepted the tablets.

Lena looked at the tablets and did not think they were deworming pills. She wondered what the doctor had discovered that called for uniform treatment. She placed her pills in the mouth and kept them beneath her tongue. She waited for an opportunity to spit them.

"Good!" The Warden said. "If you remain obedient, we will be very good friends."

"We are done for today." The Assistant Warden said, cradling the bottle of green tablets.

"Done!" The Warden affirmed.

"Everyone, follow me," the Assistant Warden said. She pushed open another of the metallic doors in the wall and walked in, bottle in hand.

It was an adjacent hall to the dungeon. Lena dropped onto one of the mattresses near her. The other girls did the same. She watched as the girls, exhausted and drugged, fell asleep within a few minutes. Lena put her head at the edge of the mattress and released the dissolving tablets onto the floor. The dim light became her saviour. She pretended to be asleep until she heard the Assistant Warden leaving the room and closing the door after her. She raised her head slowly and spied the room. The little bosses had gone. She then sat up, and looked at the sleeping girls. Awino's chest rose and fell in deep sleep. Lena sighed. She would try to talk to her some other time.

She said a short prayer for her siblings and fellow prisoners, then closed her eyes and fell back on the matress.

CHAPTER THIRTY

A call came through from the secretary's office. Mukwano received it. Arthur was uncertain whether to excuse himself or stay as his boss spoke on phone. Then he decided he would wait until he was dismissed. He had come into the VG for information, after all.

It was four days since he started working at the VG. He had been on his toes, always on the lookout in case someone should burst his cover or say something about Lena. Whenever opportunity presented, he checked for information, but he hadn't gotten anything important so far. He had barely noticed how fast the week past. Today was Thursday, and he was starting to get desperate. He hadn't heard from Lena. He could only hope that she was safe. He hoped for a time when Mukwano would leave him in his office for just about ten minutes. But that moment had not come yet. And the secretary was stuck to her desk like she was a piece of office furniture.

"Good work, Ahmed. The police are following the case... Get in touch with CID headquarter's Robert Kena.... Is the public appeal to the press ready yet? Good. I want to see the release in all major newspapers tomorrow... Great. I will send my office messenger to bring them soon. I will also do what I can with the press conference this afternoon."

"We will catch the thieves, Kigulu," Mukwano said, replacing the handset. "Now, there are parcels that need to be dispatched to the RA offices."

As Arthur moved to sit down and listen to instructions from Mukwano, another call came and Mukwano hurried to snatch the handset. It was a busy office, and Mukwano surely a busy man, Arthur thought.

"What?" Mukwano shouted into the receiver, gripping the handset while gritting his jaws. He yanked the handset away from his ear and covered the mouth piece with his palm.

"Wait outside Kigulu," he ordered.

Arthur hurried into the secretary's office and closed the door behind him. She was busy typing away at her keyboard. She smiled briefly at him as he sat in a chair by the door. Arthur returned the smile. He wondered about the sudden mood change that had come with the call. He hoped it was nothing to do with Lena. For a moment his mind told him the person on the phone must have told Mukwano they had found out one of the girls who came looking for a job was disguised as someone else. But who would recognise her? No one knew her, except Mukwano himself, who had met her just once before. But Mukwano was in office with him. So no one would recognise Lena. Lena was safe. He shouldn't worry.

Mukwano strode into the secretary's office.

"Mrs. Banya, release those two boxes in the lawyer's office to Kigulu here to dispatch to the RA immediately. And please note that I don't want to be disturbed." He hurried back into his office. The lock clicked.

Arthur stared at the secretary.

"He seems angry," he said to her.

"We all get angry sometimes, Mr. Kigulu," she said. "This is just your first week here. You will soon get used to it." She picked a batch of keys from her drawer. "Come, let's go Mr. Kigulu. When Boss makes an order it has to be executed immediately. That's how it works. Always remember that."

Arthur followed her along the western corridor to a door marked Company Lawyer. She unlocked the door and entered. Arthur remained by the door for a moment. The blinds were tightly drawn on the window and the room was dark. He heard Mrs. Banya fumble for the switch. The light revealed an extravagantly plush office, identical to Mukwano's. Arthur's eyes adjusted to the lighting. To the back of the room, stood a large L-shaped mahogany desk, complete with a large, black swivel chair. A desktop computer, draped in a protective polythene cover, sat on the shorter side of the 'L'. A three-seater sofa set in black velvet leaned back on the opposite wall facing the mahogany desk.

Tony's office was a well-equipped modern one. To the left wall stood a small Canon copier on a small table. A spiral binder and a scanner stood next to it. A tray of four china cups, a sugar bowl, and sachets of tea and coffee were set on another small table next to the sofa. By developing-world standards, this was a rich company, Arthur thought.

He entered, and moved towards the chest-level, wall-to-wall bookshelf. Law volumes lined up one of the rows. Company files in large units took the reminder of the space. A large, smiling portrait of a light-skinned man sat on top of the bookshelf. He had calm features – high cheekbones, long lashes and full lips. He could pass for a woman any day, Arthur thought. His ears were large, riding far beyond the hairline.

"So this is the lawyer Tony's office?" Arthur studied the portrait.

"Used to be."

He turned away from the portrait.

"What can I help with, madam?"

"Look, there are those two large boxes." She threw open the blinds on the window. "You will have to take them to the RA offices in town."

"Okay," he said, and moved towards the boxes.

"Do you think Tony will be able to take back his job here?"

"But how? Surely Boss will throw him in jail."

As he stared at the secretary, Arthur wondered how things were done in this company. They seemed not to give theft suspects the benefit of doubt. What if Tony returned and proved his innocence? Arthur remembered the thick blood clots in Tony's premises and fear gripped him. It was the same fear he had experienced at the premises.

"I see," he said, turning his attention to dusting the cowries and pebbles on top of the bookshelf.

"Souvenirs from his many business trips abroad," Mrs Banya said. "Over there is the founder and owner of the VG, Martina Maa." She pointed to a large portrait of Martina hanging on the wall at the back of Tony's seat.

"She looks young," Arthur said.

"The portrait is of a younger Madam, taken fifteen or so years ago. I remember because I am VG's first-ever secretary, and it was my role later on to pass to every staff member a copy of the portrait for their offices."

"I haven't seen any in our Boss's office, though."

"We had better not discuss that."

"Oh. Interesting." We had better not discuss that. Arthur smiled, wondering what she meant.

"Hmm. He ordered the removal of Madam's portrait when she was arrested. Even her door label was removed. He said Madam had committed a crime that threatened the existence of the VG. It was part of the damage control, Mr. Kigulu. You see, he loves the VG like the child he has not had. We did everything possible to hide her connection to the VG. It was important for business."

Arthur moved to Martina's portrait and looked at it closely. Mentally, he addressed the portrait: Your secretary knows a lot and she talks too much. If I press harder, I could get her to tell me a lot more. To lay bare your VG and enable me accomplish my business here in a few days.

"But Tony was always different," she continued. "He and Mukwano fought regularly over everything. I shouldn't be saying this, though." She glanced at the door and continued, almost in a whisper, "One day, they even drew guns at each other. Luckily, the RA people were within and they intervened. Otherwise, we could have had a death on our hands that day."

"I still don't understand these RA men. When I went to their offices I didn't get a chance to... you know, to meet them. What is RA, by the way?"

"Oh! You will soon get to understand who they are. As a matter of fact, you have already met them. They've been here a few times in your presence."

"I've met... what are their names again? Alug? Ahmed?"

"Those guys are very close friends of the VG. They are auditors but they also support us by linking our businesses to potential markets."

"Was Tony a bad man?" Arthur said, ignoring the information about the RA. She had already talked about the RA but had probably forgotten. All he needed was to understand exactly who they were to Mukwano.

"To be sincere, our boss is a tough one, Mr. Kigulu. I still think maybe Rhamji and Faruk stole that money, but not Tony. I think if Tony had known money was being stolen from the company, he would have stopped it immediately. Well, that's just my thinking."

"Where is he?"

"I didn't like those two men, Rhamji and Faruk, much. Maybe Tony found them out and they made him disappear." She sighed. "Eehh, that's just my thinking. I don't know."

Arthur hoped the police took his anonymous call seriously and went to Tony's house.

"Let's take the boxes to reception. I can't stay away from my desk any longer. Boss might need me," Mrs. Banya said.

Arthur received the key, waited until the secretary left, and then he locked himself inside. He was alone. The VG was certainly a rotten place. Mukwano was feuding with his juniors, wanting them arrested, wanting them out of the VG. This seemed to be a toxic environment to work in. He decided to use this chance to get as much information as he could. No more time wasting, no wasting opportunities. Who knew if he would get another chance to access this office alone? He had to get as much information as possible and get out, he told himself.

He hurried, his ears on the alert for any approaching noises. He pulled out a filing cabinet by the desk, ran through the files, and pulled out one labelled Zura Maids: Year 2. He studied it.

The first page had the word 'DRC' running across it. Arthur ran his eyes down the second page. A Mr. Dumbe was listed as the official agent of the Zura, followed by several pages of names of girls who had been sent to the DRC. Arthur felt the urge to study the names, perhaps he could identify Lena's Lilly. Identify his Molly. But there was no time. He flipped through the remaining pages – Sudan, Ethiopia, Saudi Arabia, United Arab Emirates, Oman, Malaysia, India, USA, China, UK. The list was endless, each showing an official agent and a long list of girls received that year.

Arthur couldn't believe his luck. He was certain he was holding an important document in his hands. Except the document was three years old. Lilly had been missing for only four months. And Molly had been missing for eleven years. There must be more where that came from, he thought and looked at the computer on the desk. He hesitated between going for the computer and continuing his search on the shelf. But the secretary had mentioned that Tony had been away four months now. That would mean Lilly would not be in the Lawyer's records. Perhaps he could check for Molly. But he didn't want to switch on the computer and come face to face with a screen asking for a security password.

He trembled and listened for any unwanted sound but all was silent. Soon Mrs. Banya might miss him and wonder why he was taking so long simply to move the two boxes out. Still he yanked out another file: Recruitment & Training: Year 2007, it read. He flicked through and stared at page after page of commissions paid out to about 300 local agents. Each agent had a list of girls he or she had recruited attached to their payment voucher. Some agents were paid once, others many times during the year. This was information. So agents recruited girls, and sold them to the Zura. Could that Esther woman be one of the agents? He would never know because the agents were recorded by numbers, not names. All the same, this was important information indeed.

Half way through the file, he saw a bookmark with the label 'Dungeon' on it. He quickly opened the next page: "Internal memo: girls in training." He opened the next, and the next – they were lists of girls in training. His limbs quivered like those of a kitten pulled out of the cold. His heart raced fast. Martina Arcade. There was a dungeon at Martina Arcade where the girls received training. And why would the girls be held in a dungeon if they were being trained for genuine housemaid jobs? He suspected Lena to be in the dungeon training at Martina Arcade! He hoped to God he would be able to contain his excitement about the information.

Arthur decided to make use of the Canon copier. The files would be bulky and impossible to take with him. He quickly sampled a few pages and ran them through the copier. He split up the loot into two and slipped them down his legs into the socks. He put everything back in place and rushed to where the boxes were.

He looked at his watch. He had taken less than ten minutes since the secretary left. Surely she wouldn't notice the delay. He picked the first box and left the room. His legs felt heavy with the secret they held. He hoped the papers wouldn't show or fall out of his socks. He couldn't wait to drop the boxes at the RA offices after which he would rush to his house and secure the papers. He hoped to God Lena was safe. That Maggie was still safe in the dungeon.

Minutes later, Arthur stood in the secretary's office with the two boxes by his feet.

"Ok. Do I have transport to move these boxes to the RA offices?"

"Did you say something, Mr. Kigulu?"

"Yes. Should I expect some transport means to help me get to the RA?"

"Yes. The special-hire car we used last time. It's the one we often use. I already called for it. The driver will let me know when he arrives. It shouldn't be long now. But you must wait, Mr Kigulu. I think Boss wants to give you some additional instructions for the RA people. He is still on phone."

Arthur waited. His pair of socks felt burdened. He bent on his seat and checked to ensure nothing peeped out. He wished he had not rushed Lena off to the Zura. If only he had come alone and left Lena out of it. He would have got the information anyway. He certainly had enough to expose the establishment. It was clear the Zura was enslaving girls in the name of maids. He would return to VG tomorrow, to see if he could lay his hands on more critical information.

Arthur's thoughts were interrupted by Mukwano's voice calling from his office. "Mrs. Banya, have you fetched it yet?"

Mukwano stood in front of Mrs. Banya before she could answer.

"Have you fetched it?" Mukwano asked again.

"No, sir."

"I need it delivered to RA immediately," Mukwano said. "But those letters you are working on are also very urgent. I must sign them in the next twenty minutes. Are you almost done?"

"Only two more left, sir."

"Go on. Don't leave your desk until you are done," Mukwano said. He turned and strode towards Arthur. "Are you enjoying your work, Kigulu?"

Arthur stood up. "Yes, sir." Today he had laid his hands on good information. He was confident about enjoying his job.

"Let's go look at something else that I want you to take to the RA offices. Can't wait!"

Mukwano snatched the keys from his secretary and led the way out. They walked in the direction of Tony's office, past several locked doors, past Tony's office, before turning right and then stopping abruptly before an unlabelled door. Mukwano inserted one of the keys, pushed open the door and entered the room. Arthur followed closely, studying the room. It looked like a large store; boxes of different sizes lined up against the wall on the left side of the room, and a few bags of what looked like salt lay against another wall. A number of parcels were strewn carelessly on the floor.

"She should have opened the blinds," Mukwano said. He hurried across the room and yanked the blinds away from the window. He rushed back and scanned the wall of boxes. "Somehow, I can't find the box with the green label. Go get her."

Arthur hurried away and found the secretary talking to someone on phone about food. Arthur gestured to her to hang up.

"I find it easier having my lunch from here. Boss is always calling me for this, for that. I can't afford to be away for long."

"Well. That's why I am back. He needs you right now. To find the box with a green label." He wanted to stay behind, but she beckoned him along.

They left the room in a hurry with Arthur leading the way.

They found Mukwano still examining the boxes.

"The box I had marked in green." Mukwano looked at the secretary. "Where is it?"

"Sir, it should be here." She rushed forward and studied the wall of boxes.

"Where?" He spread out his palms. "I want it now. Now!"

Mrs. Banya scurried around the room, bending down to look at each box carefully. She checked the wall of boxes, occasionally standing on a stool to take a closer look at the ones close to the ceiling.

Arthur waited on weak knees. Wild thoughts raced through his mind. Two days back, Mrs. Banya had given him some boxes she had called trash to be shredded and burnt. One or two boxes had green labels.

"What are you still waiting for, messenger?" Mukwano roared. "Don't you think you should give her a hand?"

He joined her by the wall of boxes and began searching for one with a green label. He winked at Mrs. Banya. He needed to save the woman from further harassment. After all, if things didn't go well, he had a choice to leave the Zura now that he had some good information.

He cleared his throat and said in a raised voice, "I think you have forgotten, madam. You gave me some boxes to dispatch two days ago. And one of them had a green label."

"Dispatched?" Mukwano raised his voice. "To who?"

"I made dispatches to contacts at Internal Affairs, Entebbe and the RA."

"But the RA boys claim they haven't seen it." Mukwano said. "To whom exactly did you give my parcel?"

This was easy since he had dispatched a number of boxes to the RA that day, and Mukwano knew it. "Alug was in office, sir, but he was very busy and asked me to place the parcels in the corner of the office."

"That man can be a dimwit sometimes. I will sort it out with him later. Now off with both of you."

"Yes, sir," Arthur said. "And, Banya," Mukwano said, "I will be expecting those letters on my desk shortly."

"Yes, sir."

The secretary looked shocked. Arthur followed her back to her office for a glass of cold water.

"I had to lie to save you, Mrs. Banya."

"Did you make any such dispatch Mr. Kigulu," she whispered.

"None." He smiled. "Let Alug carry that burden."

Arthur had scored a huge success. The incident sealed their friendship. He decided to try and get more information from her now that he had lied to Mukwano to save her. She owed him. After today, he wouldn't need another day within the VG.

***

Back home in the evening, Arthur called to fix an appointment with an old friend of his father. The line was busy. Arthur gave it a moment as he once again scanned through the Zura Maids papers. This was enough information to expose the company, expose the illegal trade they were hiding behind phrases like connecting maids to jobs, creating employment for the youth, and all that. He was certain Mzee Odwar would help him go forward.

Odwar and his father had studied together at Makerere University Law School. Arthur's father had excelled, and remained at the University as a lecturer. Odwar, on the other hand, had joined Police Force as a young cadet, rapidly climbing the hierarchy to Commissioner. The two had kept in touch, visiting and taking part in each other's affairs. Arthur had learnt that the two had been each other's best men. When Arthur's father died, Arthur found it natural to fill the void with Odwar. Odwar never disappointed him.

Arthur grabbed the phone and called again.

"Having problems, son?" Retired Commissioner Odwar said.

"Mzee. Happy to hear your voice," Arthur said. "I need urgent

Printed in the United States
by Baker & Taylor Publisher Services